ALSO BY GOLDY MOLDAVSKY

Lord of the Fly Fest

The Mary Shelley Club

Just Say Yes

Just Say Yes

GOLDY MOLDAVSKY

HENRY HOLT AND COMPANY

NEW YORK

Henry Holt and Company, *Publishers since 1866*

Henry Holt® is a registered trademark of Macmillan Publishing Group, LLC

120 Broadway, New York, NY 10271 • fiercereads.com

Our books may be purchased in bulk for promotional, educational, or
business use. Please contact your local bookseller or the Macmillan Corporate
and Premium Sales Department at (800) 221-7945 ext. 5442 or by email at
MacmillanSpecialMarkets@macmillan.com.

Library of Congress Control Number: 2023033636

First edition, 2024

Book design by Samira Iravani and Maria Williams

Printed in the United States of America

ISBN 978-1-250-86324-9 (hardcover)

ISBN 978-1-250-86323-2 (paperback)

1 3 5 7 9 10 8 6 4 2

For my tía Beki Schnaiderman Z"L,
who taught me the value of paciencia y humor.

1

I'M THROWING AN INDEPENDENCE DAY PARTY, which should mean a good time, but I've got a bad feeling about tonight. We're about a month and a half late for the Fourth of July, but senior year starts tomorrow—class of 2007, baby—and that makes this our last night of freedom.

An exclusive soiree on a New York City rooftop. Really, I've outdone myself. So what if "exclusive" actually means "small guest list"? And sure, by "New York City" I technically mean "working-class Brooklyn." And okay, my building is only four stories high, so the view is mostly other, taller brick buildings, but that iconic New York skyline is only a few miles away. I can't see it, but I know it's there, sparkling, full of life. Like the promise of senior year. The night sizzles with that promise— with that unquantifiable sense that anything can happen.

My best friend, Sof, marches toward me, pulling a boy behind her. "Jimmy," she says, "meet Dwayne."

"Hi, Dwayne! You got the stuff?"

Without a word, Dwayne unzips his backpack, and Sof and I peek inside. The JanSport is heavy with all sorts of illegal fireworks, and Sof and I look at the loot like two gorgeous pirates opening a treasure chest. Wouldn't be an Independence Day party without fireworks.

"Awesome." I point Dwayne toward the spot where he can start setting up.

"You sure your neighbors won't mind?" Sof asks.

"The building rules are clear: No loud noise after ten P.M." She's got her phone in her hand and I reach for it, flipping it open to look at the time. "It's only 9:04." I flip the phone closed again with a satisfying snap. "We're good."

So why do I feel a gnawing sense of unease? A vague worry that fits me like a dress that's one size too small. Sometimes, when I feel worried for no reason, I'm sure it's the residual effects of my mom's overbearingness. If my mother were here, she'd say there are too many people on this roof, that this is reckless, idiotic, courting danger, and—at 9:04 P.M.—way too late in the evening to be having fun. But my mother isn't here—she's two floors down, too engrossed in an episode of *Heridas de Amor* to have any idea what a good job her daughter is doing hosting the first party of the year/last party of the summer.

"Is that Big Rally?" Sof asks.

I follow her gaze, peeking over the roof wall to look at the courtyard below.

My eyes widen when I spot him. "He's back."

I burst through the heavy courtyard door, the hinges groaning just slightly louder than my neighbor does upon noticing me. He sits in his usual spot, an ancient Adirondack chair that

2

was once blue but thanks to weather, age, and Vitaly's near-constant use is now driftwood gray.

"Welcome home, Big Rally! How was Mexico?"

Vitaly shuts the notebook on his lap and tucks his pen into his polo pocket. "El Salvador. And it was productive."

I fight the urge to roll my eyes. It would've been so easy for him to say *great*, *nice*, or even a dorky *cool!* But Vitaly has to prove he is above a good time. Talk around the building is that he spent six weeks in *El Salvador* helping to build houses for disadvantaged families, the noblest of college application fodder. Though there is also talk that he joined a real construction company down there to make enough money to cover his first year of college. I can't be sure which story is true, but when I told my mom about how the boy from 1F had left the country to build houses and how maybe *I* could do that, too, she said, "¿Tú? ¿Construyendo casas?"

When she stopped laughing, she told me I wasn't going anywhere.

The little Moleskine notebook on Vitaly's lap begins to quiver with the subtle bouncing of his right knee. Is he impatient? Nervous? Both? Vitaly never seems all that happy to be talking to me, and I can't for the life of me understand why.

"Who spends the summer on a tropical island and comes back without a tan?"

I guess maybe it's because of questions like that. But can you blame me? He's so white I could ski off his nose.

Vitaly looks like he really wants me to leave, which is precisely why I plop down in the chair next to him.

"El Salvador isn't an island. Don't you have a party to host?"

I grin. "Come. You might have some fun for once in your life."

Vitaly holds up his notebook like a crossing guard would a stop sign. "Can't. Working."

"School hasn't even started yet. What could you possibly be working on, your valedictorian speech?"

"Something like that."

I stare at him expectantly, and he sighs through flared nostrils, resigning himself to explaining. "It's my plan for senior year."

"Plan?"

"My intentions, goals, due dates for college applications and scholarships, course load optimization, scheduling extracurriculars—"

I stop him before he starts ranking his top five pencils. "You need a party more than anyone I've ever met."

"How good of a party can it really be if you're down here with me?"

Ha.

When people at school find out Vitaly is my neighbor, they ask me what the quiet boy in class is really like. Because someone so bland in literally every sense of the word (fair skin, blond hair—he's even wearing a polo the color of mayo right now) must be hiding some magnificent secret life. But the truth is, with Vitaly, you get what you see. He's a boy doing homework, sitting by himself in a concrete courtyard on the last night of summer, actively avoiding a party.

"My party is great," I say. "I'm having a great time."

And though I am the picture of your all-American girl, your fabulous New Yorker, your effortlessly fun party hostess, Vitaly looks at me like he can see the gnawing uneasiness. My dress itches and he can tell.

Even if Vitaly thinks he knows something about me, it isn't the power move he imagines it is. All it tells me is that he's paying attention. And I'm the kind of person who likes attention.

"There's more to life than plans, Big Rally."

"There's more to life than partying, Jimena."

He pronounces my name the right way, and for some reason that hard *H* softens something inside me. Our conversation has reached its boiling point, and now I feel like taking a deep breath to cool it down. After all, I know what he's doing out here—what he's always doing out here. What he's trying to get away from. And I really *do* want him to have some mindless fun. "A party's a much better distraction than a plan."

He looks at me through the hair that falls over his forehead. He doesn't ask me what I mean about the distraction thing, and he doesn't try to deny it, either. Eventually, his notebook goes still as his knee stops bouncing and we look at each other for a long moment.

Then a shrill voice screams, "This noise is killing me!"

Both Vitaly and I strain our necks back to stare up at the lady in the fourth-floor window, her frizzy, graying bangs drifting through the late summer breeze like rising smoke.

"Hi, Mrs. Gorky!" I smile with all my teeth and wave, but it does nothing at all to brighten her mood.

"Are you having a party on the roof?" she yells.

"Aww, it's the last night of summer, Mrs. G., don't be such a cranky-poo."

Mrs. Gorky squints down at me but directs her next comment to Vitaly. "Did that little shit just call me *poo*?" She disappears back into her apartment.

"She's going to call the police," Vitaly says, standing.

"The more the merrier!" I say, popping out of my seat, too. "Let them try and arrest me! At least I'll know I went down having the time of my life!"

"Understated as usual."

I shrug and make my way back to the party.

⸻

If the cops are coming, I might as well make it worth their time.

Dwayne's got his little rockets all in a row, ready for my command. "Light 'em up!" I tell him.

Vitaly may be boring, but at least he knows what he wants out of life. He has a plan. Maybe I need to take a page out of his book. Go into this year with a clear intention. Tonight, I'm declaring my independence. I'm going to go into my senior year balls to the wall. Because this is my last year of freedom before the real world sneaks up on me.

There's the *fizz* of a lit fuse, the *thwiiip* of the launch, and then the sky above Sunset Park explodes with light. Next to me, Sof howls and whips her hair back. I squeeze her hand and peek over the edge of the roof wall. He may have declined my invitation, but the party still manages to reach Vitaly, the fireworks putting some much-needed color on his face.

"Isn't this fun!?" I shout down. There's no way he can hear me over the explosions or Mrs. Gorky's screaming. But this moment is everything. I feel light and loose and good, like someone has finally unzipped my too-tight dress.

How nice to be young and free. I hold on to that feeling, even when the sounds of sirens start to break through the fireworks. "Might be time to book it," I whisper to Sof.

"Yeah, we gotta go."

2

MY MOM IS DEATHLY AFRAID OF COPS, IN THE same way that most people are afraid of bugs or rodents. If she sees one, she will let out a little startled yelp, grip her purse close to her chest, and cross the street immediately. I don't get it. It's not like she ever does anything to get on the police's bad side. My mom has never been in trouble in her entire life. She lives by a strict set of rules, and she makes sure I live by them, too. Rules like: stay out of trouble, make your bed every morning, don't talk back to your elders, and, most importantly, never ask a cop for help.

I've broken every one of those rules tonight. Except that last one. I definitely didn't ask Officers O'Hannley and Bivens for help, and yet they insisted on accompanying me to my door like I couldn't get there myself. Before either of them has a chance to interrupt my mom's sacred viewing of her favorite telenovela, I turn to face them in a last-ditch effort to save my own skin.

"Please just arrest me."

It takes a minute for the officers to process words they've clearly never heard before. I hold out my wrists and brace for the cool metal of handcuffs. "Let's get this over with."

Cops are a drag, but they're no match for my mom.

O'Hannley ignores me and raps his knuckles against the door of 3B. I pray for the minutes to stretch as long as they can, buy me some time, but my mom is there quick as a telenovela slap.

When she sees us all standing there—two NYPD officers flanking me like drab angel wings—a million expressions flicker across her face. A flip-book of shock, awe, rage, fear. In the end, she blankets all her emotions with a bright smile that only quivers a little.

"This your daughter?" Officer Bivens asks.

It takes so long for my mom to answer I begin to wonder if she'll deny knowing me. Her fear of cops can't go that deep, can it? Spanish from the TV floats through her excruciating pause.

"English isn't her first language," I mutter.

My mom's eyes blaze with a panicked fury. If looks could kill, I'd be on the floor in a puddle of blood. "Yes, she is my daughter," my mom finally says. "What happen?"

"Nothing happened," I say, but Officer O'Hannley speaks over me.

"She threw a party on the roof. There were fireworks. Neighbor called in with a noise complaint."

I can see the wheels turning in my mom's head, working out how many buses she'll have to take to visit me in juvie. Her hand encircles my wrist, tugging me inside. "It's okay, I'm not in trouble. Right, guys?" I say, turning to the officers.

Officer Bivens starts listing all the laws I've allegedly broken, and the whole time my mom just keeps nodding, smiling, the typical show she puts on for people speaking a language she isn't fluent in. In pleasant conversation, the nodding and the smiling do most of the heavy lifting. It's a lot smoother than the alternative, which is to stop every few seconds to ask for something to be repeated or explained. And my mom definitely wants this to go smoothly.

"We're letting her off with a warning, but we don't want to have to come up here again."

In all the nodding and smiling, my mom has kept gently pulling me by the wrist, and somehow I've ended up in the center of the apartment, farthest away from the cops. My mom mutters some more words in English, thanking the police like they've just handed her a prize, not a no-good idiot of a daughter who can't even throw a successful belated Independence Day rooftop party.

"Thank you, officers. Good night, officers." My mom's smile stays firmly in place, even as she closes the door on the cops. But it melts right off the moment she turns to me.

Our apartment is small. It was originally a one-bedroom, but with the help of a family friend in construction, we put up a wall to give me my own bedroom. It makes the living room tiny, but there's enough space for a couch on one side and a small dining table against the opposite wall, the TV off in the corner. A modest galley kitchen with yellow linoleum floor tiles and a pink bathroom straight out of the seventies round out our home.

And right now, my mom is using every square inch of the place to have a complete and utter meltdown. She wails in rapid-fire Spanish, leaning on the table to stop herself from fainting and falling, and then pushes off the back of a chair, propelled by a second wave of disbelief. She pinballs to the window, terrified, then shuts the curtains, paranoid. She sinks into the couch, her rant muffled by a cushion, and then she stands again, pacing, plowing an angry path through the carpet that she vacuums three times a week. She's not even talking to me anymore. Everything she says now is a bewildered soliloquy, directed to the heavens, demanding to know what she has done to deserve such a malcriada for a daughter.

People like to say I can be overdramatic, but those people have never met my mother.

"¡¿Cómo es posible, Jimena, que me metas en tanto problema?!" she shouts. "¿Qué te pasa, estás *loca*? ¿Qué cosas estás haciendo que la *policía* vino? ¡¿Qué has hecho, hija?!"

She has so many questions, but I know they're rhetorical. This isn't about me, this is about her getting all her anger out, so I let her have her moment and wait patiently for her to finish before I say anything.

"No es posible que seas así. Dime, por favor, qué has hecho. ¿Qué pasó con la policía?"

"Una fiesta," I say meekly. "No fue nada."

"¡¿Cómo que no era nada, qué estabas . . . con drogas?! ¡¿O qué?! ¿Por qué la policía vino? Por favor, nunca más quiero ver esa policía en mi casa."

I can practically feel her blood pressure boiling in her voice. "Why are you so scared of them?"

My mom may as well be holding a broom for how expertly she sweeps my question away. "Ya después te lo voy a explicar."

No, I need to know now. She's so intense about this, and I don't understand why. "¡Dime!"

My mom sighs. It seems like her first breath since the cops dropped me off. "Hijita, es algo muy importante que tengo que decir, y nunca te lo habia dicho antes, pero desgraciadamente estamos en este país . . . ilegales."

We're in this country . . . illegally?

On the TV, the telenovela heroine lets out a cry of anguish.

It's ironic that my mom has finally taken a moment to breathe, because suddenly I cannot. She's dumped this piece of brand-new information with all the grace and subtlety of a severed horse head in my bed.

"What?"

"No quería decírtelo asi, pero . . . ya . . . ahora lo sabes."

I shake my head, the backs of my thighs finding their own way to the couch. "No sé nada."

My mom sits down too and begins to explain, how we're undocumented, how everything I thought about my immigration story is wrong, and though I hear every word, it all goes over my head. After saying everything she has to say, my mother leaves me with one piece of advice. "Mira, no le digas a nadie."

"¿Qué?"

"No confíes en nadie. Nadie puede saber. Y nada tiene que cambiar."

But how can I not tell anyone? How can she say nothing's changed? Years of lies condensed into a few minutes of truth. I can't make sense of it.

3

I CAN'T ARGUE WITH MY MOTHER ANYMORE. AND
not just because I can't form the words, but because, exhausted
from revealing the truth about my entire existence, my mom
is choosing to settle her nerves by partaking in her favorite
pastime: vacuuming. She runs the vacuum as desperately as a
heatstroke victim might run the AC, and I literally can't talk
to her over the sound. Despite her rules about staying out late,
when I go to the door, she doesn't stop me.

There is no place quiet enough to think when you live in a
big city. No place except the courtyard.

Vitaly is out here again, back in his same spot. I must've
known he would be. When he sees me, a smug smile plays on
his lips. "I don't want to say I told you so, but—I told you she
was going to call the cops."

I sink into the other patio chair and look up at the starless
sky. "My mom wanted to kill me."

I can feel Vitaly watching me. When I glance at him, his
brows have crawled to a furrow. "What's wrong?" he asks.

"Your parents are having a long fight, huh?" It's why Vitaly
comes out here. He practically lives in the courtyard.

I can see his jawbone flex beneath his skin, but he's not
taking the bait. "What's wrong?"

I sigh, scratch a spot on my leg that does not itch. What is the best way to say this? I search my nails for a hint. They're pristine, polished, and upon closer inspection, trembling. I tuck my hand under my thigh and glance at Vitaly. He isn't any help, either, but he catches my gaze so fiercely I can't pull away.

I think about what my mom said. *Don't tell anyone. Don't trust anyone with this secret.*

Well.

"Turns out I'm illegal."

Vitaly's first reaction is just what I expect it to be. Confusion colors his face, like he isn't sure he's heard me right, and then like he isn't sure how those words work together in a sentence. How can a person be illegal? But then it dawns on him, what I'm saying. Vitaly immigrated here as a kid, just like I did. I always thought we had our immigration story in common, but now it feels more like a chasm between us.

His mother works as an administrator at the hospital three blocks away. A good-paying real job, unlike my mom's under-the-table housekeeping job. Vitaly just came home from a trip abroad and I haven't been on a plane since I came to New York. Vitaly is naturalized and I am not.

To me, Vitaly is Russian American, in much the same way that I always considered myself Peruvian American. But everything I ever considered about myself is wrong. I'm only Peruvian New Yorkina at best.

"Illegal?"

"I know," I say. "I don't even have an accent." It's supposed to be a joke, but neither of us laughs.

"How?"

I shrug and relay the few details my mom told me. "We came here when I was three. Legally. It's just that, apparently, we overstayed our visa. So, I guess, we stayed here illegally? We *continue* to stay here illegally. We are illegal." It's pretty simple when you say it out loud. And the simplicity of it makes a lot of other things suddenly clear. Like why my mom and I have never once gone back to Peru to visit family. I always figured it was because flights were expensive and my mom didn't ever take vacation days. There's so much I don't know.

"And you had no idea?" Vitaly asks.

That's the question, isn't it? Did I really not know? Maybe I had an inkling. The way my mom is so secretive, the way she and her friends occasionally talk about papeles. But I only knew we immigrated here, not whether we did it the right way or not.

I shake my head. "I didn't know. But now . . . it explains so much."

I always had a sense that my mom and I weren't like everyone else. This explains why it always felt like we were hiding from the world. I thought my mom was just paranoid, but now I know she had reason to be. Avoiding cops, avoiding government buildings. The never getting a better job, never getting a car. Her fear of me ever needing to go to a hospital. I realize now with such clarity that it wasn't fear for my well-being. It was fear of all the IDs and insurance and addresses and other documentation they'd require of us. It explains everything.

Vitaly's gaze starts to feel like a heat lamp. The longer we sit here in silence, the more I worry about what he's thinking.

We aren't even friends, not really, and now I'm questioning why I even said anything to him in the first place. He's an immigrant like me, but all I see when I look at him is potential. Vitaly's got his whole life ahead of him—plans, college.

College. A rung on my life's ladder that has suddenly fallen away. Can I even go to college now? Can I do *anything*? I search Vitaly for the answers to my unasked questions, but all he does is glow with promise. Big and bright as a lighthouse.

I'm drowning.

"I'm sorry," Vitaly says. Potential and pity.

"It's okay."

"No, it sucks. It isn't fair."

It's kind, understanding, and I cling to his sincerity like a life preserver, but soon I'm dragged back into my riptide of churning thoughts. It does suck. I'm illegal. I'm pulled lower, lost in how bad this is. How much worse it could get.

Without even knowing it, Vitaly's next words haul me up. "You can fix this," he says. "Everything is fixable."

I breathe and try to believe him.

4

I SPEND THE NIGHT LYING IN BED, SUSPENDED
between sleep and cold-sweat wakefulness. When sleep does
come, in short, sporadic snippets, it's dreamless, just a dark
abyss and me, lucid and lost. Which is pretty much what my
world is going to be like. From now on I'll be wandering aimlessly through life, my dreams permanently out of reach.

Without papers, I don't really exist. I'm an alien. Persona
non grata. And if I'm no one, then what does that mean about
my life? I was always the kind of person who woke up in the
morning excited by the day's possibilities, but now, as the first
ray of sun trickles through my window, it dawns on me how
many of those possibilities have been suddenly stripped away
by the news of who—*what*—I really am.

There's no point in trying to get any more sleep, so I slump
toward my vanity to start getting ready for school. I begin my
routine by rote, slipping into a new baby-pink Juicy tracksuit.
I bought it especially for my first day of school, and now it
feels like a tacky costume. I run my fingers through my hair to
get a natural side part. Warm brown strands cascade past my
shoulders, and I tame any flyaways with Frizz Ease. The lack of
sleep has turned my typically dewy skin dull, but it's nothing a
little makeup can't fix. I have the kind of skin tone that some

of my classmates try and fail to replicate with streaky Jergens self-tanner, so I never bother with foundation. Just a couple coats of mascara and my go-to MAC Lipglass. Already, there's some shine back, and I try to bring the look over the finish line with a smile.

The full lips and rosy cheeks and sparkle in my eye usually work for me, but as I look in the mirror now, my smile falters.

I don't think I look like an illegal alien.

But then, what does an illegal alien look like? I never gave much thought to undocumented immigrants before, but when I did, what did I imagine? Was it people living on the streets? Dirty and dehydrated from crossing the border? Delivery guys on bikes? The people who dig through trash, collecting plastic bottles for recycling?

I never imagined an illegal alien could look like the girl staring back at me in the mirror. Young. Popular. Killer head of hair.

My alarm goes off and P!nk demands that I get this party started.

So I flash another smile in the mirror. Whatever's going on in my life, I can't start senior year looking tired.

"Te ves cansada," my mom says, giving me a once-over from the two-seater kitchen table.

Well, buenos días to you, too. I pour myself an extra-large mug of coffee from the pot and sit down. Every day my mom eats two pieces of buttered toast and a café con leche, which is somehow enough fuel to clean a two-thousand-square-foot apartment in downtown Brooklyn.

I used to just accept that cleaning houses was my mom's job, that it was the best she could do because she wasn't fluent enough in English, or because she didn't have the time or the money to get training for anything else. But now I see it for what it is. My mom cleans houses because it's a steady job that pays cash. She's never strived for more because she literally can't. Even if her English was perfect, even if she had a million degrees under her belt, her illegal status prevents her from moving up in the world. Not only that—it makes every decision for her. Her decision to always have her guard up, not to take even the smallest risk, to defuse any situation, to evade, to deflect any probing questions. My mom never speaks up for herself at her job. She's always "on" in front of others, her subservient smile like a spotlight she shines in your eyes so you can't see who she really is.

When she's home, though, my mom actually has a personality. She can be funny. She loves to rage against her bosses. I thought we were so close that I was the only one she trusted enough to show her real self to. But now I see how insidious this illegal status really is, because it's even infected our relationship. She's never been honest with me. Who would the two of us be if we didn't have to worry about getting thrown out of this country?

My mom has let her status rule every aspect of who she is, down to the marrow. She lives on the fringes of society. Quiet. Hidden. I think I'm supposed to feel bad for her. For us. But my anger is too close to the surface, and all I feel is bitterness.

And right now she's nibbling on toast and humming a tune, like all of this is perfectly normal. I guess it's because she's lived with this truth for years, and it's only been a day for me. My mom turns the pages of *Hoy*, and I brace myself for her to bring up the events of last night. How the cops dragged me home and she shouted and cried and revealed a secret that changed my life forever. But she only looks over the headlines of the day and says, "Esa Niurka Marcos es una trome."

Niurka Marcos is a permanent tabloid fixture south of the border, and while I don't even know if she's an actress, a singer, or a TV personality, she is always embroiled in scandal and can deliver a dis like nobody's business. A true legend.

But I have my own scandal to worry about. I can't believe my mother is just going to sit there and enjoy her breakfast like she didn't throw a grenade on my lap last night.

"¿Hiciste tu cama?" she asks.

"¡Me contaste que soy ilegal anoche!" I never snap at my mom, but she can't seriously be asking if I made my bed this morning. She sets down her mug carefully and fixes me with a stern look.

"El hecho de que te hayas enterado que eres indocumentada no significa que la vida para. Esa noticia no cambia nada."

"Cambia *todo*," I counter. But my mom only shakes her head, sticking to her guns.

"Eres la misma niña hoy que fuiste ayer. La vida continúa como normal."

I don't understand how she can say all this, talking about how finding out I'm undocumented changes nothing, how my life is the same today as it was yesterday. My world is spinning, and *this* is when my mom decides to pull the rug out from under me. She must see the questions all over my face because she does, finally, concede one point.

"Lo único que cambia es que ahora sabes que tienes que tener más cuidado."

"More careful how?"

"La policía," she says, like it's obvious. "Ay, como me asustaste anoche. Algo tan pequeño y nos pueden echar de aquí."

A new fear seizes me suddenly. I've been so worried about all the things I won't be able to do in the future thanks to this status that I didn't even consider the fact that I'm literally a crime. Just me, being here drinking coffee. I haven't considered what happens if I get caught.

"They can throw us out," I say. My mom's right. Any little thing that makes me cross paths with the cops again could end everything: another noise complaint, a random bag search at a subway station, *jaywalking*. The next time I face a cop could be the last time I see New York.

5

DEPENDING ON HOW YOU LOOK AT THINGS, senior year can be a closing chapter. The conclusion of high school. The end of being a kid. The last gasp of parties under (and over) your parents' roof. But it's also the gateway to what lies ahead. Everything you do now determines how the rest of your life goes.

Yesterday I was excited about all that. Now I only feel dread. I'm a zombie through all my classes, vacillating between asking myself a million existential questions and going completely blank. I keep wondering if the people I pass in the hall are citizens. I can't be the only one who isn't, can I?

At lunch, Sof can't stop talking about my grand Independence Day party. Everyone at this table was there, but the story is epic enough that it bears repeating. "And that's how we evaded the police," Sof says.

"How *you* evaded the police," I mutter to myself. But Sof hears. She pauses at this new glitch in the story.

"I mean, they let you off with a warning, right?" Sof says. "Not a big deal."

I nod. Not a big deal/the worst night of my life.

Luce starts talking about how the random dude with the fireworks was trying to hit on her, and then Kenz interrupts her to claim he was actually hitting on *her* and an argument instantly, inevitably, breaks out. Sof ignores them and digs into me.

"What's up with you today?"

"What?"

"You've been acting weird. And you look like you haven't slept."

"Thanks."

"Tell me."

I hold a breath, trying to figure out what to say. But for some reason, what came out so freely with Vitaly in the courtyard stays lodged in the back of my throat. Last night the wound was still fresh and I couldn't avoid it. But now that I've had time to sit with it, it's scabbed over. Picking at it is too painful.

I remember what my mom said, about not trusting anyone with this secret. That people could hold this over my head, turn on me, and then turn me *in*.

But it's not just that.

This is the kind of secret that comes with judgment. The sort of thing that can make a person look at me differently.

Do I think Sof would ever turn me in? No, of course not. But if there's even a one percent chance that my best friend might judge me for this, I never want to find out. Because that would destroy me.

"Guess I just didn't get enough sleep. Too excited for the first day." The little lie comes easy, and Sof seems to buy it. She glances at Luce and Kenz—still arguing—and groans. Far too much drama this early in the day. I agree. I pick up my tray and stand, making up a half-hearted excuse about forgetting something in my locker. I don't stop until I'm in a corner of the empty computer lab with a search engine open in front of me.

I think of what Vitaly said, his words flickering in the back of my mind like little gems of hope. *Everything is fixable.*

I start typing.

How do I fix being undocumented?

The page fills with words, and most of them say the same thing. *Lawyer.*

Of course.

6

I HEAD TO THE LAW OFFICE AFTER SCHOOL THAT
day. It's located above a Pizza Hut, and between the second-
and third-floor windows is a blue banner with yellow block
letters that spell out, simply, IMMIGRATION LAW. I'm working
under the assumption that my mom hasn't gone the lawyer
route yet. I'm sure her fear of any authority figure in a suit
has kept her from trying. But I like to think I'm a little more
fearless than she is.

To the left of the pizza place is a steel door covered in dings,
scuffs, and graffiti tags in thick permanent marker. The buzzer
has three listings, and I press the one labeled LAWYER. No
one asks me who I am or what I want through the intercom.
There's just a buzz that lets me know the door is unlocked. I
push through it.

I have no idea what I was expecting, but it wasn't a cramped
office at the top of a narrow staircase, occupied by a frazzled
young guy wiping coffee off his tie. Emphasis on the *young*.
This might be the first tie he's ever owned, and he's already
gone and ruined it.

When he sees me in the doorway, he drops the tie.

"Uh. I made an appointment. Jimena Ramos?" I check
behind me to see if I didn't accidentally bypass a secretary's

desk, but nope, it's just this office, with a sheet of paper that says TOM YANG, ESQ. taped to the door. On the desk there's a little plaque that says the same.

"Oh," Mr. Yang says. "I thought you'd be Asian."

Off my confused look, he continues, "Most of the people who come to see me are Asian."

For some reason I never even considered that there are Asian people who are undocumented, too. But now I realize how silly that is. There are probably undocumented people from all over the world who live here.

"I should really stop making assumptions on your race or nationality."

"I'm just your standard Peruvian."

Mr. Yang's face lights up. "Wow, have you ever been to Machu Picchu?"

I shake my head and Mr. Yang nods. "'Course not. If you're here, chances are you've never gone back there, right? Or maybe I'm wrong. I really need to stop making assumptions." He exhales and gestures to the chair on my side of his desk. "Please, sit."

"So, first, I just want to confirm that this is a consultation," I say. "Your website said I don't have to pay for a consultation."

Mr. Yang kind of looks like he's regretting that decision but nods anyway. "Yes, consultations are free. Now, what can I do for you?"

"Well," I begin, trying to think of the best way to broach this. "I'm sort of, apparently, illegal."

I remind myself that a lawyer is kind of like a doctor who's seen it all. He can't judge and, more importantly, can't turn me in. I hope. Mr. Yang prompts me to keep going and I do, telling him the circumstances of how I came to be in this country, how long I've been here, and how I just found out this new information about myself. Finally, I say, "I'd like to not be. Illegal. Can you help me with that?"

Mr. Yang has a strained look on his face, and I know he's about to turn my case down, so I jump in before he has a chance to. "I can pay. I babysit sometimes, and I've got savings. Plus, I was planning on getting a real job this year anyway. I mean, it was something I was putting off for a while, 'cause who wants to work on top of going to school, right? But now I don't know if I *can* get a job anymore, given my current situation. I'm sure we can work out an installment plan. A sliding scale—"

He waves both hands, cuts me off mid-sentence. "That isn't the problem," Mr. Yang says. "Kids in your predicament, well, you're kind of between a rock and a hard place."

I lean forward, all ears, like there's a big test coming up and he's about to reveal the secret to acing it. "The citizenship process takes years, for a lot of people even decades," he says.

"I'll get in line," I say. "I don't mind. Just tell me what to do and I'll wait my turn, long as it takes."

Mr. Yang bites his bottom lip and looks at me like I'm a brand-new coffee stain on his tie. "That's the thing, Jimena. For kids like you, there is no line to get into."

He's careful with his words, but they still hit me like debris. I slump back in my chair, all the blood draining from my face. "What do you mean?"

"I mean there is no path to citizenship for you. If you really want to go the citizenship route, you'll have to leave the country and apply once you're back home—"

I shake my head, confused. "New York is my home."

Mr. Yang's lips pull down. "Back in Peru."

He gives me a moment to take this in. I left Peru when I was so small that I barely remember anything about it. I have flashes of my grandmother's house, where we lived. Her blue kitchen, sneaking sugar cubes off the saucer in the center of the breakfast table.

And that's it. That's the entirety of my Peru.

"So you're telling me, the kids who were brought here when they were little, they can't do anything about it now? They can't become US citizens. They're stuck in limbo."

I keep saying *they* like it's someone else I'm talking about, but it's really *us*. It's *me*. And Mr. Yang can only shrug apologetically.

"So I go to Peru, apply for citizenship." I swallow to make my mouth feel not so dry. "How long would it take till I can come back home?"

"Well, that depends on how you entered this country to begin with. It could be ten years, but I understand you overstayed a legal visa, which makes your chances of reentry somewhat more optimistic. You have to understand, though, there are no guarantees that you'll be let back in at all, especially with this stain of being here illegally on your record."

He says so much, and continues to say even more, but the words that stick out most are *ten years*. If I left America now just to come back the right way, I would be twenty-seven before I could come home again. A full-blown adult. Ancient. My twenties are supposed to be my best years. I'm meant to go wild and make mistakes and crash and burn and try every vice and get wise and find myself and figure out who I want to be. I can't spend that precious time in a place where I'm not even comfortable with the language anymore.

"I don't know anything about Peru," I say.

"Right."

"I can't go back there. My life is here," I say matter-of-factly. "My mom is here."

Mr. Yang is very matter-of-fact, too. "Right," he says again. The word is useless. It means nothing, it gives me no answers. It takes everything for me not to reach over his messy desk, grab his soiled tie, and shake him with it. *Right, what? There must be something else!*

"Look, it's not all hopeless," Mr. Yang continues. "You could wait. Members of Congress have introduced the DREAM Act, and I hear it could pass."

"The Dream Act?"

"It would give you some form of status that would protect you from deportation."

Deportation. The word clangs in my brain, striking a chord of fear instantly. I'm back in the kitchen with my mom, finding out I'm illegal for the first time, watching my future go up in smoke. I was supposed to be worrying about starting senior year right and now I'm worried about deportation. The panic is automatic.

"Wait," I say, "I think there's a misunderstanding—I didn't choose to come here."

Mr. Yang nods like the only one misunderstanding this is me. "I didn't, like, *consent* to do a crime—this isn't my fault."

"I know," Mr. Yang says.

But for as calm and sympathetic as he's being, it only makes the panic in me burn brighter. "You're not going to report me, are you?" I'm an idiot for talking so openly about all this stuff. "You're not obligated to call the authorities, right?"

Mr. Yang shoots his hands out so suddenly I think he might accidentally knock one of the precariously stacked file towers off his desk. "No, no, gosh no. But listen—the DREAM Act. With the next administration, in a year or two, we could really see some movement on it."

A year or two. It isn't even a thing I can apply for yet.

I thought I was supposed to be near death for my life to flash before my eyes, but it's happening now, in a baby lawyer's office above a Pizza Hut. I try to focus on something to keep me from sinking right through this chair. My gaze lands on the coffee stain on Mr. Yang's tie. It will never come out. It's ruined. "So that's it?" I finally say. "My only hope is a bill that hasn't even been passed by a government that doesn't want me here?"

Mr. Yang nods sadly, but then, out of nowhere, lets out the smallest laugh. "Or you could always just marry a US citizen."

His little sensible chuckle is the only sound in the room. Everything has stilled, including my racing mind. It might be a joke to Mr. Yang, but to me it is a new doctrine. And I need him to repeat it, like a mantra. Like a law. "I could what?"

"I wasn't being serious. You're too young, anyway. How old did you say you were? Fifteen?"

"Seventeen."

"Oh. Well, not that young, I guess." He looks at me—I'm feeling clear, resolved—and the laughter on his face morphs into regret. "Ms. Ramos, I can't advise you to get married. You're young and marriage isn't something to take lightly. I've been going out with my girlfriend for four years and I'm *still* not ready to pop the question."

"Right," I say.

"And it's an especially serious thing—an offense, actually—in the eyes of the law if you're caught in a sham marriage for papers."

"Right." The word is just as meaningless coming from my lips as it was from Mr. Yang's. It sounds far away to my own ears. An echo.

"You're young," Mr. Yang stresses again, trying to reel me back in. "Just wait for the government to get their act together. Things will change. The tides are turning."

But I'm already out to sea. Marriage—what a lifeboat.

"Thank you for your time, Mr. Yang." I leap up and extend my hand. Mr. Yang stands slowly to meet it.

"Come back anytime," he says.

I'm already out the door.

7

I WORK OUT THE DETAILS OF MY PLAN ON THE
subway ride home, as intricate as anything Danny Ocean and
his band of casino-robbing criminals might come up with.
Okay, it's not actually that complicated. The plan is marriage.

Find a guy. Marry him. Get my papers.

Easy.

Mr. Yang may have been joking when he said my only path
to citizenship is one that leads straight to the altar, but I'm
not laughing. If marriage is my only option, then that's what
I'll do. And I have to do it. I did not have a cushy life by any
means. Growing up meant moving around a lot, furniture
and electronics we'd find by the curb on lucky days, hand-me-
down clothes from the kids at my mom's work, and toys from
them, too—once a year from their donation pile. It meant fur-
tive answers to people's questions and avoiding way too much
of life for reasons I didn't fully understand until now.

But growing up also made me dream of something better.
Getting out of my mom's house and making my own way. *Salir
adelante*, isn't that what we always say? Fumbling through
college and making glorious mistakes and finding a glamorous
job that would earn me the kind of money that would afford
me my own clothes. If my mom was living at a one, I grew up

promising myself that I'd live life at a ten. But I can't do that by staying undocumented.

My mom spends her life trying to be pleasant and amenable and never taking up any space. She makes herself small enough to never be a nuisance or a problem, does whatever it takes to blend into her surroundings and not attract attention. But I can't live in the shadows like that. I want to be able to be a nuisance when I need to be. I want to be someone's problem.

Maybe it's the American in me talking, but I know I was meant to do great things. Daring things. And I can start with this. Getting married may seem like a huge deal, but in the long run it'll just be a blip in the peaks and valleys of my life. A funny story I tell at many, many New York City parties. And lots of people get married young. It could be, like, a punk thing. A totally radical and rebellious act that no one would expect but everyone would admire. Maybe. Anyway, it doesn't matter what anyone else thinks. It's time to go big or go home (to Peru, via a deportation order). And I know what I've got to do.

"I'm getting married!" I say, pushing through the door to the courtyard. Vitaly's there, of course, tossing a handball against the building's brick wall. He glances toward me but doesn't pause his solo game of catch.

"You're what?"

"What we talked about? It's not a problem anymore."

"Oh?" Vitaly sounds genuinely curious. "Are you—did your mom . . . ?"

"No, I mean . . . nothing's changed. But I'm going to make it change. I just need to get married."

Vitaly catches the handball and holds on to it, forgetting the game to give me his full attention. His face pinches. "I don't understand."

"I talked to a lawyer. The only way for me to become a citizen is to marry one."

The confusion deepens into skepticism. "That can't be right."

"It is."

I can see Vitaly trying to work this out in his mind. But the immigration system is not a neat math problem you can solve with a formula. It's an abstract painting that doesn't make sense, no matter how long you stare at it and try to find meaning. The sooner he realizes that, the smoother this conversation will go.

"You're in high school," Vitaly says.

"That's irrelevant."

"This is ridiculous."

"No one said it wasn't."

"You can't get *married*."

I've never seen Vitaly this frazzled. He's still mostly his patented no-nonsense self, but he's vibrating at a higher frequency. "Have you thought this through?" he says. "Really thought it through? The ramifications of it, the risks? I know it sucks to be undocumented, but this scheme could get you into a lot more trouble than it would get you out of."

I'm learning that Vitaly comes undone when something doesn't make any logical sense to him. I try not to judge him for it—he's a facts-and-figures kind of guy—but he's going to have a hard time in life if he can't open his mind to other ways of thinking.

"It isn't a scheme, it's a plan. Kind of like your five-year plan."

Vitaly famously has a five-year plan. During career week last year, he gave a PowerPoint presentation of it in front of the class. It went all through college, ideal internships, and then the top five corporate jobs he was gunning for. It made everyone in class depressed. I mean, Vitaly could've just sat there and said nothing. He has all the makings of a mysterious, cute, smart guy if he wants. But no, he had to be the kind of person who stands at the front of the class, laser-pointing every detail of his mind-numbing future to us.

"This is nothing like my five-year plan. My five-year plan is—"

My groan is a shovel to his face. "I shouldn't have brought up your five-year plan."

"Who are you even going to marry?"

I shrug, because I don't know and also because it seems like a moot point. "Anyone will do."

Vitaly looks at me, horrified, but I look right back at him like he just gave me a good idea. "Will *you* marry me?"

His mouth goes slack. "Are you serious?"

I always imagined someone would propose to me one day. In my wildest dreams, there would be multiple infatuated men on bended knee, all at different points in my life, asking me to spend eternity with them. Of course, I'd turn most of them down gently and sympathetically.

I never thought it'd be me doing the proposing, but desperate times call for desperate measures.

I give Vitaly a once-over. Everything that comes out of his

mouth is either admonishing or boring, and his sense of style has obviously been funded by Kohl's Cash, but the blond hair frames his face nicely. And his face. I'd never seriously considered it before, since it's so often motorboating a book. But he's got a strong jawline. A bottom lip that's surprisingly plump. And his eyes are nice, too, deep blue and looking at me now with a quizzical scowl.

It's not like I love him, but I can imagine being married to Vitaly. He'd have a dependable nine-to-five and I could keep up my end of the bargain with his favorite home-cooked meal every night. If I had to guess? Buttered noodles.

So am I serious?

"Yes?"

"No!" Vitaly says, a tad too emphatically, if you ask me. "No, I will not marry you, Jimena."

"Okay, wow, harsh."

"Not only because I don't want to, but also because I don't plan on being here much longer."

I go still. Being rejected is an unfamiliar experience, but hearing this is even scarier. I reach out to Vitaly, my fingers hovering over his forearm. "Are you a danger to yourself?"

He rolls his eyes. "I'm going to Oxford next year. I mean, I applied—but my chances of getting in are very good. Extremely good. Were you not paying attention when I presented my five-year plan to the class?"

Now it's my turn to roll my eyes. "No one was paying attention to your five-year plan, Big Rally!"

"Well, I'm not sticking around here. I'm going to England for school. So . . . sorry. Can't help you out."

Well, this was a waste of time. "I don't want to marry you, either." If I'm going to do this, then it's got to be a love story. A big, sweeping, whirlwind romance sort of thing. That's the only way to make sure it looks legit. Vitaly is obviously not the guy. "Don't tell anyone at school I proposed to you."

"Wasn't planning on it." Vitaly takes a breath, looking like he just got off the Scrambler at Deno's Wonder Wheel. Poor guy. I think he doesn't like talking to me 'cause he never knows what to expect. One moment I might be trashing all his life choices, and the next I could be asking him to marry me. I almost feel bad for the whiplash, but I'm pretty sure if it weren't for our talks he'd have no excitement in his life.

"What does Sof think about all this?"

I've never talked to Vitaly about my best friend, but I'm not surprised he knows who she is. Our friendship does have a high visibility factor at school. "I haven't told her about my plan," I say. "Or my status."

"What about your mom? There's no way your mom is okay with this."

"Which is why I'm not telling her, either."

Vitaly bites back his next words, exasperation flushing his complexion. I'm not sure why he's getting so worked up about something that, frankly, isn't his problem. Almost as though he's reading my mind, he says, "I should stay out of this."

But in the next breath, he contradicts himself.

"I feel like it's my obligation to make my opinion about this known," he says. "Because no one else is aware of your 'plan,' and somebody in your life needs to tell you what a colossally bad idea it is. That responsibility falls on me." He fixes me with a long stare. "You're seventeen. Don't get married, Jimena."

I guess I should've expected this from him. If I'm being honest, I only told him my plan because he is one of the three people in the world who know my secret. Maybe I'm looking for a sounding board for my ideas. I just don't like the sounds I'm hearing back.

I shrug. "It's my only option."

Back in my room, I find a notebook with flowers on the cover that I've been saving for something special. Talking about Vitaly's five-year plan made me realize that I need to get organized about this if I expect to see results. I know he jots down all his plans; I can do the same thing.

I open the notebook to the first page and write a title across the top in block letters.

PLANS FOR GETTING MARRIED

I stare at the words. As far as a full-blown plan goes, this is pretty paltry. I don't have a whole list of actionable steps yet, but I know where to start.

Find someone to love.

8

WE CAME TO AMERICA WHEN I WAS THREE YEARS old: me, my mom, and my father. I was too young to know the facts, but this is what I've been told: My father had big dreams of making it here, in the land of opportunity. In Peru he was a graphic designer, but the job didn't afford him the quality of life he desired. My mom left her job as a schoolteacher so he could pursue his dream here.

Long story short, the best job my dad was ever able to get in New York was driving for a local car service. We moved around the borough a lot, for reasons I never questioned. Both of my parents had so many different jobs all at once that I never knew how to answer when any friends asked me what they did for a living. I'd usually go with "They work in an office." It's what every adult on TV seemed to do, and even back then, before I knew about my status, I knew instinctively to lie. Nobody else's parents seemed to have three jobs at a time.

My father left when I was eleven. I ask myself now why my mother didn't just go back to Peru after that happened. Was she waiting for him to come back? Did she need to wait for him because he'd made things complicated for her, not giving her a proper divorce? I don't know, and my mom and I don't have the kind of relationship where I can just ask her things like that.

What I do know is the story my mom likes to tell. That when I was in sixth grade, she asked me how I would feel if we moved back to Peru. I told her—in English—that Peru was a foreign country and there was no way I was leaving home. All my friends were here.

My mom must've thought that was a good enough reason for us to stay. By then I was already Jimmy, or *Yimmy*, the way my mom pronounces it. Maybe she realized she had an American girl on her hands, raised on *Saved by the Bell* and Twinkies and who no longer fit in with the cholitas back home.

I think about how different my life would've been if my mom hadn't let me make that decision for us. I'd be on the other side of the world, speaking only one language, no friction between my culture and my country's. America would've been just a memory. And I would be free.

Sixth grade.

Maybe if my mom had asked in fifth grade, my answer would've been different. But sixth grade was when I met Sof.

I'm at Sof's house now. It's been a week since I decided on my marriage plan, and I still have no idea how to make it happen. So I'm taking a break, hanging in Sof's room, flipping through magazines. Hanging out with Sof is effortless. When you've known someone for as long as the two of us have known each other, you don't have to constantly be deep in conversation. You could spend hours with your hair fanned out behind you on the carpet, communicating through two-word quotes from *The Simple Life*.

"That's hot," Sof says in a perfect monotone.

I glance at the ad she's referring to. A black-and-white Abercrombie & Fitch spread featuring three shirtless boys on a beach. "Loves it," I answer.

We're a classic pair, just like Paris Hilton and Nicole Richie. Except we both consider ourselves the Nicole in the friendship, because we both have impeccable taste.

"Did you know that Scott Speedman's first name is actually Robert?" Sof asks, reading the blurb in the Confession Corner from her copy of *CosmoGirl*.

"No way," I say, though I'm barely paying attention. I'm paging through my own magazine, not stopping to read any of the celeb stories or feature articles. My mind is too preoccupied with my lack of marital options, and would it kill *Seventeen* to publish an article about teen brides?

I wish I could tell Sof about my plan. She's so good at relationship stuff, she'd probably be amazing at finding a husband if she wanted. Maybe the hypothetical approach could work here, too. I look up at the ceiling and try to keep my voice casual as I ask, "Would you ever get engaged in high school?"

"Ew, what do I look like, Cory and Topanga?" Sof was a big fan of *Boy Meets World* up until the college years, when she lost all faith in Topanga after she skipped out on Yale for a guy. "I plan on getting married at twenty-six. First baby by twenty-eight. I need to go through my wild-girl phase in college."

I nod, the back of my head scratching against the carpet. "Yeah, no, of course." Sof is right, college is the perfect place for wild-girliness and experimentation. But I don't have time for that right now. "Do you think it's possible to meet some-one and fall in love and marry them all in a short span?"

"Well, yeah, that's different." A magazine page crinkles as Sof turns it. "Britney Spears got married to both her husbands after only knowing them for, like, a minute. She married them both in the same *year*."

I lean up on my elbow, suddenly energized by this very fac-tual piece of information. If Britney could find two guys to love in one year, and marry them both . . .

"And Tommy Lee and Pamela Anderson got married four days after meeting each other."

I am fully sitting up now, strands of my carpet-rubbed hair floating away from my head like the threads of light in a static electricity ball. "You're so right," I whisper, awed by my best friend, a legit fount of invaluable celebrity knowledge. My mind's already running away from me, thinking of the possi-bilities. I can do this. And Sof, without evening knowing it, can help. "I wanna date!" The announcement is big, and I fling my copy of *Seventeen* aside to punctuate the point. It crashes into the pink wallpaper like a bird with a broken wing then flutters to the floor.

"Huh?" Sof says.

I smooth down my hair, feeling a few fizzles and snaps of electricity as I do. "I wanna date guys. Older guys." The idea comes to me instantly, shiny and new. If I'm going to take my plan seriously, I need to date serious guys. I'm not going to find my future husband in algebra class. "I'm over high school guys. They're so immature."

"Not all of them," Sof says.

"Name one."

"Vitaly Petrov."

Of course she picks the most mature teenager in the tristate area.

"He aces every test, volunteers, participates in class, *never* has any fun," Sof says. "If that's not mature, I don't know what is. Plus, he's not bad-looking."

"You crushin' on Vitaly Petrov?"

"I don't have a crush on him," she says sternly. "But you can't deny that he's got delicate features, like a boy in a Renoir portrait. And the hair to match."

Vitaly does have a soft Renoir thing going for him. Something about his posture, or the way he never ever gets his hands dirty with sports or cars or other grimy guy stuff. Until recently he'd been growing his hair long enough to be tied back in a low, ratty ponytail. It made him look like a middle-aged divorcé who was trying to hang on to his youth by switching from classical clarinet to jazz clarinet. Decidedly unsexy. But he'd cut it short at the end of last year, and without the ponytail holder reining it back, his hair is surprisingly voluminous and thick.

I'm spending way too long thinking about Vitaly and his hair.

"He's painfully boring," I say. "Can we move on from Vitaly and get back to the matter at hand? I'm over high school guys."

Sof groans. "I hear ya, babe. So over them."

I wince and lay my head on Sof's shoulder. "I'm sorry. I didn't mean to bring up the Dog."

Sof's tiny shrug lifts my head like a sailboat on a wave. "It's cool. I gotta get over him sometime."

The Dog is Sof's ex-boyfriend, and we're not calling him that because we're trying to be mean. He insisted on the nickname. Dude is obsessed with the WWE and is determined to become a pro wrestler. He's already got his catchphrase down: *Beware of . . . the Dog.* I'm pretty sure he'll make it. The Dog is humongous, which was 90 percent of the attraction factor for Sof. She likes the kind of guy who can pick her up, shield her from an avalanche with his body, poke her eye out with his nipple anytime he flexes a pec. Not my style, but I always thought Sof and the Dog were a cute couple.

His actual name is Doug.

Anyway, the subject of high school guys is a touchy one for Sof, because she broke up with the Dog at the end of last year, thinking he was graduating and she wouldn't see him again. But it turns out he failed literally every class and has to retake senior year. So actually, she's seeing him all the time at school, but the breakup soured things between them and now they don't talk. At nearly nineteen, Sof's ex is technically not a high school guy but is definitely still very much a high school guy. I bet they get back together before the year is up.

"So," I say, wading back into our original conversation. "How do I find a guy who isn't in high school?"

Sof scrambles to her Dell laptop and flips it open. As we wait for it to boot up, she tells me that she's always wanted to try a dating site but was too chicken, but if I'm willing to do it, then she can live vicariously through me and it could be a fun, dumb experiment we can try out.

"A dating site," I murmur. It's nothing I would've thought of. I presumed Sof would list off the guys she'd met at college parties, maybe set me up with a cousin's friend. A dating site feels too formal, too forward, and it's something I probably would have agonized over if I was doing this by myself. But Sof's already on a site that looks legit. The fact that she's so gung-ho about it feels like the permission I need to dive into my plan headfirst. Plus, registration is free, so I can't in good conscience turn it down.

"You're going to need a profile," she says.

I'm ready to dictate a short but tasteful bio, but Sof is done before I know it. I lean forward to read what she's written.

Young, hot, down for a good time.

Serviceable. I would've added *Serious inquiries only!* But I guess I don't want to scare off potential suitors. "You put me down as being twenty-one."

"You gotta be twenty-one for this site. And luckily, there's this little box you can check to pinky-swear you're twenty-one. So, do you pinky-swear?"

The question trips me up. We're talking about guys on a dating site, and to me this is the first step in finding a husband. But to Sof we're just playing a real-life round of Mystery Date. This is the moment I realize how different our lives are. It's like this whole time we've been listening to the same tune, but suddenly my CD keeps skipping while Sof stays smoothly singing along to her favorite pop song.

I don't want to distract her from it. "I pinky-swear."

Sof clicks the box and finds a picture of the two of us saved in her files. In the photo, taken a few weeks ago at a party at

Kenz's, we look hot and sun-kissed. Sof crops herself out and uploads it. My profile is complete.

"Now let's window-shop," Sof says.

We browse through the profiles like we're picking clothes from a dELiA*s catalog. This guy's too short and this guy's way old, and this one guy's got a fivehead. But there is someone who makes us stop scrolling. Hot. Dark hair. Mid-twenties. And most important, his profile says he's looking for a serious relationship.

I move the cursor over the *Let's Go Out!* button underneath his profile pic.

"Click it!" Sof says. "You have got to go out with him."

So I click and Sof squeals. A sneaky smile plays on my lips, and I surrender to it until it fully overtakes my face. Sof and I may be in totally different places in our lives, but we share this distinct feeling. Like swiping a finger of frosting off a cake before anyone notices. We live for moments like this. The mouthwatering sweetness of it overpowers the guilt of lying to my best friend.

9

MY BUILDING HAS A LAUNDRY ROOM ON THE basement level. It's pretty drab—fluorescent tube lights, a pair of shoebox windows up by the ceiling that hardly let any air in—but I have the kind of very exciting news that will brighten up the place.

"I'm going on a date!" I announce, bounding into the room.

I'm surprised to find Mrs. Gorky sneering back at me. "You think I care about your date?" the old woman says. "You kids these days, you overshare everything, screaming from the mountaintops! When I was your age, I went on a hundred dates. You think I shouted the news at everyone I saw?"

If I had to guess? Yes, I think Mrs. Gorky shouted everything, all the time. But the announcement was never meant for her, it was for Vitaly, who sits in one of two folding chairs, hiding a laugh behind a paperback. I knew he'd be here because the only standing date he has is with his weekly load of laundry. My mom washes my clothes because if she didn't, everything I own would be pink. And also, I'm lazy. But Vitaly knows what fabric softener is, hence his very boring routine.

"Sorry, Mrs. Gorky. I didn't know you were in here."

"Sure, sure, why would you assume somebody who lives in the building would be in the building. Idiot."

I nearly crack my jaw biting back my words, because my mom taught me to respect the elderly. Thankfully, Mrs. Gorky's clothing is folded and waiting in her pushcart. She trudges out of the room like she's in a race with a hare.

When we're alone, I plop into the seat beside Vitaly and cross one leg over the other as I turn to him, spine straight, smile at full wattage. "As I was saying, I have a date."

"So? You date all the time."

Gasp. "Did you just call me a slut?"

Honestly, I only joke with him like this because the color his face turns is my favorite shade of pink. But I'm not here to make the poor boy suffer (that much). "I'm joking, Big Rally! This will be the first official potential suitor on my path to marriage-slash-citizenship."

"Congratulations?"

I ignore the snark in his tone, because this news is too exciting to be overshadowed by him or anyone. After a few back-and-forth messages over the course of two days, Keith and I have decided to officially meet. Vitaly thought I couldn't make this work. But here I am, proving him wrong. I'm so excited I can hardly sit still, so I jump out of my seat and try not to bounce in place.

"Someone from school?"

I smile because while Vitaly is keeping his tone casual, his question suggests that he's deeply invested in my plan. "I'll have you know I found him on a dating website."

Vitaly groans. "This is a bad idea."

"He's a mature—terribly hot—young gentleman—"

"Such a bad idea."

"—whose interests include fitness, finance, and spirituality—"

"Maybe the worst idea."

I cock my hip and spike a hand on it. "Why are you being such a sourpuss? I'm getting things done, setting things into motion, things are moving along swimmingly, et cetera, et cetera."

"Because dating websites are practically the Wild West. The people on there—you don't know their motivations. You can't trust a person's profile. Especially not when he's a guy. Trust me, I know—I'm a guy."

I snort. "You're not a guy."

This, more than anything I've said yet, makes Vitaly stop to really look at me. "What is that supposed to mean?"

"You're not a *guy* guy. I mean, you're not the type of guy who's going to be on a dating website. You're not even the type of guy who dates. Why *don't* you date, anyway?"

"Because dating would pull focus from my schoolwork."

"But you'll have schoolwork in college, too. Are you not going to date then? And what about when you have *work* work? How will you ever meet anyone?"

I'm pretty sure I've just punched a bunch of holes into Vitaly's entire "pulling focus" philosophy, because he takes so long to answer. Finally, he mutters something about "finding a good work-life balance" by the time he's an adult or some other nonsense.

"You can't always have your nose to the grindstone, Big Rally. Wasn't it Shakira who said, 'Life happens when you're making other plans'?"

"I'm not sure that quote is accurately attribu—"

"But she's right."

DING. The dryer stops spinning, and Vitaly is all too happy to end this conversation with me and tend to his laundry. He leaves his paperback splayed face down on his seat. I peek at the cover. *Extremely Loud & Incredibly Close*? I can do that.

Vitaly opens the round door while simultaneously grabbing the room's one cart. We both take a deep breath as the tiny space fills with the fresh smell of Downy. He rolls his dry clothes a few feet to the counter against the wall to begin folding. I watch him for a bit. He is so precise in his movements, smoothing a shirt over the scratched and dented Formica until there is not a single ripple or ridge in the fabric. He folds like it's meditation. So he doesn't notice when I swipe some clothes from the cart.

"I'm going to give you another shot," I say. "Will you, or will you not, marry me?"

Do I feel ridiculous wearing a pair of Vitaly's boxers on my head like a wedding veil? No, they're freshly clean. And the bouquet of loose socks in my clutched hands really completes the whole look. Vitaly turns as white as one of his newly laundered sheets, though.

He swipes his underwear off my head and shoves it into the bottom of his cart, where he can pretend it doesn't exist. "Never," he says.

I really shouldn't torture him (much).

"You're driving me crazy," Vitaly says, eyes firmly on his next fold.

"In, like, a sexy way?"

"In, *like*, an annoying way." He stops folding so he can give me his full attention. "Did it ever occur to you that you're not mature enough to be getting married?"

"Rude."

"Well, it's a big commitment. It's kind of the biggest commitment there is. I guess I just find it strange that you're so thrilled at the prospect of making a huge life decision like that when you're not even eighteen yet."

"I'm thrilled about a *date*," I clarify. "Not marriage, per se. I mean, yeah, I'm young, but if this date leads to love and that love leads to marriage and that marriage leads to citizenship, then that's awesome, isn't it? It's romantic."

Vitaly turns back to his clothes. "'Romantic' is not the word I'd use for your immigration scheme."

"You call it an immigration scheme, I call it a girl on a quest for freedom."

At this, Vitaly has the audacity to snort. Actually *snort*. "What?" I say.

"Nothing, it's just ironic. Freedom through marriage."

"What do you mean?"

His sideways glance tells me it should be obvious. "Marriage is a cage."

"Damn, boy. Tell me how you really feel."

"I just wonder if anyone can truly be happy and married at the same time."

I stand there, lips parted, just watching Vitaly fold for a minute, because I really never knew he was this cynical. "But love and marriage. They go together like a—"

"Love isn't a theme song," Vitaly cuts in. "Love can mean heartbreak. It can be unrequited. It can feel like torture. Love makes you think with your heart instead of your head, which leads to terrible decisions, which could then lead to your life spinning out of control."

"Whoa, whoa, whoa, you don't want to fall in love because it'll make you *spin out of control*?"

Vitaly shakes his head like I didn't hear him right or, probably, like he didn't mean what he said. "I'm sure that, one day, the feeling of spinning out of control might be something I want to experience, but for the path I'm on right now, it would be too big a risk."

I lean my hip against the counter, right between him and his cart, closing the gap between us. "'Risk' isn't a bad word."

I can see him doing some risk assessment right now, mulling over my words as he crisply folds a pair of cords at the knees, then the thighs. He pats the fuzzy fabric into roughly the shape of a three-ring binder. "I'm talking specifically about contentment," Vitaly says. "Happiness. I just don't think I'm going to find it within the confines of a marriage."

He reaches past me to grab more clothes and pointedly ignores the shocked look on my face. "Okay, but marriage can equal friendship," I say. "A partnership. Someone who's there for you through everything."

"Marriage can equal resentment. Settling. Someone who holds you back and makes you miserable and keeps you trapped."

My lips have nowhere else to go, so I bring them back together in a closed line. I don't think we can possibly be coming at this from two farther ends of the spectrum. What he's saying shouldn't be that shocking—he is a seventeen-year-old boy, after all. It's only rational that he wouldn't want anything to do with marriage right now. But he's not just reflexively recoiling at the thought of marriage—he's clearly given this a lot of thought.

My parents were a bad model for love and marriage, seeing as how my dad skipped out on us. But Vitaly's parents are obviously as bad a model for love and marriage just by staying together.

I'm seeing Vitaly in a new light, and it's not just the blinking fluorescent tubes above us. I had to know that this boy—who does his own laundry and takes meticulous care folding it—thought about more than just courses and exams. But I never considered that those inner thoughts might veer toward something dark. Well, not dark, exactly. Sad. It breaks something open in me, something that longs to reach out and show him that not everything ends in sadness. And even if it does, well, there are always beginnings.

But we're not those kinds of friends. No matter how close we may be standing, or how much of his intimate apparel is on display. There's no hiding the stark expanse between us. Certainly not under this harsh lighting.

Vitaly keeps folding his clothes, but the method is haphazard now, his T-shirts looking more like rhombuses than perfect squares.

"I'm sorry," he says. "I don't want to be a downer. People get married all the time and they're probably not any worse for wear. I just want to make sure you're looking at this from all the angles. Do you think, honestly, that you can get married right now? And make it last? While you're this young? Without long-term relationship experience?"

Every question he asks feels like an added plate on a weight stack at the gym. But he doesn't see me struggling under the bulk and just keeps piling.

"And can it really be true romantic love if you also have an ulterior motive? How can you trust someone from a dating site with your freedom? How will you trust your own feelings about him when you stand to benefit so much?"

The conversation feels dangerous. It's too close, the kind of existential stuff I would only ask Sof, and only when we're really high or after I've had a good cry. Frankly, it's giving me a headache. I push off the counter.

"It's just a date," I say. But I can't muster quite the same enthusiasm as when I first walked in here.

10

LATER THAT WEEK, ALL I CAN THINK ABOUT
during last-period trig is my date with Keith. I have no idea
what his last name is, so all I can do is imagine myself as *Mrs.
Keith*, which, yes, is a little premature, but I need to keep my
eye on the prize.

As soon as the final bell rings, I meet Sof outside school
and the two of us head to my place so she can help me get
ready. "Mr. Brightside" blasts from my boom box as Sof
applies liquid liner to my eyelids. She keeps asking me questions about Keith as though I've already met him, but our
dating site messaging was just empty flirting. I really don't
know much more than his first name. So I keep saying it.
Maybe it's a nervous tic. Maybe it's a prayer. The point is,
Keith is all we talk about.

"Keith," I say, like the chime to end a communal meditation.

"Keith!" Sof says, like the eureka moment in a brainstorm
session.

If I'm gonna lure this guy into a whole marriage situation,
my hair and makeup need to be flawless. Sof doesn't know
my endgame, but she's a firm believer in a full face of makeup
for every occasion. Weddings! Funerals! Breakfast! Makeup!
Makeup! Makeup! She and I are different like that, but

tonight, I need the whole shebang. So when she dusts enough finishing powder on my face to make me cough, I let her.

To her credit, Sof is taking the task as seriously as Picasso with a brand-new canvas. Well, hopefully not *Picasso*—I don't need my eyes looking like they're two different sizes. Warhol? No, too many clashing colors. Seurat, maybe. Yes, Seurat is perfect. Keith will see me as a beautiful, cohesive vision but upon closer inspection will notice that I have a lot of good points.

"Keith," I say, like a new flavor I've never tried before.

"Keith," Sof says, like a punch line.

I'm wearing my favorite low-rise boot-cut jeans under an emerald-blue satin slip dress. It's kinda heavy on the cleavage, and I'm wondering if it's too much. This whole thing is going to be a delicate balance of trying hard while looking like I'm not trying at all. I never had to try hard with guys before, and second-guessing my every move is doing my head in, making me way more nervous than I've ever been before a date.

I'll throw a skinny scarf on. It's getting chilly, anyway.

Sof secures my hair bump with a couple of bobby pins and then stands back, appraising me. I look her in the eye, wanting to ask her not just how I look, but whether this is a good idea at all. If she knew what I was doing, would she cheer me on, or smack me upside my beautiful hairdo to knock some sense into me? I want her to tell me that this is fine. It's no biggie. But that isn't a fair expectation of her. She doesn't have the whole story.

"Keith?" I say, like a first responder setting foot in an all-too-quiet cult headquarters with dozens of empty Kool-Aid jugs littering the floor.

"Keith," Sof says, like a doctor announcing a life-changing diagnosis. She squeezes my shoulder.

It's go-time.

I picked this café because coffee seems like a perfectly acceptable date activity, plus it's centrally located in Manhattan and close to multiple subway stations in case Keith is a total dud and I want to book it. He's there first, sitting at a table in the corner. When he notices me, the look on his face is exactly what I was hoping for. He breaks into a slow smile as he stands.

"Jimena?"

"Hi."

"Look at you," he says, eyes roving over me. Suddenly I'm not sure about my outfit, but he must see that uncertainty, because he quickly tries to course-correct. "I mean, you look gorgeous."

I flash him a smile. "Thank you."

There is an awkward moment where we stare at each other, then gesture to our seats. I sit but he remains on his feet. "Let me get you a drink. Coffee?"

I nod. I'd typically get a fancy, syrupy latte, but I'm going for a more adult vibe tonight. "Milk, two sugars?"

Keith heads to the counter. I was worried he wouldn't look anything like his profile pic, but to my astonishment, he looks even better and only slightly older than twenty-five. Square chin, bright eyes, five-o'clock shadow. His hair is black and freshly cut, if a bit over-gelled. And he was reading when I got here, which obviously means he's smart. I glance at his book on the table.

Best Cars 2007.

Okay, not Shakespeare, but general interests are important, too.

Keith comes back and sets our drinks down. "So. Your profile says you're twenty-one, but I gotta tell you, you look like you're still in high school."

I clear my throat, pause to think. This is just the first of many lies we're going to start this relationship with, and I need to get used to it. "I have good genes."

"Nice," Keith says. "Tell me about yourself."

The story of myself is that I'm your typical all-American high school student in search of a green card. I really should've spent more time inventing a backstory than imagining myself as Mrs. Keith.

"I'm studying for a degree in interior design," I blurt out. Who knew I was so good at lying? But I don't know how long I can maintain this superpower. I need to deflect the attention off myself and onto him. "So, you're into fitness."

"It's my passion." Keith's forehead crinkles with sincerity, his biceps flexing subtly. "I hit the gym every day after work."

"What do you do?"

"Finance."

He does not expand on this, even though "finance" isn't exactly a job title or even a job description. Or maybe it is—I don't know how things work in the adult world. I don't know anything about finance. Or jobs. Or the best cars of 2007. I'm gripped by a sudden fear, because what will we even talk about, going forward? I'll have to keep lying to Keith until we're both so invested in each other that a few little white lies won't be able to tear us apart. I'll come clean to him down the line and he'll understand why I had to make a few things up, and our relationship will be stronger than ever. It has to be.

"Where do you go to school?"

"Hunter," I say, lightning fast, the only college I can think of. But Keith's barely listening. He's staring at my dress, which is a good sign. Maybe the metallic sheen of it will hypnotize him.

"So, your profile said you're looking for something serious."

Keith nods. "I'm a relationship guy. I'm a boyfriend guy. I'm the guy you bring home to mom."

Not my *mom.*

"Is this silk?" He grazes the fabric on my lap, smoothing the dress between his thumb and index finger.

"Uh, satin. I'm a relationship person, too."

"Oh yeah?" Keith takes a sip of his coffee.

"Yeah, love being a girlfriend. What was your longest relationship?"

Keith shifts in his chair, causing his leg to accidentally knock into mine. But it stays there, denim on satin. "You really are beautiful. Has anyone told you that?"

My laugh is a reflex, a cover-up for the subtle tension building between my shoulder blades. I know I should appreciate the compliment, but it doesn't feel like one. "You're not too bad yourself."

Keith smirks. "I'm a metrosexual, I admit it."

I know it just means he likes to dress up and look pretty,

but he seems a little too eager to shoehorn the word "sexual" into our convo.

"So, your longest relationship?" I ask again.

"My longest relationship?" He has to think about it. "Two years."

"Amazing," I say, forgetting the meaning of the word. "Did you ever talk about marriage with your girlfriend?"

Keith's manicured eyebrows rise, which makes me reframe the question. "I mean, like, how serious were you?"

"You really want to talk about my ex?"

I shrug. "No, but, like, how open to the idea of marriage were you?"

Keith chuckles. "I haven't even finished my coffee yet and you're already proposing?"

"Of course not." I laugh, too. "But seriously."

"Seriously. You. Are. Stunning." Keith's hand migrates under the table until it's gliding up my thigh, beneath the satin, and I react like it's a spider crawling up my leg. I jump back.

"What are you doing?" The volume of my voice, I recognize too late, is high. High enough to get the barista to look over at us.

Keith sits back. "What?"

"You're being kinda handsy. Like you said, 'I haven't even finished my coffee yet.'"

Keith looks offended, which in turn makes me feel crazy. And also like I've blown it.

"Yeah," he says slowly, pushing his chair away from the

table. "I don't really see this going anywhere. I don't date high school girls who are obviously lying about their age."

Shit. "And I don't date creeps who've never seen satin before!"

The little bell over the door chimes on his way out.

So that's Keith.

11

IT'S ONLY ONE DATE. THE FIRST, ACTUALLY. AND everyone knows the first time you do something doesn't really count. It's a mulligan. Practice. I tell myself to shake it off, that I never actually expected to meet someone who could make me weak in the knees. But I also never expected someone who would touch them.

No matter how much I try to rationalize the experience, play it down like it doesn't really matter, it's that moment—the one with Keith's hands on me—that quiets my inner pep talk. I spend the entire subway ride home thinking about it, how close the date was to going sideways. I'm choosing to go out with older men that I don't know. Men who could be dangerous.

It's only one date. The next one has to be better.

I'm still bummed when I reach my stop, and now I'm walking down the street being sad in a killer outfit. I can feel strangers' eyes on me. And I know that's not just all in my head because a guy outside a bodega whistles at me and asks, "Why you looking so sad in a dress like that?"

I stop in front of him, hands on hips, and ask point-blank, "Do you wanna marry me?"

The guy whistles again, only this time in disbelief. "Too pretty to be that crazy," he murmurs.

Even the catcallers don't want me. Can this night get any worse?

I reach my building, but home is the last place I want to be. My mom is back from work by now, and I really don't want to answer her inevitable questions about my dress and overly made-up long face. So I cross through the lobby until I'm outside again, in the courtyard.

"Nice dress."

Why is he always here? We live in one of the biggest cities in the world—surely there is a bingo tournament at a retirement home he can be moderating right now. "'Nice dress'?" I repeat. "Is that sarcasm?"

"No," Vitaly says. "It's . . ." He considers my dress, searching for words, but he gets lost somewhere along the lush terrain of my cleavage, and the boy looks like a stand-up comedian who's forgotten all his jokes. Though he recovers quickly enough. "Was there a party?"

Poor Big Rally. He only ever hears about parties after the fact.

"I was on a date." I plonk down on a patio chair. "It's this thing you do when you're interested in someone and want to get to know them better."

Vitaly pulls up a chair, ignoring my little dig at him. "The dating-site guy? How did it go?"

"Not great."

I'm giving him an opening to rub this dating website failure in my face like I know he wants to. To tell me, in so many words, *I told you so.* But Vitaly doesn't do any of that. His brows only settle low, his gaze intent on me. "What happened?" he asks.

Vitaly's always so serious. He looks at me like this is an important question and my answer will be important, too. Of all the boys I've dated, I don't think any of them have looked at me like that. I could lie and not tell Vitaly anything real about the date. But maybe I'm honest with him because I know he's really listening.

"Dude touched my dress."

Vitaly reacts like I said something much worse. "He did *what?*"

"It's fine."

"I don't think it is."

"I set him straight." I glance at my nails. They're painted blue to match my outfit. The color matches my mood. "It was a bad date. But at least now I'm more prepared for the next one."

"You're really going to keep doing this?"

"I have to."

I can tell how disgusted he is by the whole thing just by the way he pushes off his chair. "Jimena, you can't do this."

"Okay, *Dad.*"

"There's gotta be a better way. You know how dangerous this is?"

Now I'm the one to stand, just to be on even footing with him when I give him a piece of my mind. As if I haven't thought my plan through. As if my future isn't worth fighting for, no matter the cost. "It's not dangerous."

I know that only twenty minutes ago I was considering

just how dangerous my plan is, but I can't help feeling a little defensive. It's automatic. Because I really don't need a disapproving not-so-macho savior type looking at my life from a safe distance and explaining it to me. He thinks he knows, because he's an immigrant, too, but we are not the same. He doesn't live in my reality. He can't grasp the kind of shit I'm going to have to wade through to find my happy ending. Not even a happy ending, I'll just take freedom. Something every other American takes for granted.

"You don't actually believe that," Vitaly says.

Talking to him, I'm reminded of why no matter how often we see each other around the building, we're not actually friends. The know-it-all killjoy aspect of his personality runs deep. He might be book smart, but that doesn't mean the boy knows anything about the way the world actually works.

"You're just going to keep dating creeps?" Vitaly asks. "Until you find the king of all creeps and then marry him?"

"I'm not going to marry a creep."

"Any guy who wants to marry you is a creep."

"Thanks."

Vitaly's cheeks redden but he presses on. "I mean any guy who wants to marry a minor is going to be a creep, Jimena. I don't think I'm saying anything out of turn here."

I throw my hands up and shrug. "Most guys are creeps, anyway. The point is, I can take care of myself."

His little flame of unearned indignation starts to fizzle out, like he finally realizes there's nothing he can say to change my mind and he has to reluctantly accept the plan. I take a moment, too, and try to see Vitaly through a different lens.

One where he comes off as a concerned classmate and neighbor who's just trying to look out for me.

"I know you can take care of yourself," Vitaly says. "But you shouldn't have to. I'm just saying, if you need help, I'm here."

"Well, I don't need help," I say, that last bit of indignity clinging to me like stubborn lint. "Although . . ."

"I won't help you look for creeps," Vitaly starts, but I cut him off with a shake of my head.

"You can tag along, maybe." I'm sounding out the idea before it's fully formed. "I mean, if we're being totally honest, this whole thing *is* a little dangerous."

He seems more than a bit annoyed at having his own argument thrown back in his face, and I'm sorry if we're going in an endless loop here, but what if Vitaly's right? Not about my plan being bad—my plan is brilliant and is definitely going to work—but what if one of these guys I go out with *is* bad news? Like I said, I can take care of myself, but it wouldn't be the worst thing in the world to have Vitaly there as backup. Backup brandishing a textbook, sure, but backup nonetheless.

"You want me to tag along on your dates? Like . . . as your chaperone?"

"Ew, no, you really have no idea how regular people date, do you? You'd be there like a bodyguard." Major stars have bodyguards and they aren't damsels for it. "You could wait for me outside."

"I could *wait for you outside*?" He says it like I just offered him a job without pay. Which . . . well . . . "I have better things to do."

"I wouldn't call homework 'better' per se." Probably

66

shouldn't tease him while I'm asking for his help. I can tell I'm losing him, so I pull out the big guns. The guilt trip. "So first you won't marry me and now you won't even help me out? Are you really going to let me go out and date the big bad men of the world all by my lonesome? Come on, Big Rally, compromise a little."

I can tell that I'm getting through to him, and now I just need to cross the finish line.

"Please." I reach for him and my fingers brush against the golden hairs just above his wrist. It's supposed to be a sign of friendliness, an olive branch to forget our little pseudo spat. It's supposed to show my sincerity. I do not expect the current that flows from his skin up through my fingertips. It's only a moment, this touch, but it's long enough to leave friendliness behind. Which is when I realize I should pull my hand away.

I don't know if Vitaly felt the same thing I did, but his gaze flicks from his forearm back to me. His mind seems set.

"Okay," he says.

With the way my date with Keith went, I didn't expect to finish the night happy. But I smile. With Vitaly's help, I can really put my all into my plan. He has my back, and I didn't realize how much I needed that until now.

12

BY THE NEXT WEEK, I WALK INTO THE CAFÉ WITH
purpose. Same setting as my last date, but I'm not going to let
my experience with Keith color my outlook for today. I have a
new strategy, I'm optimistic, and there's no way this date can
be worse.

I march over to the counter and smile at the barista. "Small
iced caramel latte, skim milk, whipped cream, four pumps of
caramel, please."

He takes my money and starts on the drink. "I like your
hat," I tell him. I'm in a good mood. Nothing's going to get
me down tonight.

He sets the cup between us on the counter. "It's part of the
uniform."

"Well, you make it work!" I take my drink to my usual
table. This is only the second time I've been here, but I decide
this is going to be my spot. If things don't work out with my
date today, I'll bring the next one here, and so on, until I
find my husband. My cheeks burn just thinking of that word.
It's hard to take it seriously when my closest association to it
comes from a deadbeat dad and my doll-playing days with
Barbie and Ken.

But this is never going to work if I let myself get embarrassed over a word. I have to fight the ridiculousness of it all and take this mission seriously. Hard to do when I can feel Vitaly judging me through the window.

He's not thrilled about it, but he is here, so I have to give him credit for following through on his promise to tag along. He's sipping his scalding black decaf coffee on the bench just outside. The coffee is in a tiny paper cup, which makes Vitaly look like he's at a child's tea party. In his other hand he holds open an AP Physics workbook, engrossed in it like it's a spy novel.

It's a good thing I got him to come out. The boy needs to feel the breeze on his face more. I catch his eye. He nods solemnly. I give him a few quick baseball hand signals that mean nothing, just to confuse him. He looks properly confused, then goes back to his studies.

My strategy this go-round is all about being the one with the upper hand. The one in control. No sensory overload electric-blue satin to invite unwanted touching. I'm in the same clothes I wore to school. But aside from that, a big part of being in full control this time is that I'm way out of this guy's league.

Keith was too good-looking, too confident, probably accustomed to flirting by way of unwanted advances. I need a guy who looks like he's never made the first move in his life. A guy who has probably never gone out with girls like me. A guy I can intimidate.

"You sure about this one?" Sof had asked when I matched with him. She'd stared at the picture a long time. "He is . . . how do I say this delicately . . . seriously not cute."

Exactly what I was looking for.

And anyway, I'm not so vain that I can only date hot guys. It's what's on the inside that counts. If I'm going to be out here looking for a husband, then I have to be a grown-up about it. I'm above such childish things as mutual physical attraction.

Plus, as far as I could tell, this guy has zero muscle mass. If he tries anything, I know I can take him.

The bell above the café door chimes and Marvin walks in. Through the window, I can see Vitaly's reaction in real time. He stops reading his workbook, stops sipping his coffee, and just openly gapes at my date. I ignore him.

There are only so many things a dating profile can tell you about someone. What I know about Marvin is that he is a full decade older than me. He works in IT. He likes giraffes. But you can tell a lot more about a person by meeting them in real life. I'm glad I didn't overdress, because Marvin didn't, either. His sweater has holes in it and he wears jeans that are two sizes too big, secured over his waist with a braided leather belt. In the grand scheme of things, his lack of fashion sense doesn't matter. As far as I'm concerned, the most important thing about Marvin are the four sparkling words written in his bio: *Looking for a wife.*

It's like he was talking directly to me. "Hi, Marvin?"

In lieu of hello, Marvin sneezes. "You got a coffee already."

"Oh yeah," I say. "I got here a little early. Do you want to get anything?"

"I don't like the flavor of coffee."

I nod, even though I truly don't understand the words coming out of his mouth. "Tea?"

"I'm saving up for a new computer."

I'm not sure if this is a non sequitur or if he's seriously refusing to spend a couple of bucks on tea for the sake of his computer fund, and my eyes flash to the window, as though Vitaly can hear this exchange and explain it to me. But he's still just staring at Marvin, uselessly. Why did I ever think inviting him to my dates was a good idea? I feel like a mannequin in a store window. No, worse, an animal in the zoo. No, worse, a dead goldfish, floating upside down in a fishbowl.

"A computer," I say, grasping onto this conversation topic like it's a railing on the *Titanic* and the ship is starting to go vertical. "Tell me all about it."

But Marvin shakes his head. "I'd rather not."

It's only been a couple of excruciatingly awkward minutes, but it dawns on me that I have nothing more to say to Marvin. Am I *too* intimidating for him? Did my surefire strategy backfire? Outside, Vitaly watches. He should be doing the valiant thing and turning away from this dumpster fire, sparing me an audience. Instead, he draws a leg up onto the bench so he can pivot fully to the window and get a better vantage point.

I turn my attention back to Marvin. He's breathing through his mouth. I try it, too, as a calming technique. "So, do you have any hobbies?"

"Of course I do," Marvin says. The words float out of him, flutter down to the ground, and die. He stares at me with freakishly large eyes.

"Can you tell me what those hobbies are?" I nearly shout at him.

"I'll do you one better," Marvin says. "I'll show you."

He takes an object out of his fanny pack. It's round and fits into the palm of his hand. Irrationally, the first thought that pops into my mind is *engagement ring*? But then, in one swift motion, Marvin flicks his wrist and a yo-yo nearly takes my nose off. I reel back and gasp, and maybe thinking I'm impressed, Marvin smiles for the first time.

The window muffles Vitaly's laughter, but it's forceful enough to make coffee dribble down his chin.

"If you think that's good, watch this," Marvin says.

The barista with the hat that really isn't that cute, to be honest, is watching my date now, too, and I try to telepathically ask him to call security.

The date was dead on arrival, but because I'm a good person, I keep it on life support for another seventeen minutes. Long enough to learn that Marvin is also good at rolling a quarter over his knuckles, and that he's been looking for a wife for years, to no avail.

Unfortunately for him, he'll have to keep looking. "So, this was fun," I say. "But I think we should probably just . . . stop."

Marvin sighs, already standing. "Yeah, you aren't really my type."

The bell chimes once again as Marvin leaves, and somehow, I feel even worse than I did after my date with Keith.

13

VITALY STILL THINKS IT'S FUNNY TWENTY MIN-
utes later at a burger place around the corner. We're here for
a post-date debriefing. The last thing I want to do is talk about
my second disastrous date, but Vitaly, ever the nerd, thinks it's
important to review. It's dinnertime anyway and I'm hungry,
so I grudgingly go along with it.

But Vitaly is too busy laughing to talk *or* eat his food.
Laughing is the wrong way to put it, though. It's more like
he's trying to hold in his laughter. Like laughing is an alien
concept that isn't natural to his kind, and if he does too much
of it he might have an allergic reaction. Maybe he *is* having
an allergic reaction. His face is beet-red, he's having trouble
breathing, and as much as he's trying to hold it in, the laughter leaks out of the corners of his eyes in fat teardrops he has
to wipe away with his knuckles.

Finally, he gathers enough breath to wheeze out, "The yo-
yo," before dissolving into a puddle again.

I smash a soggy fry into the blob of ketchup on my paper
plate like I'm putting out a cigarette. "It's not that funny."

"Yesitis." A single wheezing word.

The restaurant is pretty full, and most everyone is too

engrossed in their own business to care about ours, but the people at the neighboring table are starting to stare. I try to angle myself so I'm facing away from them, my arm swiping the sticky edge of the table. "I'm so glad my mess of a life is amusing to you."

Vitaly sniffs, makes a real effort to compose himself. Then lays it on thick with a sobering fact. "That guy was wrong for you. You knew it the moment you looked at his profile. And the moment he walked into that coffee shop. And if not then, then definitely the moment he pulled out his *yo-yo*." I can tell the word tickles the back of his throat, and Vitaly takes a bite of his burger like it's an antihistamine.

"You might think it's a joke, but I'm serious about this. I'm doing all this to find a husband. And I *will* find him." But I can't even look Vitaly in the eye as I say it. I only glance at the snuffed-out fry pinched between my fingers, oily and sad and flaccid.

"Okay," Vitaly says. "But you were never going to marry him."

"Why not?"

"Because this isn't just one date, it's a lifetime—or until you have your papers and get divorced, if we're being honest with ourselves. You should be attracted to the person you're going to be looking at every day for the next few years. Can you imagine looking at that guy across the breakfast table for the foreseeable future?"

I try to imagine sitting across from Marvin on a Sunday morning, the *New York Times* spread between us, me with the culture pages, him with the business section, a steaming pot of coffee sweetening the air. But of course I can't.

Maybe it's because he's in front of me, but the only person I'm picturing across my hypothetical breakfast table is Vitaly, sitting as comfortably as he is now, except in sweatpants and a white undershirt. His hair's still mussed from sleep, and he's bringing a mug to his mouth, his lips turning up at the corners with a lazy Sunday smile.

"Tell me I'm wrong," Vitaly says now, his words a sharp pin that pops my daydream soap bubble.

I blink, shift in my seat. "Yes, you should be attracted to whoever you end up with. But looks aren't everything. I care about the way *I* look because it makes me feel good. Even when everything else is going to shit. But I know what guys see when they look at me. Someone pretty and vain and dumb. I know what it's like to be judged only on my looks. I wouldn't do that to someone else."

Though his eyes still glisten and his cheeks are still ruddy, I think all the laughter's finally leaked out of Vitaly. "I'm sorry, I didn't mean to imply that you . . ." He seems unsure how to finish that sentence and buys some time by wiping his mouth with a napkin. When he does speak again, it's on a totally different tangent. "For the record, that's not what I see when I look at you."

I lean an imperceptible mile forward, tuning out the voices in the restaurant, the smell of the greasy food, tuning out everything until it's just the bright blue sky of Vitaly's eyes. I want to know what he really thinks of me. But maybe because my instinct is to tease, or because I want to get back to the lightness of the laughing boy from earlier, or because I'm actually too afraid to know what he really thinks of me, I say, "You don't see someone pretty?"

Vitaly looks anywhere but at me. "That's not what I said."

"That's kinda what you said."

He sighs and starts playing with his napkin. "You're pretty, Jimena, you already know that. You're beautiful." Now Vitaly bites his burger like it's a muzzle. But he can't take it back.

Beautiful.

It's nothing like when Keith said it. That time it made me freeze with alarm. Now it's like a spark that warms me up. "Beautiful" makes "pretty" seem small by comparison. The word has a heft to it, crams itself between us like a brand-new guest at the table that Vitaly and I both have to acknowledge. The word strikes us dumb.

So I ask him a question I know he has an easy answer to.

"Will you marry me?"

"No."

I'm smiling around my milkshake straw when a knock on the window makes us jump. Sof waves at me, though not without tossing a bewildered glance Vitaly's way. She circles to the entrance and doesn't stop until she's standing between us at the edge of our table.

"Jimmy!" she says. "What are you doing here?"

I look at Vitaly for an answer, but he's no help. "Hey! Nothing, just out for a bite."

Vitaly lifts his half-eaten burger, as though for proof, and

Sof eyeballs him before turning back to me. "Didn't you have a date with that guy?"

"Yeah, that didn't turn out so good. So, now I'm out with Vitaly." I quickly correct myself. "Not *out*. He was just here at the same time, so we're eating together. Just like you're suddenly here at the same time. Why are you here?"

"I was at the Sephora and I saw you through the window."

I guffaw. "So random."

Sof nods in agreement but she still looks at us strangely, like it's her who's supposed to be sitting in Vitaly's spot. "So, I guess we'll talk later?"

"Def," I say. I watch Sof go, feeling crummy for lying to her once again.

When I get back home, I find the notebook where I wrote down the contents of my marriage plan and add something to the list. Vitaly probably thinks I'm too thickheaded to listen to what he has to say, but I'm actually very open-minded. Within reason. And he kinda made a good point.

I look down at what I've written, satisfied and ready to keep going with the plan.

Find someone to love who doesn't totally repulse you.

14

THIS LATE IN OCTOBER, SOF AND I LIKE TO GET pumpkin spice lattes before school. We stand on line at the Starbucks two blocks from campus. Across the street, I can see a group of half a dozen Hispanic men standing on the corner. They're always hanging out there, with their work boots and backpacks, some of them with tool belts slung around their waists. I know what they're doing there. It's like an open secret—I think most people know. I wonder if Sof does, though. Would she say they're loitering, or does she know they're waiting to be selected, picked up by a random van belonging to some construction company looking for extra hands for hire?

I have seen those men every time I come to this Starbucks, and though I knew they were undocumented, I never gave them much thought. I did not pity them, and I did not judge them. In retrospect, I think I was trying to avoid thinking about them on purpose. Like if I asked myself too many hard questions—about how I felt about them, about how they were similar to me—it would've scratched an itch in the back of my head that I wanted to leave alone. It would've made me face a truth I wasn't ready for.

When the line at the register moves forward, I realize Sof

has been talking this whole time. She's looking at me expectantly. I'm at a total loss. "Sorry, what?"

"I said we need to talk Culture Club trip ideas!" she says.

Right. Culture Club is a totally useless extracurricular that requires you to visit museums around the city. Thanks to the club, I know the difference between Monet and Manet, Magritte and Matisse, Miró and Mondrian. Like I said—completely useless. But everyone knows the only reason to join is for the year-end field trip. Only seniors are allowed to go, which makes it a popular club among our classmates, but Sof and I joined as juniors, enduring a whole year of the world's foremost masterpieces on display in New York just so that we could beat everybody to the two open spots on the club's trip-planning committee. We get to pick the destination. It's kind of a big deal, which Sof is taking really seriously and which could not be further from my mind.

"I think I already know which place you're going to pick," Sof says as we move up in line. "Which—I think—is exactly the same place I'm going to pick, so let's say our choices at the same time, 'kay?"

There's a lot going on in my life, but that doesn't mean I can just neglect my responsibilities as Culture Club planning committee co-chair. Plus, the trip could be a nice distraction. Just what I need to remind myself that I'm still a normal teenager, despite my current circumstances. "'Kay!"

Sof and I gear up to say our choices, and I know we're going to say the same thing. We're always in sync. A classic pair, like Marissa and Summer on *The O.C.*, except we both consider ourselves Summer because we both have impeccable taste.

"Orlando!"

"Montreal!"

Sof and I stare at each other, dumbfounded. "Can I help you?" asks the woman behind the counter.

Yes, she can help me understand why my best friend just came out of left field with a suggestion to visit *Canada* (???). "Venti pumpkin spice latte with a caramel swirl and whipped cream on top," I say.

"Venti pumpkin spice latte with a shot of *French* vanilla," Sof orders pointedly.

We go off to the side to await our drinks and get some answers. "Why did you just say Montreal?"

"Jimmy, I thought . . . we both . . . I've been talking about Canada nonstop for like the past month."

I try to unscrew my face, but the mounting confusion won't let me. "Yeah, you've been talking about Canada, but I thought that was just a perfectly natural curiosity about our neighbors to the north. Like, 'Who lives in Canada?' And 'Why?'"

In years past, Culture Club has been to Boston, Pittsburgh, and Colonial Williamsburg, and Sof and I were going to blow everyone away with our choice of Orlando. We were going to see the whole world at Epcot! It wasn't in the budget but we'd planned for that, too, cutting most of our scheduled museum visits and replacing them with fun fundraising activities. Or, I guess that's what I thought we were planning.

"No, Jim, I have been talking about how hot Frenchmen are and how we didn't have to travel all the way to France to see them because there's so many of them just walking around in Montreal."

"They're not French, they're CANADIAN. What about Orlando? Disney World!"

"Disney World is for children, and we're about to be adults. As head of the trip-planning committee, don't you want to do something different? Something daring? I want to go to another country. See some *actual* culture. And make out with French guys. They must have double-jointed tongues with all the French they speak."

I pinch the bridge of my nose, just in time for Sof to career into another topic I don't want to talk about right now.

"You never gave me the deets on that ponytail guy you went out with."

I know it has taken all her strength to use "ponytail" instead of "ugly" to describe Marvin, and I'm touched by her effort. "Ugh. It was not good."

"I tried warning you," Sof says. "I don't know why you're doing this to yourself, Jimmy. With the hot older guy, I totally got it, but then when you went for the Ponytail I thought, 'Wait—what?'"

"I'm just trying new things," I say. "And I'm also a very charitable person who believes men with ponytails deserve to go on dates, too." Though, I wonder if maybe Vitaly was right when he said I wasn't serious about my plan. I would never have gone out with Marvin if I wasn't serious. But then again, was it just self-sabotage? Did I pick someone awful as a cop-out so I could force myself not to go through with this marriage plan?

As though she can read my mind, Sof brings up Vitaly. "And what were you doing with Big Rally?"

Our drinks are ready, and it gives me a few seconds of cover before I can come up with a good answer. I can't tell Sof that he's my date chaperone because that's weird. "We were just eating." It sounds defensive, even to my own ears. And Sof hears it that way, too. I don't know if it's my statement that makes her eyes go wide, or a brain freeze headache from the huge sip she just took.

"You were on a *date*?"

"Girl, where at all did you hear the word 'date'? Vitaly was there at the same time I was. It was completely random, just like you showing up there was completely random."

"Okay, but the second you decided to sit down and eat with him, it *became a date*. How do you not realize that?"

I would honestly like to get back to talking about the trip. I need to convince Sof that Orlando is the way to go. Not because it's better (of course Montreal is more exotic than Orlando, and it's the closest place to New York where they speak a different language, making it a true culture clash), but because—well, here goes nothing. "I can't go to Canada."

Sof remains flabbergasted. "Can't or won't?"

"I don't have a passport." It's a solid reason, and the truth. I don't add that I don't have the proper documentation to get a passport. That I wouldn't be allowed back into the US if I leave. That the thought of border control detaining me in front of the whole club gives me hives. But Sof acts like it's nothing.

"Oh, don't worry about that, it only takes, like, max two months to get it done. You have plenty of time."

She's already making concrete plans as we head out. "Can't

you just see us sneaking out of our hotel room? We'll find a bar downtown and use fake IDs to get in. Or maybe the drinking age is lower there, like in England! We'll wear matching black berets and little red neckerchiefs to attract the Frenchiest of the fake Frenchmen. They'll ask us if we need a light—we are definitely trying cigarettes in French Canadia—and then we'll say 'oui' and the French Canadian boys will light our cigarettes with the tips of their own. We'd cough, yes, but the smokiness is essential to set the mood, you know? And pretty soon we'll be making out with the French-ish as romantic smoke swirls around us and jazz music fills the air. Doesn't that sound incredible?"

I can't deny that it does. Way better than Mickey ears.

I glance at the men across the street again. A pickup truck has just arrived and some of them are angling to get a spot on the truck bed, but the driver is handpicking whoever he wants. My heart aches for them.

No matter how much I think I'm living this life that Sof is going on about—the travel, the fun, the dimly lit bar where we're making out with French guys—it is suddenly so clear to me that my reality is a lot closer to the one the men across the street face. The impermanence of where they are, the uncertainty of where they're going.

Sof keeps talking, oblivious to the men. In the back of my mind, I make plans to casually forget to get a passport form and fill it out in time.

15

I THOUGHT OPERATION GREEN CARD WOULD
really start to kick into gear by the end of October, but I'm getting no traction on the dating front. I've decided to stop telling Sof about my suitors, and I think she's forgotten about my dating site profile. She's fully immersed in the flurry of senior year, busy with Culture Club trip planning, filling out college applications, studying for the SATs and Regents. She's too busy to notice that I'm nowhere near that thrilling whirlwind.

I probably should be studying, but I'm at the coffee shop. It's slow tonight. So slow that I feel obligated to make small talk with the barista as he makes me my drink. "Waiting for a date," I tell him. He glances at me briefly, then goes back to concentrating on my order.

It's the same guy behind the counter every time. The two of us don't usually speak, but still, we already know a bit about each other. Like, I know his name is Cary because of his name tag, and judging by the number of times he's seen me here for different dates, he must, on some level, know that I'm on the hunt for a husband for a green card marriage.

Cary hands me my medium butter pecan coffee and I thank him. "I have a good feeling about this one," I say. Cary, bless him, gives me a bemused but encouraging smile.

The bell over the door chimes and I turn to find my date standing there.

"Jimena?" Drew says.

I smile. "You pronounced my name right."

"It's just Jimenez, but with an A at the end, right?"

Point 1 for Drew.

"You already ordered?" he asks. "I would've gotten it for you."

Generous? Well, that's Point 2. I wait beside him as he orders his coffee.

Keith taught me that looks ultimately don't matter. Marvin taught me that, actually, they matter more than I thought. I'm not sure what Drew will teach me, but judging by his profile pic, he's a compromise. Not the hottest guy I've ever seen, but also nowhere near unattractive. And though his profile doesn't mention anything about looking for a serious relationship, at twenty-one he is the youngest guy I found on the site, and the fact that he's even on it at such a young age has to mean he's serious about relationships.

We go to a table and Drew pulls out my chair for me. Point 3 for Drew. He takes a sip from his drink, which looks like something I'd order—pink strawberry swirls and plenty of cream. He hasn't stopped smiling since seeing me, which makes me smile back. I don't want to get my hopes up, but so far the date's starting off strong.

"You're so . . ." He gestures awkwardly at the whole range of me. "You're very nice to look at."

A bit awkward in the delivery, but exceedingly complimentary. Point 4 for Drew! If he gets to five points in under five minutes, I might just propose.

"Thank you." In return, I lob him a compliment, too. "I like your shirt."

Drew looks down and grins wide. "Oh this? It's from my favorite video game, *Wizards of the World*. Do you know it?"

In my stack of *CosmoGirl* articles about how to date successfully, one bit of advice always stood out: Show interest in their interests. So I shake my head and lean in. "What's that?"

That's when Drew launches into the entire history of *WotW*. No questions about me or my interests, just twenty-three straight minutes of ghouls and goblins and a magic centaur ruler in love with a wench who has a magic hoo-ha.

When he pauses for air I speak up. "No."

Drew looks at me like he's remembering for the first time that I'm actually here. "What?"

"I would've loved for this to work out, but sadly, no." I slide out of my seat, toss my empty paper cup in the trash, and leave.

Outside, Vitaly falls into step with me. "I could've told you it never would've worked out."

Such a know-it-all. "Yeah? Why?"

"His shirt," Vitaly says. "That game is like a cult. He was never going to stop talking about it."

I guess that's an unexpected benefit of having Vitaly around. He can warn me about the nerd culture I'm oblivious to. "Marry me?"

"No."

"Wanna go somewhere?" I'm too wired from the roller coaster of once again getting my hopes up only for them to shoot back down like daggers, straight into my heart. Plus, the date ended super early and the night is still young.

"Sure."

The thing about the city is that everything costs money. All I see around us are restaurants, bars, coffee shops, and stores, and Vitaly and I are both broke. But then I spot a crowning jewel of cheap—nay, free!—thrills. "Let's go over there."

The playground is tucked away inside Union Square Park. But because of the late hour, it is mercifully devoid of children.

Still, Vitaly seems hesitant to enter, like someone might call the cops on him for being a grown guy in a playground. Or he's just got a case of his usual skepticism at discovering a place designed for fun. I try to picture Vitaly as a little boy in Russia, swinging from the monkey bars. Can't do it.

I head for the slides. There are two of them, divided by a two-inch bumper, and I go up the steps and crouch through the metal arch that seems designed to keep little bodies safe and my body out. I slide down and my feet touch the ground two seconds later. "I think I may have outgrown this." But I don't get up. There are so few places in the city to truly lie back, so I do it here, my head resting on the cool stainless steel.

Vitaly watches me, hands in his peacoat pockets. After a moment he comes to sit on the slide next to mine. And then, after another moment, he lies back, too. Just beyond the playground, which sits in a sunken part of the park, shrouded by trees, there's light coming from apartment windows and streetlights, there's foot and vehicle traffic, and there's not a bit of quiet, or anything like stillness. But all the sounds of voices and car engines mix together until it's the sort of ambient noise we New Yorkers stop noticing after a while.

The threat of winter looms in the air, but I'm relishing the fact that I can still enjoy the outdoors for a little bit longer. And that at least there's another body here for warmth. I turn my face to Vitaly, who is staring up at the starless black sky. This close, I spot the tiny scar at the top of his ear, and the memory pops into my head of the last time I noticed that scar.

A smile sneaks its way across my lips. "Remember that night in the summer? When we were thirteen?"

It's dark, but Vitaly flushes red like a stoplight. The muscles in my stomach tighten, because I feel both sorry that he's all embarrassed and just a little thrilled that I can elicit that sort of emotion from him. I must admit, saying something to make him blush is my absolute favorite game. I have to bite my lip to keep from full-on grinning.

In typical Vitaly fashion, he flees so fast from the topic he lands at a completely different one. "So, did Sof ever ask you what we were doing together at the burger place?"

"Yeah. But she mostly just wanted to talk about Culture Club." I've tried not to think about Montreal, but I can't help it. Damn Sof for making me spend so much mental headspace on Canada of all places. "What's it like to travel?"

Vitaly turns his face to me, his expression betraying his question. "You really want to know?"

I sweep a strand of hair behind my ear. "Mhmm."

"It's nothing special."

"You don't have to lie just to make me feel better."

He seems to struggle with this, taking his time debating whether to keep lying or to be honest. "It's incredible," he finally says, an apology laced between the words. "There's a whole world out there. And New York is great, but it's just a tiny fraction of it."

I nod and try to tamp down the pang of jealousy blooming in my chest. Jealousy and longing.

"Sof wants the Culture Club to go to Montreal." It's supposed to be a fun surprise, so I shouldn't be telling one of the members, but Vitaly does me the favor of acting the opposite of excited.

"Canada?"

"She wants to try somewhere more exotic this year."

Vitaly lets out a scornful "*pfft*" that I think I'm correct in translating as *Canada? Exotic?*

"I know."

"What are you going to do?"

I shrug, but my shoulders are trapped against the slide's bumpers. "Skip the trip."

"Why don't you tell Sof about what's going on? She'd change the location."

"Because people have really strong opinions about immigration. People . . . I mean, people hate illegal immigrants."

Vitaly doesn't insult my intelligence by trying to argue that fact. "But Sof's your best friend. She's not going to hate you."

"Maybe. I don't know. I just don't want to tell people."

"You told *me*." It isn't a question, which is good, because I wouldn't know how to answer it if it were. But I see his eyes cloud with murkiness, a storm is rolling into his mind, and I realize instantly that Vitaly is taking this the wrong way—that maybe he's thinking, *You told me because I'm no one to you.*

That isn't it at all, and I don't want him to think that for another second. "I told you because I felt safe telling you."

All this time I didn't know why I'd shared my status with Vitaly, but when I say this out loud, I know it's the truth. And now I've done it; I've said something that makes *me* blush instead of him. I turn my face toward the sky and hope he doesn't notice, and we stay lying on the slides, our city blaring around us.

16

THE NEXT MONDAY, SOF AND I STAND IN FRONT
of the Culture Club to announce the location of the senior trip.
It has already been approved by Ms. Shea, our faculty adviser,
though I hope to sneak in a vote to see if anyone would prefer
Disney World to maple leaves and universal health care. But as
soon as Sof mentions Montreal, the decision is made. The club
erupts with approving cheers. Well, most of the club. Logan
Discka and Luke Park sit on top of their desks in the back of
the class, mouthing the words "What the fuck?" at each other.
Logan and Luke are, shall we say, unequivocally dim, but they
are the most popular boys in school. If those two knuckleheads
don't want to go to Canada, that could swing the entire club
my way. I latch on to them.

"Logan, Luke?" My voice rises over the excited murmurs
simmering throughout the classroom. "Do you guys have
concerns?"

"Yeah," Logan says. "What's in Montreal?"

The club seems to think this is a good question, because
they all swivel in their seats to face Sof and me, suddenly wondering the same. Sof doesn't have an answer, so she makes me
come up with one. "Jimmy, tell them what Montreal has."

I respond truthfully. "Montreal has poutine."

Logan and Luke howl simultaneously and high-five each other.

"Poutine is a *food!*" I clarify, feeling all my hopes and dreams slip from my grasp. "It's soggy fries!" But the club is back to being completely on board. In the front row, Vitaly's eyes meet mine, soft with sympathy.

I wallow for the rest of the club meeting.

"Hey, before you go!" Sof waves me down just as I'm trying to book it. "We gotta start on our college apps."

"What?" My mind is still on the Montreal trip.

"UCLA, remember? We have to start working on our applications. Wanna meet up this weekend to fill them out together?"

Sof and I made a pact to go to Los Angeles for college together. She would pursue her dream of eventually landing a role on a reality TV show, and I would see what Rodeo Drive was all about. But I don't even know if that's possible anymore. Either way, it's definitely not something I have the brain space for right now. "I can't this weekend. But yeah, soon."

"'Kay," Sof says. "Lemme know when."

―――

At home that night, I ask my mom about college over dinner. I clear my throat and rake the rice on my plate with my fork. "Ya es tiempo de empezar my applications para college."

My mom looks kind of skeptical, which is not the response a parent should typically have when their child brings up college applications, but nothing about my life is typical. "Estaba pensando en Los Angeles. Para estudiar," I say.

And now my mom actually looks kind of affronted. Like maybe I've insulted her somehow? She puts down her fork and clasps her hands together, still making sure to keep her elbows off the table. "¿Y por qué quieres ir hasta Los Angeles?"

I shrug, because I really don't have a very good reason for wanting to go across the country. "Sof quería ir . . ."

"Sof es Sof," my mom says. "Tú no tienes que hacer todo lo que hace tu amiga. ¿Cómo vas a pagar la matrícula en otro estado?"

I swallow, and I realize how unprepared I am to answer my mom's questions about out-of-state tuition. The answers I once had are no longer relevant. But I try them anyway. "Hay financial aid . . ."

"No para algien como tú."

Financial aid is one thing—I know I can't ask for federal money, or loans, but, "Scholarships," I blurt out. "Scholarships no tienen nada que ver con el gobierno."

"Te van a pedir un número social."

It's so obvious, and I should've given it even a moment's thought before bringing it up with my mom. Of course I'd need a Social Security number for loans or scholarships. Probably for out-of-state schools, too.

"¿Si te piden tu social, qué vas a hacer? No lo puedes arriesgar."

My mom is right. I can't risk it. And any hope I had about college sinks deep into my gut, never to be seen again. I don't know if it's this, on top of the Culture Club meeting earlier, but pinpricks of tears sting the corners of my eyes. It's all bullshit. The fact that I have to deal with all this, that every dream

I had for my life is up in smoke, that I'm out here looking for a husband to solve my problems. I feel like a mouse in a lab—in a maze—having to navigate risks and land mines, all while avoiding these shadowy figures who are out to get me. I'm being saddled with all this through no fault of my own, and it. Is. *Bullshit.*

The tears threatening to spill aren't sad—they're full of rage and frustration.

"I don't get why you couldn't just go through the proper channels when we immigrated here. Now I have to pay for all your mistakes."

I say it in English because it's the clearest I can be with my feelings. Because I don't know how to say "proper channels" in Spanish, and though the word for "mistakes" should be easy, it totally eludes me right now. Because I don't even know if "pay for your mistakes" makes sense in Spanish or if it would just sound like some nonsense idiom. Because I don't want to have to translate every single word in my head first and potentially talk myself out of saying what I really mean in the moment.

I can't just sit here with my mom's gigantic doorstopper copy of *Inglés sin Barreras* every time we wanna talk. I'm jealous of my friends who can just talk freely with their parents. I know most teens and parents don't understand each other, but this is on a whole different level.

My mother doesn't understand me. Not fully. Maybe she grasps something from the context, my tone of voice, but when I speed through a string of words in a language she's not fluent in—it's not enough. I may as well have spoken to an empty room. But she doesn't have to pick up a single word to know that whatever I just said was disrespectful.

"¿Piensas que sabes más que yo? Es hora de que entiendas cómo son las cosas. Tienes que aceptar que no todo va a salir como lo soñaste."

In so many words she tells me I'm a child who knows nothing, that it's time for me to wise up and accept that I'm not going to realize my dreams. That's one thing about English; it's a lot more succinct. She could've just said the words "Grow up" and saved herself some breath.

I hate having a language barrier with my own mother. I'll always have to parse through my words, translate, find alternatives when I'm unsure of something. Sometimes, I wonder if my mother will ever know how I'm truly feeling, no matter how hard I try to tell her.

The lines in her forehead begin to smooth out and she sighs. She tells me that I can put college on hold and start making money, that she can find me under-the-table jobs that can provide security. She's trying to paint it like a safe, dependable future, but all I see is a lifetime living off the grid, no vacation days, no upward mobility, no benefits. No hope. I've seen that life on my mom, and I don't want it.

I push my plate away and stand. "Ya no tengo apetito."

17

STANDING AT THE COFFEE SHOP'S CONDIMENTS
bar, I check all the milk thermoses until I find the skim, then I
pour till my cup nearly runneth over.

"I know you try to avoid whole milk, but studies show that
whole is ultimately better for bone density," Vitaly says.

It is starting to become clear why he has never ever been on
a single date. Throwing around words like "studies show" and
"bone density" in casual conversation is definitely one way to
kill a mood. "You sure I can't marry you?"

Vitaly rolls his eyes but he's smiling. "No."

He pours a tiny bit of milk into his take-out coffee cup, and
I grin, triumphant. A couple of months ago he would've taken
his coffee black as mud. But my delicious taste is rubbing off
on him. It's only a matter of time before he adds a bit of sugar,
and who knows, maybe one day he'll go totally off the rails
and try some whipped cream.

"I'm sorry about the college thing," Vitaly says.

I told him about the conversation I had with my mom two days
ago, my college hopes officially dashed. That, plus the announcement of the Montreal trip, have been a double whammy of bum-
mers. But self-pity is not good for my complexion. The only way
to get past an overwhelming tide of disappointment is to line up

an overwhelming number of dates. I've scheduled to meet with a new suitor every day for the next week. I figure one of them's gotta stick.

Vitaly plucks a wooden stirrer from the collection and draws circles in his coffee. "I never actually asked you what you envision for yourself, in terms of your future. What did you want to study?"

His question shouldn't stump me, but it does. College was never about studying for me. It was about getting away and meeting new people and partying and sororities and picking a major under duress during my floundering sophomore year so I could graduate. "I don't know."

Vitaly interrupts his methodical stirring to shoot me a bemused look. I'm not sure I appreciate it. There is an unspoken implication there that if I'm fighting for a future, I should have a clear vision of what it will look like. But I don't. I have no idea what I want to be when I grow up. I just know I want the freedom to find out. I want to stumble through life and fail at a million things and live recklessly in my twenties before eventually settling down in my thirties—hopefully knowing what I want out of life by then.

"And what about you?" I say. "You know I wasn't paying attention during your whole five-year-plan presentation, but if I recall correctly, there wasn't any specific job in there. Just a vague position at a Fortune 500."

The boy goes back to stir mode, even though his shots of decaf and bone-density milk could not be more acquainted with each other. I stand there and sip my drink slowly, waiting for an answer.

Finally, Vitaly sighs. "Okay, so I don't know exactly what job I want. But the 'what' is not important. All I need is something that's going to pay well, something I can rely on until I retire. I want to clock in at nine and leave at five. Good benefits. 401K. Simple as that."

I stare at him, jaw practically on the floor, because who in their right mind dreams about a nine-to-five? "You're killing yourself to go to Oxford just to live on autopilot?"

I may not have a very desirable future, but it still sounds better than what his looks like.

"I just don't want to struggle," Vitaly says. "I'm not interested in wandering around aimlessly looking for something I'm passionate about. Passion doesn't usually go hand in hand with stability. This path may seem boring to you, but I know I'm not going to get lost along the way, so long as I keep my eyes forward. No detours."

"No adventure."

I feel kind of bad for challenging him on his neatly packaged life plan. So I impulsively pluck a packet from the bins of sugar and hand it to him as a peace offering. He doesn't tear it open and pour it into his coffee, but he doesn't reject it, either. He slips the sugar packet into his pants pocket, and I take one and do the same.

"Are you going to prom?" I ask him.

"That came out of nowhere."

I sip my coffee, lick some foam off the top of my lip. "You need some fun in your life."

"Prom's not for months."

"Want to go together?"

The poor guy is at a loss for words. He opens and closes his mouth like a fish on land trying not to die.

"If I'm not seriously dating anyone by then, I think we should go together," I say. "Let me do you this one kindness."

"As, like, a favor to me?" Vitaly says it like he's all offended, a pity date, but let's be real—he should be so lucky.

"Sure," I say.

"Fine."

"Great."

"Um, excuse me? Jimena?"

Vitaly and I turn at the same time to find Allen, my date. Who knows how long he's been waiting?

"Happy hunting," Vitaly murmurs. He goes out the door and I lead Allen to our table.

My overwhelming string of dates is overwhelmingly disastrous.

I tell Allen all about my interests, my values, my hobbies, and Allen asks me how much I weigh.

My next date, with Pace student Rufus, is only slightly better, but I lose all interest when he tells me I don't look like I read books.

Fedora-wearing Daniel spends most of our date staring at my boobs. It is not discreet. Both Vitaly in the window and Cary behind the counter notice, and the two offer up a thumbs-down when they catch my attention.

Marcus doesn't stare at my boobs, but he also just plain doesn't pay any attention to me whatsoever, too busy texting on his phone while simultaneously asking me a list of standard first-date questions.

Brett is okay. Boring, but inoffensive, and that's light-years better than all the dates that came before him. We chat pleasantly for a while, but then someone walks into the coffee shop who steals all my attention. He looks like he's college-aged, a backpack slung over one shoulder. But it's not who he is or what he looks like or where he goes to school. The most interesting thing about him is the shirt he wears. It is black with bold red letters, and the words on it take my breath away.

UNDOCUMENTED AND UNAFRAID.

Time stops a little. I feel a kinship so strong to this stranger that my fingers buzz in my lap, almost like they want to reach out to him. I want to ask him a million questions, about how he stopped being scared, about how he's living in a country where he isn't recognized as a member of society. I want to know his secrets, I want to know how he's navigating through this world with such ease, like he isn't swimming against violent currents. But I am frozen to my seat.

His shirt tells me this guy is like me, but he and I have one glaring difference that separates us. I'm undocumented and very afraid.

18

SOF WANTS TO WORK ON OUR COLLEGE APPS after school, but I convince her to go to Kings Plaza instead. It's been a while since we've been to the mall, and I think we both need the mindless shopping excursion. She's been busy with school stuff and I've been busy with dating for my green card marriage, and it's nice to take a break from all that and browse the cheap jewelry at Claire's.

"What do you think?" Sof says, holding a dangly blue bauble to her lobe. "Too *Girl with a Pearl Earring*?"

"Not enough *Girl with a Wineglass*, if you ask me."

Sof snickers and gives me a deranged smile like the girl in the painting, and we both crack up. We amuse ourselves with our little Vermeer jabs, but there's no denying he's the most talented of the old masters. I guess Culture Club has been good for something after all.

"I've been looking over our application essays," Sof says, moving on to a display of necklaces. "I think yours is pretty much done, honestly. It just needs a few touch-ups."

"Yeah?" I try for nonchalance. We'd written practice college application essays for English class last year. Nobody really took the assignment seriously, but I had what I thought was a surefire topic at the ready. My American Dream. It was all about being an immigrant and how I'd be the first person in my family to attend college here. I forgot I'd given it to Sof to keep with her essay, for when we'd eventually apply together. "I was thinking of writing a new essay. That was just a practice one."

"Well, the deadline's coming up. I think it's good enough as it is."

I nod and wonder how to get off this topic. How did I get to a place where hanging out with my best friend can feel both like a lifeline and a time bomb? Sof is my person. She's the only one I have inside jokes with about obscure artworks. We're like Meredith Grey and Cristina Yang, except we both consider ourselves the Cristina of the duo because we both have impeccable taste. And yet, at any moment, she might step on a conversational land mine, and suddenly I freeze up, trying to avoid having to lie to her once again. The necklace aisle in Claire's is not the place to tell her that we aren't going to college together. So I bring up something that's safe, something I know she'll want to talk about.

"Any idea who you're taking to prom?"

"That's months away," she says. "But of course I've been thinking about it." She launches into her list of candidates, guys she has crushes on and guys who'll do in the clutch.

"What about the Dog?" He took Sof to his senior prom last year, and she couldn't stop talking about it for weeks. I only bring him up because yesterday I spied Sof doodling a poodle on her spiral notebook, and she only ever draws puppies when she's thinking about the Dog. The margins of her loose-leaf papers were decked out with bulldogs whenever the two of them were in a fight, old English sheepdogs at the height of their happiness, and for the periods of longing—after break-ups but before getting back together—the poodles.

The side of Sof's mouth twitches with a smile. "He texted me a few days ago."

I shove her so hard she lets out a yelp. "What?!" I squeal.

"I didn't say anything because I don't know what it means."

"Lemme see."

She fishes her phone from her purse and flips it open for me.

Sup. The Dog's message is simple, but his intentions are loud as a bark. "He wants you bad."

"I knoooow." The word stretches from her lips the way her love story with the Dog surely stretches through space and time. I don't know if they're the real thing, but they've been on-again, off-again since we were sophomores, and it wouldn't surprise me if they kept going like that for the next decade. "But I don't need a boy in my life right now. It's senior year. I need to look forward. As Kelly Clarkson says, I'm Miss Independent."

I can't relate. But whatever she decides to do with the Dog, I'll support her. I'm rooting for the two of them. "Throw the guy a bone."

"I dunno, I need time to think." Sof shakes her head like she's trying to clear it. "What about you? Still over high school boys?"

"They are the last thing on my mind."

"But prom. You can't go stag."

I could tell Sof I already asked Vitaly. But she'd want to know why, and I don't have a very good answer for her. Why *did* I ask him? I'm trying to picture it now, him in a tux trying to bust a move. But I think if he set foot on a dance floor, he might spontaneously combust.

"Did you ask Vitaly Petrov?!" Sof's eyes go wide and so do mine, because *how the hell does she know?* "It's all over your face!" she says.

Have we reached the telepathic stage of our friendship? How has she not figured out my illegal secret at this point?

"You get that faraway look on your face whenever you think or talk about him!"

"Okay!" I admit. "He's my friend. I told him that if we were both dateless by the time prom rolled around, I'd let him take me because I'm generous of spirit and kind of soul . . ." I trail off. We both know I am neither kind nor generous. And judging by the look on Sof's face, she isn't buying what I'm selling.

"Why won't you tell me that you like him?"

"I do not like him," I say, really stepping on the words. It's the truth, and I have no idea why she's grilling me about this. She only saw us at the burger place that one time. "I promise you."

Sof sighs. "It just feels like you're hiding something."

And that's the thing about best friends. They know.

Sof picks up a charm bracelet and looks around before surreptitiously slipping it into her bag. She holds an identical bracelet for me to steal, too. But I place it back on the rack. My days of casual shoplifting with my best friend are behind me.

The look in Sof's eye, it's like I'm a stranger to her. And any hope I had that I'd convinced her I'm not hiding anything is good and dashed.

19

I DON'T EVEN REMEMBER THIS NEW GUY'S NAME,
but I'm very bored. Outside, Vitaly sits on the bench in front
of the window, bundled up in a ski cap, gloves, and a scarf
wrapped around the bottom of his face. He's reading a classic
novel that is definitely not on the AP English syllabus.

What a loser.

I'd rather be hanging out with him.

"Hey . . . guy . . . this was fun," I say, standing suddenly.
"But I gotta go."

"Oh, okay." My date clumsily stands, too, and we both
walk to the door. We say our awkward goodbyes, and Vitaly
waits for him to leave before getting up from the bench. "Not
a match?"

I shake my head. "Let's go."

It's coat weather, yuletide season, first-snow-crunching-
underfoot time. But Vitaly and I defiantly munch on snow
cones. We found them at the bottom of the freezer in a grocery store and tossed their crinkly plastic wrappers in a trash
can on the street corner. Vitaly's is blue-flavored, mine is red.

"In Peru this is called raspadilla."

"You have to try Russian ice cream. It's called . . . it's called—" He snaps his fingers, then waves them around, trying to grab hold of the word. "I forget, but it's amazing."

I slurp some more red. The only time I ever hear Vitaly speaking Russian is when he's with his parents. It's easy to forget he speaks another language. He doesn't have a foreign accent, doesn't even have a Brooklyn accent. Just like I don't.

"Do you remember when you first realized you were talking more in English than you were in Russian?"

Vitaly chomps on ice and nods. "I don't remember what I said, but I must've asked my mom a question in English— something that I easily could've asked her in Russian. And my dad smacked me upside the head and asked why I was making my mom work so hard to have a conversation. And from then on, that was the rule. Only Russian at home."

I don't remember when the divide happened. Only that one day I knew every word in the Spanish dictionary and the next my mom was looking at me like she couldn't decipher a single word out of my mouth. I'm losing more and more Spanish every day. Like Vitaly, who no longer remembers the name of his favorite ice cream.

We walk in silence for a while, finishing our snow cones.

We aren't really going anywhere at all, just wandering below Fourteenth and randomly choosing which direction to turn when we reach a corner. The glow from busy stores and restaurants spills onto the streets, the trees sparkle with string lights. It's cold out, but it's also beautiful.

I thought spending time with Sof was what I needed to take

my mind off things, but honestly? This works better. With Vitaly there are no conversations I need to avoid. Our post-date talks are easy, and just the breath of fresh air I need to recharge.

When we reach the corner, Vitaly swallows the last drop of blue, then crumples the soggy paper cone in his fist and tosses it in a city trash can. "Which way?"

I point east for no good reason.

Vitaly follows my direction and it's almost like he's trying to prove he can be spontaneous. It's so adorable I could pinch his cheeks. And maybe I should because . . . "You look dead."

He stops in his tracks. "What?"

"Your lips." They're very blue. "You look like a corpse."

"Gee, thanks. You look . . ."

He stares at my mouth, trying to come up with an insult, but I brandish my most winning smile. There's a reason I always pick red snow cones, and it's because they make me look the opposite of dead. My luscious cherry lips are swollen from the cold and I smack them together, waiting for Vitaly to take his best shot. But the boy is good and lost.

It's funny, he looks frozen and dead, but the longer his gaze lingers on my mouth, the more alive I feel. And warm. I could swear there's a heat flushing up my neck. And does he really look that dead, anyway? The blue of his lips actually brings out the blue of his eyes. It's really kind of . . .

It's really kind of . . .

I get lost somewhere in the blue, and suddenly it isn't so cold anymore because my insides feel liquid, melting.

"Marry me?"

The temperature drops again in the time it takes Vitaly to deliver his typically swift standard answer. It arrives in a solemn, cloudy puff. "No." He sniffs and starts to walk again. "You have a problem."

Not what I was expecting. "Excuse me?"

"You haven't had any success with your scheme yet."

I catch up to him. *"Plan."*

"Right, plan. You're—for all intents and purposes—a pretty good catch. You should at least be getting some second dates."

"It's not me not being able to get a second date," I say. "It's the guys not being worthy of second dates because *ew*."

"Well, yeah, that's part of the problem. There's no reason you shouldn't be able to find someone who's more suitable for you. What if we take a mathematical approach?"

I can't believe how many times I have to explain to him how human dating works. "Big Rally, you can't fix a date with math."

"I'm serious. With the right analytics and the information provided to us by these guys' profiles, I could narrow down your dating pool to people you'll actually want to see again. Because the way it is now, your dates are soul-crushing."

"They are not soul-crushing."

Vitaly stops. "I have box seats to your dates, Jimena. Trust me: They're soul-crushing."

I take a moment to ponder this. Maybe Vitaly's right. The dates have all been uniformly terrible. And if he's willing to do homework to make my life easier, why shouldn't I take him up on it? He *is* the smartest person I know.

"Okay, go wild."

Vitaly smiles, excited as a geek with extra credit.

20

TWO NIGHTS LATER, VITALY'S AT MY FRONT DOOR, laptop, notebook, and charger stacked in his hands. But he isn't here to pick me up. We need a place to plug in, and we're going to do this thing in my room. There's just the small matter of getting past my mom.

"Quién es?" she asks from the living room.

"El vecino."

"'El vecino'?" Vitaly repeats. "Not sure what that means, but it makes me sound cool."

"An impossible task." I grab the Neighbor by the forearm and try to quickly usher him through the apartment, but my mom is remarkably quicker.

"Oh, hello, Vitty." A glowing smile flashes over my mom's face. I have no clue if this is a nickname she's already established with Vitaly, or if she simply doesn't realize that's not his name. But my mom's smile is a master class of charm offensive, and Vitaly accepts his new name like he was born with it.

"Hi, Mrs. Ramos."

"How is your mother? You say hello to her?"

"She means say hello on her behalf," I explain.

"He knows what I saying." My mom shoos away my explanation with a flick of her wrist.

"She's good, thanks. And I will."

"¿Desde cuándo se conocen?" my mom asks me. The thing about knowing a second language is that you can have a private conversation right in front of the person you're talking about.

"Desde que somos vecinos. We really should get going."

"¿Hacer tarea?"

"Yep." This is definitely a type of homework.

"¿A solas? ¿En tu cuarto?"

"Ma, like I said, *solo somos vecinos*." It's important to reiterate the fact that Vitaly is first and foremost my neighbor. He may be a classmate, and also my date chaperone/bodyguard, and possibly my prom date if I don't have a husband by then, and definitely a boy, but if my mom is going to let us cross into my bedroom, "neighbor" has to be his only descriptor.

"Qué chico tan desabrido," my mom says, giving Vitaly a not-so-discreet once-over. I have to bite back my laugh at her assessment of him. It's the same word you'd use to describe unseasoned boiled chicken. "Pero esos ojos son . . . eléctricos."

Is she seriously swooning over his *electric eyes* right now? I pull Vitaly's arm and my mom finally lets us through, but not before ordering me to keep the door open. Naturally, I close it fully like I didn't hear her.

Vitaly has never been in my apartment before, let alone my room, and he takes a moment to look around. I think I have a pretty typical room for a girl my age. There's golden twinkle lights lacing the wall behind my bed, torn magazine ads taped up above my desk, four-by-six photo prints of me and my friends everywhere. Vitaly steps up to a few of the pictures, studying them closely, and it makes me suddenly self-conscious. The photos are a record of my popularity. Maybe also of my vanity. I wonder if Vitaly sees them that way. He prob def has noticed that there are too few books in here. Ugh, inviting him over was a bad idea.

I should've tidied up before he showed. There are clothes piled on my desk chair and magazines on the floor. The top of my dresser is overflowing with loose bits of things I should've trashed a while ago. At least I had the forethought to toss a wayward bra in the closet minutes before he rang the doorbell.

I don't know why I even care what he thinks my room says about me. When I was younger, I never had any friends over. Whatever apartment I lived in, I knew they weren't more than glorified shacks. I was always ashamed of how strange my living space was compared to other people's. How little we had. This apartment is huge compared to the others I've lived in. Sof comes over all the time. But with Vitaly, it's like he can look at everything I own—my garbage and treasures—and see straight into my soul.

Not that I actually care that Vitaly's getting a private showing of my inner sanctum. I shake my head because that sounds so wrong, and now Vitaly isn't looking at the things in my room, he's looking right at me like he can read my mind. But then his glance drifts past me, settling on something on my bookshelf.

He picks up the binder and opens it with the kind of reverence and curiosity that would be better reserved for my underwear drawer. But this is Vitaly, and he cares more about school supplies than whatever's in my dresser. The binder holds various Student of the Month awards from elementary school; old (good) report cards; my first-place finish for knowing the multiplication tables the fastest in third grade; a photo of me, Sof, and a few of our friends on the Winter Formal court last year; a book report from seventh grade that I kept because Mrs. Steiner marked the cover page with a glowing paragraph about how far I'd come with my vocab skills.

"What's all this?" Vitaly asks, careful not to bend the plastic sheet protectors as he turns the pages.

"I've been doing research on what kind of documentation I'll need to show officials. For when I'm ready to become a citizen. They'll want proof that I'm an upstanding, good person. A model student . . ." Deserving of being in this country. Of staying.

The binder is still open in Vitaly's hands, but he's stopped turning the pages in order to watch me. And do my eyes deceive me or are his going kind of glassy? I know I'm not the most exemplary student. I'm not on the honor roll or in all AP classes like he is. Suddenly my paltry achievements seem pathetic in his hands. *A picture from Winter Formal? Multiplication tables champ?* Is that really all I have to show this country? Vitaly's looking at me like I just pinched him in the heart or something.

Pity was the number one reason I never invited friends over in the first place, and I guess I still have a chip on my shoulder about it because I snatch the binder from him, probably too harshly. I cram it between books on the shelf. Not only do I hate the pity, I hate how I'm reacting to this whole situation. I hope I didn't just make things more awkward than they already were. I don't do awkward.

"Make yourself comfortable."

Vitaly nods, though he doesn't make a move. "Where should I sit?"

My one chair is a mess of clothes, so I point to the bed. I always tell my mother not to make it, that I'll get to it eventually, but she makes my bed whenever I'm not looking, like an unfunny prank. Right now, I'm grateful.

I take Vitaly's power cord—why does everything sound so wrong in my head all of a sudden!—and plug it into the outlet next to my nightstand. "Before we start, I did some homework, too." I swipe a loose-leaf paper from my unzipped backpack on the floor. "This is a list of things I am looking for in a perfect partner. I thought it might be useful for your data. There's data involved, yes?" I clear my throat, not waiting for his answer lest he launch into mind-numbing math-speak. "Number one, good sense of humor."

Vitaly opens his mouth to say something, but I stop him before he can start. "I know, you probably thought I'd put 'really hot' right at the top, but once again, I am not the vain monster you make me out to be."

"I was only going to say that your list isn't necessary. I already did the work."

I slump down next to him on the bed. "Well, what an absolute waste of the two minutes I spent on it."

Vitaly flips his laptop open and rests it on his knees. It's an old model, and it hums loudly the second he turns it on. *That's what she said.* I officially hate myself for the dumb *Office* reference. I need to get a grip, I don't know what's going on with me. Am I somehow freaking out that Vitaly's in my room? He should be the one freaking out. He's the one who hasn't met a room he can't be awkward in. Yet here I am, stiffly sitting beside him on the edge of my bed, the only sound in the room the laptop's disapproving hiss.

Vitaly's document finally loads. The first slide fills the screen with big purple letters.

WHY CAN'T JIMENA LAND A GUY?

I lean in and squint to get a better look at the subtitle, even though its font is at least twenty points big.

A STRATEGY TO HELP JIMENA GET
TO DATE NUMBER TWO.

I turn to him, still fully squinting. "You made a PowerPoint presentation about my ineptitude at dating? Is this a joke?"

"I never joke about PowerPoint, Jimena."

I reach for the touch pad, and the laptop wobbles as Vitaly shifts his legs. I glance at him, wondering if he's not comfortable with me touching his stuff, but he avoids my gaze, so I go ahead and scroll. Section 1 is titled, *Who is Jimena Ramos?* Below that, he's written:

Objective: Find more suitable matches by comparing
and contrasting known personality traits.

Key points about Jimena:

- Bold, blunt, impulsive. Jimena says exactly what's
  on her mind and likes to act first, think second.

I whip around to face him. "Who do you think you are?
This is so . . . so . . ." There is no one word to describe what
this is, but it's cold, analytical, judgmental, and I don't like it.
"You made a list of all my faults?"

"Not faults," Vitaly says, "traits. I tried to make it as objective and precise as possible."

"Yeah? Well, this reads like my last report card. Do you
honestly think you know me well enough to list my personality
traits in neat little bullet points?"

Vitaly slowly juts his chin at the screen, prompting me to
keep reading.

- Argumentative, hardheaded, and stubborn, but
  will ultimately listen to reason.

Point taken.

Vitaly clears his throat. "You know what? Maybe this was a
bad idea. You're right, it's weird that I wrote all this, and it's
even weirder that you're reading it now, so we don't have to
d—"

I shush him and keep scrolling. A few minutes ago I was
wondering what Vitaly really thought about me. And this document is full of just those thoughts. I may not like it, but if
I stop thinking about myself for a minute, I realize that this
could actually tell me more about Vitaly than it could about

me. If I want to know what Vitaly sees when he looks at me, all I have to do is keep reading.

- Determined and optimistic to a fault. Even with numerous obstacles in her way, Jimena will only see them as small speed bumps.

- Nimble and capable. Jimena is able to straddle multiple worlds—her public-facing life at school, her home life, and her inner life, without letting any of them intermingle.

- A dreamer. Jimena's vision of her own future is hazy, but she will stop at nothing to fight for it.

- Jimena possesses the resilience and emotional maturity of someone older than her age.

- Intelligent, charming, and somewhat free-spirited.

"Only somewhat?" I say, but I keep my face turned toward the screen to hide my smile. The PowerPoint isn't that critical and cold, after all. It's actually, weirdly, kind of intimate.
And then I read the next bullet point.

- Guarded.

It's just one word, but compared to all the other points, full of adjectives and explanation, this one word feels loaded.

And it gives me pause, not because I don't agree, but because I do. Before I knew I was undocumented, I was an open book. I faced the world head-on, unafraid. But living with my new-found status means hiding it. It means privacy and fear and not letting people in. I didn't think anyone could see through the facade. But Vitaly does.

I fight every impulse to deny or be snarky, because he'd probably see through that, too, wouldn't he? It's funny how being called guarded can make you feel so exposed.

Vitaly taps on one of the many browser windows he has open. "I had to create a profile on the dating site you use. Opposite sex, so I could browse the guys, and before you ask, no, I will not show—"

I bulldoze his hand away from the keyboard. He tries to fight for control, but I grip the heavy laptop like it's the last cashmere sweater at a Black Friday sale at Loehmann's. Vitaly makes an attempt at grabbing it, but barely. He can't restrain me. He could probably tickle me, but I'm not sure he's familiar with the concept. And the moment his fingers graze my fore-arm, they fall away like they've been electrocuted.

Vitaly is no match for me. Or should I say, *Petrova Vitalia* is no match.

I gape at the profile pic. A bodacious blonde babe from stock image heaven who, according to her profile, loves Beaches! Puppies! and Cuddling!

"Okay, get it over with," Vitaly sighs.

"You could've just left your interests blank—that's an option," I sputter.

"Have at it."

"Are these your real interests? Do you enjoy cuddling?" I whimper.

"Had your fun yet?"

"Why did you—?" I say, wheezing. "Her name is basically your name backward."

Vitaly launches into a very pragmatic explanation of the whys and hows of Petrova Vitalia's conception, but I hear none of it. It's a good thing there's the bed, because I'm weak and collapse onto it, howling, out of breath. Dying. Lifetimes pass before I sit back up again, my face pillow-puffed from trying to muffle my delight. Vitaly, on the other hand, has aged. He's all frown lines.

"I'm trying to help you, you know."

"I know."

"A thank-you would be nice."

I lean my temple on his shoulder. I hope it's enough to convey that I really do appreciate all the work he's putting into this. That he had to expect that I'd say something about Petrova—that I wouldn't be me and we wouldn't be us if I just let something like that slide. That I haven't felt free enough to laugh like that in a long time.

When I pick my head up, I notice a drop of wet on his shirt, a stamp of one of my joyful tears. I dab it. "Thank you."

Vitaly's shoulder, strong and rigid, softens under my touch. The laptop is squarely back on his lap, and he brings my attention to our project, pulling up a new profile for me to see. This one belongs to a very real person. Cute, clean-cut, young.

"His name is Cameron," Vitaly says. "The age gap between the two of you is only five years, which isn't too glaring, and puts him in the sweet spot where most guys start looking for long-term relationships. He's a self-described introvert but is looking for someone who can bring him out of his shell and widen his horizons. Plus, he mentions that his parents are his model for a successful relationship. They married young and are still together."

"You think I'd be good with him?"

Vitaly nods and pulls the PowerPoint back up. "There are a lot of different approaches we can take to your dating life, but I wanted to start with the law of Opposites Attract." He points to the slide and I read.

> If we apply the Opposites Attract principle, Jimena would be well-suited with someone who is reserved, premeditative, and mild-mannered. A partner who can help unload some of her burdens even when she insists she can carry them herself. And someone secure enough to let her shine. Jimena is a burning flame. She should be with someone who won't try to dim her.

I turn to Vitaly but I don't know what to say. I'm struck by what he wrote, by how he sees me. And it makes me see him—makes me see a lot of things—in a new way, too. Like how I've wrested a computer from him and rested my head on his shoulder, but it's only now that I'm hyperaware of the way our bodies are touching. The length of my arm, my leg, flush against his. The laptop breathes like an extension of us. Vitaly's so close I can feel his body heat. And as sure as I feel his, I know he can feel mine, too.

He clears his throat. "So, what do you think?"

What do I think? I think about what he wrote about me. *Do you really see me like that? A burning flame?*

There is a question I usually ask at moments like this, where a pause has gone too long. When he looks at me and all I want to do is make him blush. But I don't ask him. Maybe it no longer feels appropriate. Or funny. Maybe I'm tired of hearing no.

So instead, I say, "Cameron means shrimp in Spanish."

Vitaly gives me a close-lipped smile. "Don't mention that on your date."

21

IT'S ROPE-CLIMBING DAY IN GYM CLASS. YOU
need a good excuse to avoid rope climbing, but if Ms. Tubek
hears too many of them, she's less likely to be amenable.
That's why being at the front of the line is imperative. I don't
come to school to sweat in unflattering regulation T-shirt and
shorts. And I have no intention of falling on the mats while
our perpetually angry gym teacher stands over me and yells,
"NEXT!"

My friends and I secure the first four spots in line, excuses
at the ready.

"Sorry, Ms. Tubek, but I've got lady troubles," Sof says.
Euphemisms for "period" always work best, because if you're
too embarrassed to even say the *word*, just imagine how embarrassing it would be to do strenuous work while *on* your period.

Kenz is next: "Aunt Flo came to visit."

Then Luce: "Riding the crimson wave, miss."

By the time I step up, Ms. Tubek is ready for me. "Let me
guess, you're all on the same cycle?"

I shake my head. "Broke a nail."

Ms. Tubek stares me down and I stare right back. It's a
game of chicken at this point. She could call me out on my lie,
but she's too familiar with my group of friends at this point. If

she forced me to climb, they'd stage an instant protest, all with faux outrage that the "administration" isn't taking our "medical emergencies" seriously. There'd be whining, and heartfelt promises that they'd call their parents/the media immediately, and doesn't Ms. Tubek know that Luce's cousin is a lawyer with the ACLU, for goodness' sake?

"Three laps around the gym, all of you," Ms. Tubek barks.

I join my friends by the bleachers and we proceed to take our stroll. The place might smell like rubber and sweaty mats, but gym really isn't so bad once you take the work out of it. This is practically a walk in the park, and the only thing that's missing is a latte, honestly.

The next person on line either had a bad excuse or none at all, because they're already flat on their face. "NEXT!" yells Ms. Tubek.

My friends chat about how Miles Ugwu was caught smoking in the boys' bathroom, and I try paying attention, but my focus keeps wandering back to the people waiting to climb the rope. Specifically, to the boy who's fifth in line. His tube socks are pulled all the way up to the middle of his shins, his T-shirt is tucked into his shorts, and he's using all his upper body strength to hold a giant tome of a book. He moves mechanically forward whenever the line does, never lifting his eyes from the pages.

I can't stop thinking of him sitting next to me on my bed last night.

Burning flame.

It isn't a straightforward compliment, per se. On the surface, it's actually a very strange way to describe someone. And yet, every time I think of it—the fact that he sees me like that, so vibrant, so vital—that flame sparks to life inside of me.

"Earth to Jim," Kenz says.

I suck in a breath, like I've just been roused from sleep. "Huh?"

"What are you staring at?"

"Nobody—nothing."

A thud. "NEXT!"

"She was checking out Vitaly Petrov," Sof says. I turn to look at her just as Kenz and Luce divert their gazes to Vitaly. "Jimmy likes him."

"NEXT!" Ms. Tubek bellows as another body hits the floor.

"No, I don't." My voice is indignant, authoritative, the final word. But inside, I am flayed. "He's my neighbor. And he occasionally helps me with my homework."

"Don't play it off like you guys don't have a history," Sof says. Her next words are meant for our friends, but her gaze stays hooked on me. "Vitaly was Jimmy's first kiss."

At this, Luce and Kenz officially abandon the whole walk-around-the-gym concept, even though we haven't even made it a full lap.

"*What?*" Luce asks.

"Hold up," Kenz says. "I thought you and Zach were each other's first everythings."

You tell your best friend your deepest secrets and she just spills them all over the gym floor. I don't get why Sof is trying to weaponize this blip in my history. Maybe I shouldn't have ignored her incessant texts about college apps and deadlines. But it's not like a dumb first kiss is anything to be ashamed of. "We were thirteen and bored," I explain calmly, *not* defensively.

Sof takes up our stroll once again, and while Kenz and Luce clearly have more questions, they follow her lead.

"I always thought Vitaly was gay," Luce says over her shoulder.

"NEXT!" yells Ms. Tubek.

"He's not gay," I say. Though in all the time we've spent together, Vitaly has never once tried to get in my pants, which is gentlemanly, to be sure, but also deeply inexplicable.

"You sure?" Luce asks. "He's never had a girlfriend. And he's the only teenage boy I've ever seen who has a good haircut."

"Luce, a good haircut does not a gay boy make," I start, but her attention—and apparently everyone else's in the gym—is suddenly soaked up by the latest person climbing the rope.

I turn to see who they're all looking at. Vitaly climbs quicker and higher than anyone has yet. Apparently lifting heavy books has given him the necessary upper-body strength. Now his biceps stretch the sleeves of his T-shirt, and here I am, dumbfounded to discover that Vitaly even *has* biceps to begin with.

"Is this the Ned Flanders effect?" Sof says.

"The Ned Flanders effect?" Luce asks, her eyes tracing the length of Vitaly's arms.

"It's when a public nerd turns out to be a secret hunk," Kenz explains, awe in her voice.

Vitaly flicks the red ribbon at the top of the rope and then lowers himself just as gracefully. I'm not sure what I just witnessed, but all I know is Vitaly went up in the air a dork and touched the ground a superhero. Guess a summer building houses does a body good.

"Okay, you wanna date Vitaly, you do you, girl," Kenz whispers.

22

IT'S BEEN A WEEK SINCE VITALY CAME TO MY
apartment. Now we stand at the condiment bar, fixing our
drinks. He passes me the whole milk after pouring himself
some, and I pass him what's left of my last sugar packet, only
using one and a half sugars this time instead of my usual
two. We work silently to measure out the right balance of
ingredients—him to make his coffee sweeter, me to make
mine a little less likely to induce a heart attack. I thought he'd
be spending this time giving me pointers for my impending
date, but he seems kind of off tonight.

I watch him out of the corner of my eye. His cheek looks
sunken. He must be biting the inside of it. But then he catches
me staring. "What's up?" he asks.

"You nervous or something?"

"Why would I be nervous?"

"I don't have the faintest," I say.

"It's going to go well, I think. I'll be right outside if you . . ."
He trails off, which makes me wonder even more about what
he's thinking.

Is he nervous because he's the one who set this date up?
Maybe he's afraid that it'll fail, making all his hard work and
his opposites-attract hypothesis pointless. I want to tell him

that it's not a big deal, but Vitaly just nods and leaves without another word.

We both take our respective usual seats. I watch through the window as Vitaly sets his drink down to dig a folder and pen out of his book bag. Where are his gloves? I make a mental note to give him one of the pairs my aunt sends every year. Peru is famous for its fingerless gloves, so Vitaly can work on math homework or translate a poem into Russian and still stay warm.

He may be (clearly) nervous about this date, but I'm not. Either it goes well and leads to a second one, or it'll suck like all the rest, which I'm getting used to anyway. Am I hopeful the date will go well? Of course. I have hope for all my dates. But am I also keenly aware for the first time of how strong Vitaly's jaw looks as he opens his mouth to take a sip of his coffee? Of how soft his lips appear as they press against the plastic lid of his cup?

Definitely not.

I'm so distracted by Vitaly's—frankly lewd—drinking display that I almost forget what I'm here to do. But then I see his gaze follow someone into the coffee shop. And it's only then that my attention diverts to my date.

He smiles wide when he sees me. "Hi, I'm Cameron."

For the first time in my marriage plan, my date shocks me. I'm shocked by the fact that he's cuter than his profile picture. I'm shocked by the fact that we have similar opinions on things

(Times Square isn't as bad as people make it out to be, and NYU, his school, takes up way too much of downtown). Shocked by the fact that we're having a normal, pleasant conversation where the questions go both ways and the answers pique both of our interests.

Of course, I still have to lie a little bit. I don't want to weird him out by revealing my true motivations behind this date, or even my age. But it's going well enough that I can imagine a second date, and a third, and a whole slew of them in a lead-up to the moment of honesty where I will come clean. My lying will have tested our trust for each other, but ultimately it'll make our relationship stronger. And doesn't every relationship have those little tests of trust anyway? Why couldn't this one be about my age and—yes—my illegal status in the United States?

When we're done with our drinks, Cameron goes to the counter to get us a couple of pastries. That's when I finally notice Vitaly behind the glass, looking like he's been trying to catch my eye for the past forty-five minutes. In complicated non-baseball hand signals, he seems to ask if the date is going well. I shoot him a quick thumbs-up. But my view of Vitaly is blocked when Cameron slides back into his seat again.

"I know you said you wanted something sweet, but they only had one plain croissant left." Cameron places the pastry on the table.

"Really?" I look over to find Cary wiping the crumbs from the display case.

"It's almost closing time," Cameron says. But he doesn't check his watch, doesn't even comment on how maybe we should finish things up. The night feels young, like we can move our date to its next location, keep it going.

"You think there's any bagel places still open?" I ask. "I could really go for a cream cheese on an everything bagel."

"Okay, I know this is controversial," Cameron says, "but I just don't like the bagels here."

I stop chewing on the piece of croissant I tore off. To be sure, not liking bagels is not a red flag in and of itself, but Cameron's choice of words sets off alarm bells. "What do you mean, 'here'?" I ask cautiously. "Where else can you find bagels?"

Cameron laughs. "Bagels exist outside of New York."

Do they, though? "Pretty sure they were invented in a Brooklyn basement." My tone of voice says I'm joking, but inside I'm chanting a very serious refrain. *Don't ruin this date just because he has blasphemous opinions on bagels, don't ruin this date just because he has blasphemous opinions on bagels.*

What I don't say, because it obviously should go unsaid, is that bagels from outside of New York are a joke. But I'm not going to stop dating a guy because of something as stupid as him preferring LA bagels. I won't give Vitaly the satisfaction of telling me I'm sabotaging my own dates. I can learn to love Cameron despite the fact that he has terrible taste in breakfast breads.

"I just prefer the ones back home," Cameron says.

"Where's home?"

"Toronto."

I stare at him, unblinking. Compared to all the pleasant little shocks I've had throughout our date, this hits me like a stun gun. And now I get why we've just spent the last hour talking about New York. I was speaking about it with the love and reverence of someone who considers it home, while Cameron spoke about it with the excitement and fascination of a tourist. I guess in the back of my mind I must've known he wasn't from here. I just thought he was from some small Podunk town in the middle of nowhere, like Chicago or something.

Not *Canada*.

"Oh," I say when I can talk again. "Cool."

By the time the whole croissant is gone, Cameron has told me how great Toronto is, and how he has no interest in becoming an American on account of our whole obsession-with-guns thing. He keeps talking until Cary tells us he has to close up.

I won't break up with Cameron because he's wrong about bagels. But I will break up with him because of where he's from. He seems to sense something is off when he walks me to the subway station on the corner.

"You sure I can't walk you down?"

Another glaring sign that he's a tourist. No New Yorker's gonna walk you down into the subway. "I'm good, thank you."

Cameron nods, though he seems more doubtful than ever. "Hey, everything okay? You got kind of quiet for the last ten minutes there."

"Yeah, everything's great. I should probably get going, though."

"Oh, okay, sure. Hey, it was great to meet you. I had a great time."

My smile is tight. "I did, too."

"Can I see you again sometime?"

This is the moment where I know I should come clean. But I just can't work out how to break it to him that despite an unquestionably good date, I can't give him a second one. I'm bummed, but in the last few months I've become an exceptionally good actress. "Sure," I say, knowing I'm never going to see him again. "I'll call you."

I go down the subway stairs and wait a bit until I'm pretty sure Cameron's gone. When I climb back up to the street, Vitaly's at the top of the stairs, waiting for me.

"Well?"

I sigh and paste on a smile. "Canada foils my plans once again."

Vitaly winces as he takes this in. "Cameron is Canadian?"

I nod, trying to play it off like it's one of life's big jokes. Just my luck that I'd put all my eggs into this one basket and the basket isn't a US citizen. I'll have to adjust my marriage plan in my notebook when I get home.

Find ~~someone~~ an AMERICAN to love
who doesn't totally repulse you.

"I wasted your time," Vitaly says. "I'm sorry."

"You couldn't have known."

"I found him. I set you up. I should've vetted him better." To himself, he says, "I can't believe I missed that."

"Hey, it's really okay," I assure him. "It's just another date."

"But you seem sad."

My heart squeezes a little at hearing that. I thought *I* was upset, but Vitaly's taking it hard. I'm crushed because I got my hopes up, but Vitaly's sad because he's the cause of it. I don't want him to think he let me down.

"Tonight doesn't have to end on a bad note," he says. "Let's go somewhere."

Our post-date routine feels like a relief. I look around. "Everything's closing."

"I know a place."

23

WE'RE STANDING OUTSIDE A WAREHOUSE-LOOKING
place back in Brooklyn, and it is closed. In fact, everything
around here is closed. But Vitaly takes out his keys and uses
one to unlock the door. "What is this place?"

Instead of answering, Vitaly leads me through the door and
flips the switch. The fluorescent bulbs come to life in a slow-
moving wave, splashing the concrete walls with bright white
light. The floor is covered in a bunch of blue mats. "Again, I
have to ask: What is this place?"

"I work here," Vitaly says. "On the weekends." He gestures
to the wall as he takes off his coat. There are rows of framed
eight-by-ten photographs hanging there, and I scan the faces
in them until I find Vitaly's. In the photo, he wears what looks
like a red karate gi, and he's standing behind a line of similarly
dressed toddlers, who look like they are prepared to kick my
ass. It is the most wonderful picture I've ever seen.

I cannot wipe the smile off my face when I spin around,
and Vitaly looks like he can't contain his smile, either, though
he's clearly trying to.

"You teach kids karate?"

He shakes his head. "It's a Russian fighting style called

sambo. And yes, technically I teach them, but I like to think they really teach me."

Vitaly with the earnest jokes. I take another peek at the picture and see that no, it's definitely not a gi, because I don't recall karate uniforms having little short-shorts. And Vitaly's got *thighs*.

"How come you never told me you teach tiny babies how to kill?"

"You never asked."

I gawk at him, because I really can't believe this. "Big Rally. You contain multitudes."

He walks over to one of the mats, but before stepping on it, he starts toeing off his boots.

"What are we doing?" I ask.

He turns to me, and I swear I've never seen him smirk before, because I would've remembered the way it makes his whole face light up with devilish mischief.

"We're gonna fight."

━━━

Usually, I don't like anyone to see me sweat. Never even liked it with my most talented boyfriend, Ryan, and sweating was the whole entire point. But I am *dripping*. My hair is up in a knot that flops around like a drunk girl on a mechanical bull, threatening to fall at any moment. It feels like most of the strands have spilled out anyway, sticking to my neck and the side of my face. I am nothing more than a flushed bag of skin on its last breath.

But I get the sense Vitaly can do this for hours. He bounces on the balls of his bare feet, fists up, circling me. And while I'm trying to gulp in as much air as I can, the boy is *laughing*. A great, big, open laugh that makes his torso constrict. I can tell because he stripped down to a white tank that clings to him like it's painted on. There's smoothness but also dips, lines, ridges.

The Ned Flanders effect indeed.

"Remember what I taught you," Vitaly says.

Remember? I can barely remember how to breathe right now. I blow a strand of hair off my forehead and try to focus. But his tank.

"Just one," he says. His laugh makes his Adam's apple bob, and I notice a bead of sweat roll over it. I lick my bottom lip. "Just one punch."

I really shouldn't laugh—I need to reserve my breath—but I can't help it. The fact that he thinks I can land a punch. I haven't been able to land a punch this entire *time*. My legs are burning. A slight breeze might knock me over. But okay, he wants me to land a punch, so here goes.

I swing, and as Vitaly ducks out of the way, he uses the opportunity to dole out the world's lightest jab, right in the dip of my waist. I dissolve into a fit of giggles. Vitaly tries to catch me but I take him down, too. We land on the mat tangled together, me flat on my back, Vitaly catching himself on top of me. We're face-to-face, still giggling like idiots, then letting our laughs taper off, then breathing in and out.

Vitaly hovers over me. My body tingles with heat and . . . something else. Anticipation, maybe? It's like the tension between two batteries held tip to tip, millimeters apart. There is that pull of them coming together, and that pop of release, of them coming apart. I stay as still as possible, because I'm not ready for what comes next. Not the pull or the pop. Vitaly doesn't move, either, not his forearms on either side of me, not his knee pinned between my legs.

What am I afraid of? Afraid of this moment ending? Afraid of what happens next? I decide to push away the fear. But when I move, it breaks the spell. My fingers reach for him just as Vitaly shifts off me. *Pop.*

He scrambles to his feet and clears his throat before offering me his hand. "We should probably get out of here."

We're the only two people on the B68. We decided on the bus instead of the subway because the stop is right outside Vitaly's work. It's slower, though, and we'll need a transfer, but I don't mind. Not even when the driver pauses at every stop, despite there being no passengers on the curb waiting to get on.

"Why sambo?" I ask. Tonight I learned so much I didn't know about Vitaly, and greedily, I want more.

"It's kind of a long story."

I lean forward. "Tell me."

Vitaly sits perpendicular to me, his back against the window, while I sit facing front. His choice. I try not to overanalyze it, but I think he's trying to maintain some distance between us.

"My dad taught me sambo when I was a kid."

"Doesn't seem like a long story."

The corner of Vitaly's mouth turns up in a smile without any joy behind it. It seems kind of bitter, actually, and now I kind of feel guilty for making him talk about something he clearly didn't want to talk about. But Vitaly pushes on.

"It was his way of making it acceptable to kick the shit out of me."

Everything in me goes cold. "What?"

"Anytime I was acting up, he'd want to give me a lesson. But he was mostly just slamming me to the ground and stuff. He gave me this scar." He plays with the cartilage at the top of his ear, the ragged ridge of scar tissue I've always wondered about. "But thanks to all his 'lessons,' now I'm the one who can beat *him* up if he ever tries anything, so . . ."

"Vitaly." My heart aches hearing this. I wasn't expecting it, and I think Vitaly surprised himself, too, telling me all this. I know his parents fight, but I didn't know it went beyond shouting.

Vitaly scratches his chin with his thumbnail, and his gaze settles on a random spot on the bus floor. "He's the reason I applied to Oxford. I want to get as far away from him as I can. And my mom, she's never been willing to leave him, but if I go to England, she'll follow me there. My dad wouldn't upend his life for me, but my mom . . . I know she will."

I nod, not really sure what to say, but wanting him to know that I hear him. I'm here. Without a word, I place my hand over his. His knuckles are so cold I really do need to get him gloves. But for now, I'll have to warm them up myself. When I slip my fingers through his, he lets me. He looks at our linked hands for a long while and I can't tell what he's thinking, but he's focused, decisive almost. It seems like he wants to say something but he's having trouble getting it out.

"My parents really screwed me up," he says. "They're bad for each other. Really bad. And I never understood why my mom didn't just leave. But I guess it's because their whole lives are so tied up in each other. If they weren't married, they could just break up, you know? But the fact that they're married is the thing that makes it so hard to walk away. I never want to be in a situation like that. I never want to be stuck." His words come out haltingly, careful about what he's trying to say, but wanting to get it all out just the same. His eyes meet mine to see if I understand.

And I think I do. He's been telling me all along. I just never thought his feelings about marriage were really relevant to me. But I know now that they are.

"You're not changing your mind about marriage," I say.

Vitaly nods and his gaze drifts back to the floor again. But he doesn't let go of my hand. I don't let go, either. Even though I know I have to.

24

IT'S A RARE NIGHT THAT I SPEND SITTING AT HOME
watching telenovelas with my mom, but I don't have any
new dates lined up, so here I am on the couch, watching two
women argue over a galán. My mom doesn't shoo me away to
go do schoolwork. I think she's happy to have me home after
so many nights out.

Every telenovela has a main villain, and it's always a woman.
She's evil in an uncomplicated way, all too happy to yell at her
servants, or pull someone's hair, or kick puppies. And by the
end she always winds up in an accident that leaves her horrifi-
cally disfigured, poetic justice for her unchecked vanity. I gotta
say, novelas are sort of a comfort watch. You know everyone's
roles and that the good guys win and the bad ones fall into
a vat of boiling oil. But something that always trips me up is
when the villain throws around the word "ambiciosa" as the
biggest insult. Like daring to be ambitious is the worst trait a
person could possibly have.

I never thought being ambitious was a bad thing, but now
I wonder if there's such a thing as being too ambitious. Do I
want too much? Maybe it's my American way of thinking—a
delusion that I'm entitled to everything I want and that I can

have it all if I just work hard enough. Well, it turns out I can't, no matter how hard I try.

Me and my mom used to watch novelas together all the time. The shows are all the same: heavy on the petting but still chaste enough for family viewing. It's mostly just men grabbing women by the elbow and spinning them around and cornering them against walls and proclaiming undying love in husky voices.

Growing up watching this stuff, I thought love was so intense. But then I started dating, and my own experiences taught me that love was simple. More often than not it was boring and frustrating and annoying. But never intense.

"Qué hombre tan guapo." My mom's talking about the blond male lead, who looks and acts like a hair model in a shampoo commercial. "¿No crees?"

I get lost staring at the TV, until the galán my mom is referring to transforms into Vitaly, his hair whipping in the breeze. "Sí," I agree. "Es handsome."

I haven't talked to Vitaly since the bus ride home three nights ago. I also haven't been able to stop thinking about him.

I like him. There's no use in denying that anymore. I never gave a name to my feelings for him, but the point is that those feelings were there, since the beginning. I always wanted to talk to him, even before we were really friends. I'm instantly happier whenever I see him. I love saying things that make him blush, because pink looks really cute on him. And I think I could go on a million dates but I would always, without question, rather be spending my time with the boy on the other side of the window. But I especially know that I like Vitaly because right now my stomach twists at the thought that I can't be with him.

Selfishly, I want him. But Vitaly is not an option for me. He's off the table, right when I finally realize I really want him *on* the table.

My mind has been muddled for the last three days, trying to sort things out, but nothing is any clearer. Do I let go of my stupid marriage plan just because I like him? But then what—date Vitaly until he leaves for college in England? What would be the point? It's not like I can get on a plane and follow him.

I want Vitaly and I want to get married and I want to be free. And I can't have it all.

I've been too ambiciosa and now look at me. Worse off than I was before I started on my marriage plan.

And even if I ditch my plan, it will always be there, looming. Whether I get married now or in my twenties or forties or sixties, it is still the only way I can do anything with my life. It's the only way I can get an ID, travel, work. I can put off getting married, but I'll need to do it eventually.

I sneak a look at my mom and I wonder how she does it. I feel so alone right now, in my private little pity party. But my mom's been lonely for years. She's been away from her family, she hasn't been in a relationship since my dad. She is so completely isolated. All she has is me.

For the first time since I learned about my status, I don't feel a complicated cocktail of anger and frustration toward her. I feel like we're in this together.

"¿Por qué me miras así?"

She's caught me looking at her and I don't want her to read

my expression, so I turn back to the TV and swallow the lump in my throat. "No reason."

I'm not giving up on my plan. But getting married was supposed to grant me access to everything I want. Now it's just getting in the way of being with someone I really like.

I fucking hate this. Being illegal is taking too much from me.

I feel my mom's hand on my cheek before I realize what she's doing. "¿Oye, por qué lloras? No te pongas triste. Siempre se casan al final, no te preocupes."

I bite my lip, nod, and let her keep thinking that it's the breakup of the couple on the screen that has me crying. I breathe deep but tears still blur my vision. My mom puts her arm around me and draws me closer. "Ya, no es para tanto," she says gently, changing the channel to *American Idol*.

Tomorrow I'll get over it. I'll get back on track, back to the plan. But for now, I allow myself a moment to mourn something that never had the chance to exist in the first place.

25

I LOVE SOF'S FAMILY, SO WHEN SHE INVITES ME
over for dinner the next night, I accept. It's just the distraction
I need right now. Sof's house is big—two floors and a basement,
exactly like the kind of house you see on sitcoms. The kitch-
en's even got an island, which is pretty much unheard of in my
neighborhood. Six of us gather around the dining room table.
It's Sof's mom and dad, Daniela and Lalo; her twelve-year-old
brother, Brandon; and her grandmother, Carmen, visiting
from her apartment around the corner. Tonight, dinner is sushi
takeout. There's a big platter on a lazy Susan at the center of the
table and we spin it around, plucking pieces with chopsticks.
Carmen is the only one who doesn't touch the fish, preferring
the miso soup.

"¿Pescado crudo?" she mutters next to me. "¿Quién come
pescado crudo?"

I chew to keep from laughing. Everyone else picks at the
sushi rolls, ignoring Carmen's complaint about eating raw fish.
Brandon and Sof only know the most basic Spanish words, but
I can answer her.

"Mucha gente. Ceviche es pescado crudo también."

"No, muchacha, ceviche está cocinado en el limón. Y tam-
poco me gusta."

I love Carmen. I like to think of her as my grandma, too. I talk to my own abuela on birthdays and holidays, but we haven't seen each other since I was twelve, the last time she was able to come visit. Best summer of my life, eating the papas rellenas she made for me.

"Yes, more Spanish at the table!" Sof's dad says. "Jimena, when you going to teach my girl more Spanish?"

"I think the ship has sailed on that one," I say.

"Dad, lay off Jimmy," Sof says. "If you wanted me to know Spanish, you shoulda taught me yourself."

"Sofia tiene razón," Carmen says. "No sabe mucho, pero en este caso sabe algo."

I nearly choke on my Coke, and Sof nudges me with her elbow. "What did she say?"

"She says she loves you a lot." Sof doesn't need to know that her grandma has, to put it kindly, little confidence in her.

"So, what were you girls working on before dinner?" Daniela asks.

"Fundraising ideas for the Culture Club trip," I say. Helping to plan a trip I won't be going on is a special kind of cruelty I'm inflicting on myself, but I'll do it a million times over if it means avoiding uncomfortable convos with my BFF. "I think we should have a bake sale."

"And I think we should do a bikini car wash like they do in every teen movie," Sof says.

Her little brother makes a gagging noise and her parents look dubious. "A *what*?" Lalo asks.

"I'm against the bikini car wash idea," I say, knowing Sof's parents will have my back. "Teen movies aren't real. I mean, who do we know that even drives a car?"

"People drive cars," Sof says. "I'm gonna drive a car soon. Dad's gonna give us lessons, right, Dad?"

"Us?" I echo.

"Your mom doesn't drive, right?" Sof's dad says. "Don't worry, I got you."

There's a new pit in my stomach as I'm roped into yet another unfulfillable promise to Sof. If I agree to driving lessons with her, then we'll have to take the road test together, too. I can't get a license, and I'm not about to sit through a whole driving test with a real-ass instructor, either.

"I'm never driving," I announce a little too loudly. "I'm afraid of cars."

Sof cocks an eyebrow. "Since when?"

"My cousin once tried to teach me and we almost got into this big accident, and ever since then I can't get in the driver's seat of a car without breaking out in hives."

"You have a cousin?" Sof asks.

"Yeah, I have cousins," I say, like who doesn't. "He lives in Texas, you don't know him."

The lies roll off my tongue so easily these days that Sof accepts them, no more questions. I breathe a tiny sigh of relief. Land mines successfully sidestepped.

Sof's family, like mine, is from South America, but that's where the similarities end. Both her parents immigrated as young people. Lalo came as a child and Daniela came to study with a student visa. I know they eventually became

147

naturalized citizens, and I never questioned it before, but now I marvel at how they were able to do something that eluded me and my mom. I wonder what the process was like for them to obtain legal status. Was it difficult? Expensive? Arduous? How many documents did they have to fill out? How many interviews did they have to go through? Did they even need interviews? Did they have to take a verbal exam? Did they apply with lawyers?

But I swallow down all my questions, because I know as soon as I ask them they'll be lobbed right back at me. Questions like, *Why are you asking about this stuff? Haven't you been naturalized? Why are you worrying about citizenship?*

Sof pokes me with the clean end of her chopstick and I snap out of my reverie. "Huh?"

"My mom was asking you about the president. Do not feel obligated to answer her."

She could've been asking about seahorses for how confused I am. "The president?"

"I was just saying that you girls will be eighteen soon," Daniela says. "You'll be able to vote."

Why is this dinner going so sideways? Everyone else is having a pleasant time talking about upcoming elections and driving lessons, but I feel like a contestant on *Jeopardy!* with a negative balance and a broken buzzer.

"I haven't given that any thought." I hope this is enough to shift the topic to something more manageable, like space exploration or equine medicine.

"You'll have to do absentee ballots when you girls are in California," Lalo says.

Are you fucking kidding me? Now the college thing again? How have I stepped on every single land mine today?

Sof tilts her head toward me, whispers, "We need to talk about that."

I nod, but Sof's dad is in the middle of asking me another impossible question. "Jimena, you a Democrat or Republican?"

"Hmm?" I munch on my yellowtail far longer than I need to.

"Dad," Sof groans.

"I'm trying to convince Sofia to register as a Republican."

Sof rolls her eyes and Lalo begins a rant about how Republicans are the only ones who care about small business owners like him. It is so strange to me, how we can come from a similar place and background and still have startlingly different views on this sort of thing. I mean, before I knew about my status, politics bored me. But now I have more of a vested interest in the way people are running this place. Not that I can do anything about it. I can't vote. I'm not recognized as a member of society. Sof's never been political, and I don't see that changing anytime soon. She can afford not to be.

"We get it, Dad. *They took our jerbs*," Sof says, doing a perfect *South Park* imitation. Instinctively, I giggle, but inside I go cold. I think she's just making a joke. I hope she is. I don't know how Sof truly feels about this issue, but it's clear how her dad feels. Maybe Sof doesn't agree with his politics, but she's also not refuting them.

I am consumed by a sinking feeling—a *knowing*—that even after all these years of having dinners with me, offering to teach me to drive, watching my friendship with his daughter, if Sof's dad found out about my status, he'd want me gone. If he knew I was illegal, I don't even think he'd say, *I still don't believe illegals belong here, but you should be able to stay*. I think he'd say, *I still don't believe illegals belong here, and I'm sorry, but you should've come to this country the right way*.

This issue is so black-and-white to some people that they barely see me as a person. But this dinner is the big heartbreaker. Finding out that even for someone I love, like Lalo, I'm just one of the millions of illegals taking food off his table.

The old version of me would've happily taken the chance to debate him on an issue we disagree on. But the new me keeps quiet to protect myself. I watch Sof eat her sushi while I focus on remembering how to breathe.

I need to avoid, deflect, spin. I need to ask something else, shake something shiny in front of their faces—smoothly, effortless—without anybody even noticing my sleight of hand. All so they don't see me crumbling under the pressure of the easiest questions.

"The only election I'm thinking about right now is for prom court. My vote's going to Sof, of course."

Sof tries to keep the biggest grin off her face, to little effect. "Stopppp," she says, batting her eyelashes. Which is my cue to keep going. And I do it happily, going off on a prom tangent. It's a performance, but I'm getting good at it.

After dinner I help clear the table and wash the dishes. There isn't much to do, but my mom would be mortified if I didn't help clean up, and I guess I'd be mortified, too. Sof leans against the counter, on drying duty.

"Thanks for dinner." Even though it's been a juggling act of lies, hanging with Sof and her family is still better than yet another miserable date.

"Yeah, been a while since you came over," Sof says. "You're not going out with any more of those dating website guys, I hope."

It hadn't been my best idea, creating that dating profile with Sof. I busy myself with the dish in my hand. At least I can honestly say, "I never want to go on a dating website again."

"You've been bringing up prom a lot," Sof says. "If you really want a date that bad, you should just hire some rent-a-boyfriend off Craigslist or something."

I hand Sof the wet dish, pivoting my whole body toward her. "Rent-a-wha—?"

"My cousin Miggy did that when he needed a date to *his* prom. And you know Miggy was not going to get anyone to go with him unless he paid them."

I stare at her, mouth agape. Not because I don't believe no one would go out with Miggy (I've met him) but because I'm wondering if the solution to all my problems is really this simple. I've been banking on a genuine whirlwind love connection all this time, when all I actually need is someone who'd be willing to be in a fake relationship for the right price.

Of course. I've been thinking about this all wrong. This isn't a love story, it's a business transaction. My marriage, in the eyes of the US government, is going to be a clerical thing anyway. Papers and proof and documents. Why should my means of finding a partner be any different?

"That's so . . ."

"Desperate," Sof says. "I know."

But the word I would use is "genius."

When I get home that night, I make a few adjustments in my notebook.

an AMERICAN
∧
Find ~~someone~~ to ~~love~~
marry. ~~who doesn't totally repulse you.~~
Doesn't matter who at this point.

And then I get to work.

I've been thinking about my plan all wrong. A part of me can't believe I've been so naive. If I want to get married quick, I need to take love out of the equation. I mean, if we're being honest, I don't *actually* want to get married. I'm seventeen, for crying out loud! Getting married for real right now is ridiculous. Getting married for fake is where it's at.

The new plan is to find a guy. Get married. Get my papers. Get divorced.

Easy.

I stay up hours past my bedtime, hunching over my computer screen like it might swallow me whole. I follow a trail of search engine results that take me to message boards that seem created just for people like me. There are people there, of all ages, looking for the same thing I am: a green card marriage. There are even personal anecdotes from people who have gone through with it and come out the other side. Some have regrets, but a lot more say it's the best decision they ever made. They explain how their life opened up. How it feels like they can go out into the world and breathe for the first time.

One thing is abundantly clear: If I do this, it's going to cost me. But I have savings. And I can't think of a better way to spend them than on my freedom.

Seeing this option feels kind of like relief. I won't have to look for a Prince Charming. I won't have to weigh their looks against their personality. None of that matters anymore. My Mr. Right could be Mr. There and Willing to Do It. My marriage could be as bureaucratic as the reams of documents I'll have to fill out for it.

So I start a new post in the personal ad section of the message board. I don't include any distinguishing details, no name, no paper trail. I'm clear about what I want and why, no more lying. And in the subject line, I put my mission statement in all caps.

GIRL, 17, SEEKS HUSBAND

26

THE NEXT WEEKEND, WE'RE AT MoMA ON A Culture Club field trip. Kenz, Sof, Luce, and I walk through the museum together, our elbows forming a tight-knit chain. But eventually we separate. My friends slink away to another section of the museum and I stay in this wide-open white room, fixated on a sculpture. It's a bicycle wheel upright atop a wooden stool. At some point I notice Vitaly through the spokes, staring at the sculpture, too.

"How is this art?" he asks.

"It's art because it's in a museum."

He snorts, but I'm not trying to be funny. "You don't like it?"

He pinches his lips together, and I take it to mean, *What's there to like?* "There's no skill here. Did the artist even work on this? Because it looks like he just went out and bought this stuff. It's not as if it's even nice to look at."

"That's kind of the point." It sounds snooty even to my own ears, so I try to explain. "Duchamp wasn't trying to make art that was beautiful. He was interested in art as an idea. What does it mean to make something without putting years of work into it? Can it still be of substance? He's making the claim that part of the art is in the packaging of it. The title you give it, the setting you place it in. It's about the tension between the viewer's interpretation and the artist's meaning. He's saying that art is so much more than what everyone accepted it as for centuries. His work challenged people's notions about art, made them uncomfortable. He redefined what art *is*."

Vitaly isn't looking at the sculpture anymore. He's looking at me. And I have to turn away. I hate that I can't even look at him now without my stomach doing a little flip. "If I cared about art—which I don't—I'd care about Duchamp the most."

"Noted." Vitaly rounds the *Bicycle Wheel* and comes to stand next to me as I observe a Dadaist painting on the wall. "Are we okay?"

"Yeah." I scan the name and date beside the artwork. "Why?"

"It's just, I haven't seen you since the—"

The bus.

"—the Canadian," he continues. Vitaly looks equal parts confused, hopeful, hurt, guilty. It makes my insides twist to think that he feels like I'm avoiding him because he did something wrong. When really, it's because I like him and I need to stop liking him. He does not fit into my plan. And I don't fit into his. The only way I can think of to stop liking him is to spend less time with him, which, right now, I'm failing at.

"We're grand." I paste on a grin.

"Okay. Good. Sorry again about the Canadian. I'll do a better job vetting the next guy and may—"

I wave him off with a flick of my wrist and move to the next artwork on the wall. A paper collage. "Don't worry about that. I'm done with the dating website. Going in a new direction."

I can see his face morph from relieved to skeptical in under a second flat. "What direction?" he asks, wary.

"I found a website where people go looking for green card marriages. Posted a personal ad."

I examine the collage until I almost go cross-eyed trying to find a hidden meaning behind it, though I know there isn't one. And while I don't look at Vitaly's face, I can tell what he's feeling by the way he holds himself. Still but taut. I can't stare at the art piece any longer, and it's killing me that Vitaly isn't saying anything. The normal human response would be to say something. A reaction I can work with, but his silence is a slow needle through the heart.

When I finally turn to him, I wish I hadn't. His face is etched with alarm, and beneath that, disgust. "So you're just going to drop the whole pretense of dating someone? Falling in love? You're just going to buy yourself a marriage?"

"I know it's not what you picture when you think of marriage, but I think I've been looking at it all wrong. Trying to build a relationship from scratch wasn't working. And it was taking too long." I glance around the white room, but most of Culture Club has moved on to the next gallery. "This way is better."

But Vitaly isn't convinced. The alarm seeps deeper into his skin, scratching lines in his forehead. "Jimena. What are you doing?"

"I don't care if you disapprove. This is the only way."

"You know it's not the only way." He's whispering, but it's urgent, exasperated. "You don't have to get married at all. It's not like ICE is banging down your door. You're not getting deported. You could just forget all this and worry about senior year and wait for the laws to change. Or wait to get married the right way. Why are you doing this *now*?"

It's a gut punch, that after everything, he still doesn't get it. "I know it seems like you and I have nothing in common, but that's just the details," I say. "The backbone of who we are— the building blocks? We're basically the same. We live in the same place, in the same building, we're the same age. We've been in the same classes practically our whole lives. Sitting next to each other. Same shitty education, same opportunities. Our lives"—I gesture between the two of us—"are on parallel lines. But soon those lines are going to diverge. You're going to keep moving forward, and I'm going to stay stuck."

A woman passes by, and I'm reminded of where we are. This is the wrong place for this conversation, but it can't be avoided. I take a step closer to Vitaly and speak so only he can hear me. "I can't do *anything* with my life," I whisper fiercely. "I can't get a job, I can't get a license, I can't go anywhere, I can't even form meaningful, honest relationships without my stupid legal status getting in the way." I don't know how else to put it. I don't know how to make him see how stifling my world became the minute I found out I'm undocumented. How it's worse every day, thinking about my future and only seeing it blotted out. How, before I know it, that bleak future is going to be my whole existence.

"I'm being *haunted* by this. Can you understand that? It's like my illegal status is a ghost and it won't leave me alone. I'm haunted by this thing and suddenly *nothing* in my life is the same. I don't see things the same. I can be sitting in class, trying to actually pay attention, but the ghost is in my ear telling me there is no point to anything. Do you get it?

"You work so hard for your future—you've got your next five years mapped out. What if somebody took that away from you because of a mistake your parents made when you were a kid?" I search Vitaly's eyes, hoping I'm getting through to him. Because one of the things that makes people hate undocumented people like me is that they just don't understand how hard it is, to live like this. Vitaly sees me as just another girl— like everyone else. But I'm not like everyone else. I would do anything to be like everyone else. "I'm not going to wait for my life to start."

I don't know if I've gotten through to him. At least he doesn't look so disgusted with me anymore. But now he looks pained. "You shouldn't need to do this," Vitaly says.

"Yeah, well, I don't have that luxury."

We let a few moments pass between us until we're both facing the gallery wall, pretending to look at masterpieces. I decide to be bold with the next thing I say. "What's the real reason you don't want me to do this?" It's a question and a dare. I want him to be honest with me. I want Vitaly to tell me to stop looking for a partner. That he's right here. I'd quit my whole plan if he just said that. In the light-year it takes him to respond, I find myself full of hope, bursting with it.

"Because it's dangerous."

It's not what I want to hear. It's kind of a broken record at this point. "I'd still just be meeting up with random guys."

"It's different," Vitaly says firmly. "The guys you were going out with had profiles, pictures. They weren't anonymous avatars from the dark web. Don't act like this isn't dangerous."

"I'm not being naive. Don't tell me I'm being naive."

"You're playing with getting married like it's a game," Vitaly says. "You need to take it seriously. You need to grow up."

I draw back. "Fuck you."

"Excuse me." It's one of the museum guards, come to stand between us. "You need to keep it down." When I notice him, it's like the color comes back into the room, a blur of paintings and people in their coats. We're in a room full of fragile things and I'm so worked up, like I'm holding a sledgehammer.

"I'm sorry," I mutter to the guard. Vitaly turns to look at the *Bicycle Wheel* again. All I see is his profile, but his cheek burns like it's been struck. When the guard goes, I say in a quiet voice, "I don't need to grow up. You need to loosen up." It comes off sounding like the most childish thing a person can say. And I feel like an idiot, being told off by him, trying to make him see something he was never going to see.

"You know what, this was a weird setup from the beginning. I don't need you coming on my dates anymore." My voice threatens to crack, so I keep it low, blink, focus on the sculpture. I don't look at Vitaly, but I can hear him. He exhales, long and slow.

"I don't understand."

"You don't have to understand. It just is."

"Are we still talking about the art?"

"I have to go." I cross into the next gallery without turning back. I don't understand, either. How I went from holding his hand the entire bus ride home to wanting to get as far away from Vitaly as I can.

27

AT BREAKFAST THE NEXT MORNING, ALONG WITH
the café, toast, butter, and mermelada, there is a new item on
the table. When I sit down, my mom holds it up for me to see.
"¿Qué es esto?"

I should be shocked that she found my notebook—my *marriage plot* notebook—but I'm not. I left it on my unmade bed,
open to the page where I'd written my plan. And to use the
SAT analogy format, my mom is to an unmade bed what a
moth is to a flame.

"'Find an American to marry,'" my mom reads off the
page. "Explícate."

"Es una idea." I shrug, feign nonchalance. But I watch my
mom carefully. I need to know what she thinks.

My argument with Vitaly at the museum shook me. What
if he's right and this is a bad idea? What if I'm not thinking
things through in a rational way? Not my fault—according to
biology class, my frontal lobe is not fully developed yet.

Maybe I subconsciously left my notebook open on my
unmade bed on purpose. Without Vitaly, I need a new sounding board, and since she's the only other person who knows
about my situation, that job falls to my mom. Whatever she
has to say, I think I need to hear it.

"Me quiero casar," I tell her. "Para conseguir mis papeles."

I want to get married to get my papers. *Push back. Punish me.*

My mom sets my notebook back down on the table, ironing out the top page with the flat palm of her hand. "¿Por qué quieres casarte ahorita? Eres joven. Hay que *enjoy your life*."

She's saying exactly what I wanted her to, but it feels ridiculous coming out of her mouth. She wants me to hold off on getting married so I can enjoy my life? Like she's enjoying hers? Afraid at any moment her employer might ask for her Social Security number? Afraid to go to the hospital? Never letting anyone in, literally and figuratively? "I don't want my life to be like yours."

When I talk to her in English, I'm pulling my punches. It's a way to say things to her that I don't really want her to hear. But this she understands, and I feel terrible for the way it comes out.

"¿Ma, estás contenta?" I ask. "¿Con tu job? ¿Tu vida?" It's something I never bothered to ask my mom, if she's okay with the way her life turned out. But I'm doing whole backflips not to end up like her, and I've never even tried to find out if the life I'm rejecting is really that bad. I mean, she provided for me. Gave me a roof over my head and food to eat, and toys to play with. The two sides of me are at war: The Latina part of me is deferential and respectful and grateful for everything my mother has done for me to make sure I have a good life, but the American side of me wants to keep asking questions and demanding answers and feels entitled to the same equal rights and opportunities that everyone else has.

"¿Esto era tu sueño?" I ask my mother. Was this her dream?

"¿Ser una empleada? Claro que no. ¿Pero sueños? Yo

soñaba en tener una vida buena. Poder mantenerme yo misma. Una vida con dignidad."

No, she never dreamed of being a maid, but then, she also never longed for much. And I realize that maybe that's just my American upbringing, dreaming lofty dreams for myself, always striving for the bigger and better. Most people don't live the lives they always dreamed of. Most people end up somewhat disappointed, don't they?

My mom is content with what she has. A job, a roof, a daughter.

But all I see is someone who has shut herself out of life. My mom has found her place in the world and convinced herself it's warm and safe, but all she's done is dug a grave. It's nice enough—she gets TV here and always has her breakfast essentials—but no matter how comfortable she gets, we both know the air's going to run out.

This isn't about dreaming big anymore, it's about living.

My mom has been able to successfully deny that we're getting buried, but I can't ignore it. And now that I know it, it just keeps getting darker and darker.

I can't live underground.

"I'm getting married. Y eso es eso."

I'm putting my foot down. But there's a tiny tremor to my voice, and I can only look at my mom through my lashes as I say it.

I brace myself for the histrionics, the waterworks, the meltdown. I'm her little girl! She might ground me. She might lecture me. But all she does is sigh. A tiny release of breath that practically knocks me over.

"¿Y con quién te casarías?"

She asks who I would marry, like it's a party game ice-breaker and not my number one priority.

"Con cualquiera." *Anyone.*

"Pues." My mom sweeps a cupped palm over the spotless tabletop. She dabs at invisible crumbs. "Si eso es lo que quieres hacer . . ." *If that's what you want to do . . .* "Hazlo." *Do it.*

Not only is my mom not objecting to my plan—if you squint, she's actually kind of giving me permission. My mother, who is so strict with everything about my life, is cool with me getting married to any guy off the street.

But then it's so suddenly clear. My mom isn't strict with me because she's a stickler for rules. She's only ever been trying to protect me—us—from being caught. Strictness is just how she achieves that.

"Solo ten cuidado." She tells me to be careful in the exact same wording you'd use for a toddler holding a glass of water.

She is letting me go through with my plan.

A part of me is hurt that she isn't trying to stop me. Shouldn't she be protecting me from having to make a life-altering grown-up decision? But the fact that my mom is encouraging this only confirms my suspicions. My mom is not as content as she claims.

If she's so okay with me doing this, then it must mean we're in deep. The air is starting to get thin. And this is the only way to dig ourselves out.

Once I'm in my bedroom, I find a new email in my inbox.

Hi, I noticed your ad and I thought I'd reach out.
If you're looking for a romantic relationship, I'm
afraid I'm not your man. But if you're interested in a
mutually beneficial partnership with a finite start/end
point, I think we can help each other out.
A few basics about me:
I was born and raised in Ohio, and have been living in
New York for the last four years.
I'm a foodie, but sadly, allergic to peanuts and
shellfish.
And I have a Labrador named Roscoe.
Your plight touched me, and even if this doesn't work
with me, I hope you're able to find the person with
whom it does.
We can talk if you're interested.

—Michael

I read the message a few more times, slowly, then quickly, then stopping at every line for closer inspection. I think I stay on the word "whom" for a full five minutes. It's the kind of word that tells you a lot about a person. High society educated brainiac much?

Michael sounds promising. It is too soon to think anything might come of this, and it's only one email, but my guts are a jumbled frenzy of nerves because all I can think is, *This is happening.*

28

I'M NOT GOING TO THE COFFEE SHOP THIS TIME.
This date is a totally different animal from the others I've been on. Less get-to-know-you casual hang, more let's-make-a-deal business meeting. But I'm not going to be a dummy about it, either. It still needs to be somewhere public. So I tell Michael to meet me in Union Square. The park is always stuffed with people, and it has multiple subway entrances in case I take one look at Michael and decide to bolt.

I'm close to the little playground Vitaly and I went to that night we sat side by side on the slides. I almost wish he was here right now. Not because I need him to protect me or anything, but so that he can see how responsible I'm being, going above and beyond with these extra precautions.

I had three hours to kill between school and meeting Michael, and while I could've spent the time doing homework, I couldn't focus on anything but this date. Well, this meeting. Anticipation courses through my body, making everything from the tips of my fingers to the ends of my hair buzz. But I can't say whether it's the excited or nervous kind of buzzing. For the first time, I'm going to be on the level about who I really am. I won't have to lie about myself, or flirt, or try to convince him to keep dating me. With Michael, my status is not a secret. My plan is finally starting to feel like it's within reach.

Michael's email runs through my mind again. I know it by heart, and I keep coming back to two words in particular. *Mutually beneficial.* What does that mean? Maybe he isn't straight and he needs a sham marriage to prove something to family? Is it an inheritance thing, where he can only collect a trust fund once he's married? I dwell on the phrasing like it's a brain teaser, puzzling out all the myriad things it could possibly mean.

I'm staring into space, thinking about those words, when someone walks into my line of sight. I see his shoes first, coming to a stop in front of me, and then I take in the rest of him. He wears a quilted black jacket a decade out of style, casual work slacks, and his figure blots out the dying January sun. "Hi," the man says. "Are you Shirley?"

I stare at him for a beat too long. "Yes." Fake name, another layer of protection. Take that, Vitaly. I pull down the sleeves of my bubble coat. In my email correspondence with Michael, I told him to look for a girl in a red jacket.

"I'm Michael. May I join you?"

I nod quickly and scoot over, even though there is plenty of room on the bench. Michael sits, and neither of us says anything for a few seconds. I take the lull as an opportunity to decide, right then and there, based on nothing but looks and instinct, whether anyone will ever believe us as a married couple. It shouldn't be my first thought upon meeting a guy, and yet, increasingly, it is.

Michael has a weak jaw, mousy hair overdue for a trim,

and nice eyes. I'm definitely not attracted to him, but for the first time since I started on these dates, I don't have to be. He's already made it clear that he isn't interested in anything romantic.

"So," Michael says, "where should we start?"

I shrug. "This is kind of new for me."

"Well, we can try to get to know one another. Tell me something about yourself."

I hesitate. My ad was anonymous. I want to make sure nothing can be traced back to me. I'm keenly aware of how careful I have to be about this, which in turn makes me more than a little paranoid. Even now I can't shake the feeling that I'm being surveilled somehow, that someone out there is gathering proof that this relationship isn't real.

I think I let too much time pass since Michael last spoke, because now he says, "If we do get married, we should probably know something about each other."

There's a pair of moms passing in front of us with strollers just at that moment, and both of them turn to look at us as soon as Michael says the word "married." I catch one of the young mom's glances for a split second before she turns away, but it's enough to see exactly what she's thinking. That I look like a teenager, clutching the backpack I'd set on the bench beside me, a buffer between me and this older man. And why in the world am I talking about marriage with him?

If that mom can be skeptical of us with just one passing glance, how will we look sitting next to each other at an immigration agent's desk as he quizzes us on the legitimacy of our union?

"How old are you?" I ask.

"I'm thirty-three," Michael says.

Ancient. Older than any of the guys I've been on dates with. I try to keep my poker face on so as not to betray the sour feeling in the back of my throat. Michael already knows how old I am, because of my ad, so I offer a different fact about myself. Well, a semi-fact. "My name's not really Shirley."

He smirks. "I figured."

"So, what made you look at my ad?"

Michael links his fingers together, placing his hands over his knee, looking like he's about to give me a very thoughtful answer, when a shrill cry comes from the playground behind us. He pauses, waiting for the children to stop shrieking. This is so not a place for a business meeting.

"You know what? I'm freezing," I say. "Want to go somewhere else?"

"Sure."

I glance around. It's mostly just stores. The coffee shop is a couple of blocks away, but what if Vitaly's there? A teeny part of me doesn't even want barista Cary to see me with this guy. That's when I spot the W across the street.

A hotel is probably not the most appropriate setting for this kind of thing, but I can see the lobby from here, floor-to-ceiling windows right on the corner of the block. It's practically still out in public. And the plush armchairs inside look regal and comfortable. I nod toward it. "Let's go there."

29

OUTSIDE, THE SUN HAS FULLY SET, AND INSIDE, the hotel lounge is fancy and dimly lit, full of velvet chairs and plush sofas and highball glasses on low marble tables. It's such an adult space, and I've never felt more like a kid.

As Michael looks over the drinks menu on the coffee table between our armchairs, I account for the people in the room. There's the concierge, a couple of people manning the check-in desk, and two men in blazers at the other end of the lounge. There are people here, holding me to my public-space rule, but they are far enough away for Michael and me to speak freely, without having to whisper. I unzip my coat but I don't take it off. It's nothing, but to me it feels like one more precaution.

"So, back to your question." Michael sets the menu down. "I found your ad because I was looking for it."

The distant nerves I'd been feeling earlier, about the government on my tail, come brimming to the forefront. Dread prickles my skin as I wait for Michael to say he's some sort of undercover agent tasked with looking for girls who post green-card personal ads.

"My friend did something like this—helped a girl in a similar situation to yours," Michael says. "He married her, and stayed married to her until she got her citizenship, after which they divorced. He said if he could do it again, he would in a heartbeat. But it's pretty difficult to do twice without Homeland Security catching on."

I lean in, fascinated by the existence of this underground world. I wish I was sitting across from this friend of his so I could interview him. I have so many questions. But the bottom line is: This half-baked plan of mine can work. *Has* worked before. And suddenly it doesn't matter that I'm not attracted to Michael or that I'm nearly half his age.

"You said in your email that this would be mutually beneficial," I say. "Did you mean it would be, like, spiritually fulfilling? To help someone out like this?"

A crease forms between his eyes, making me second-guess my question, and then a chuckle bursts from his thin lips, making me doubt myself even more. "I mean financially."

Oh. Of course. *Financially*. I guess this is the moment of truth.

Michael sits back, looking more at ease now that the topic of money has been put on the table. "Did you have a number in mind?" he asks.

I shake my head.

"I was thinking ten thousand, cash."

The number rings in my head like a clapper in a bell. I vibrate with the shock of it. "Ten thousand *dollars*? That's a lot of money."

"Really?" Michael says. I can't believe he has the gall to be more surprised than me right now. "It's within the normal range for this kind of thing."

Normal range? Why does he even know that? For the first

time I ask myself something I probably should've asked the moment I made my ad. *What kind of man does this?* What kind of man not only looks for ads like this, but responds to them?

That sour taste in my throat that I've been trying to swallow this whole time spreads. It's on the roof of my mouth, the lining of my esophagus. I'm kind of disgusted with Michael, but I'm disgusted with myself, too. He may have responded to my ad, but I'm the one who placed it. I'm party to this whole seedy husband-finding arrangement. I glance out the window, the way I would at the coffee shop whenever a date started to go off the rails. But Vitaly isn't on the other side of the glass.

"Ten thousand is a steal if you consider your reward versus my risk," Michael says. I can't tell if he looks offended or if that's just me projecting my own feelings onto him.

"Risk?" I say.

"I would have to commit to two years of being married to you. I'd need to rearrange my life to make it appear as though we're living together. There's the time we'd have to spend together to get to know each other, the pictures we'd have to stage as evidence of our relationship, the interviews. Obviously, the risk of jail time and the fine."

"Jail . . . fine?" I am an echo chamber, unable to do anything but parrot his words back at him.

"Five years and up to two hundred and fifty thousand dollars if we get found out."

Michael's words swim between my ears, making my head spin. I feel a sort of motion sickness. I knew about these things, vaguely. But I never allowed myself to really delve into the repercussions of my plan. I'd gone into it with blinders on, hoping for the best and ignoring everything that could blow up in my face. But this is getting too real. And now I can't help asking myself questions like, *If I get caught in a sham marriage, will I be deported right away or put in jail first?* And, *Where the hell am I going to get ten thousand dollars?*

I'm not sure if I accidentally ask that last one out loud, but Michael answers it. "We can talk about the price more, but you can pay in installments."

The whirling thoughts dizzying up my head quiet down with that one word. "Installments" is the kind of word that belongs on a spreadsheet. An invoice. It doesn't belong anywhere near an interpersonal relationship. I know I wanted to erase all romantic components from my plan, but the combination of those two things—*installments* and *marriage*—makes my stomach churn.

My vision starts to go fuzzy. I grab onto the armrest and start to stand. "I need—"

Michael's calloused fingers are around my wrist, like the cold metal of handcuffs. "Where are you going?" he asks.

There's a flash of panic in his eyes. Maybe it's a reaction to my own rising alarm. Or maybe he's concerned that his big payday is about to get up and walk away. I don't know why he needs all that cash. I don't want to know anything else about him. All I know is that I need to get out of here. I try to pull my hand free of his grasp, but all that seems to do is pull Michael up to standing.

"Why are you running away?" he asks in a steady voice that hums with an undercurrent of urgency. "You know, anyone else would demand a lot more from you than just money.

You're lucky I'm not a creep. Unless . . . is that what you were hoping to pay me with? Instead of cash? You did put your age in the ad. Were you trying to attract the type of guy who's into jailbait?"

And just like that, my flight response turns into a fight one. I yank hard on Michael's hand, until his face lurches forward, meeting my fist in an uppercut. It happens so quick—the squelch of skin, the crunch of bone, the howl coming out of him. The men in the corner gasp.

I can't believe my punch actually had an impact. I didn't need Vitaly here to save me, but I still silently thank him for teaching me this new skill.

"You broke my nose!" Michael growls. "She broke my nose!"

I stumble back, my thigh clipping the overstuffed armchair. Someone who works for the hotel is there suddenly, looking unsure whether it's the high school girl who needs help, or the man with blood dripping over his mouth. I don't know if it's the adrenaline or the nerves, but I'm shivering. I want to explain, but I can't get the words out. And what would I say anyway? *He was trying to extort me?*

The guy in the hotel uniform tries to calm Michael down, press a cloth napkin to his nose, but Michael squirms away, shouting, "Call the cops!"

That's all it takes for me to get out of there. First it's a brisk walk, but then I give up the ghost and go full speed, past the hotel guy before he can reach me, ignoring the businessmen pointing at me, until I push through the door. I run so fast my tears fall sideways, leaving a trail to my ears.

30

MY FIRST KISS HAPPENED WHEN I WAS THIRTEEN years old, on a summer night when I was bored out of my mind. That particular day in July felt like the longest in the world. My mom couldn't pay for any sort of day camp. I begged her to let me be a junior counselor—other girls in my class were doing it—but my mother put her foot down and said I was too young to work.

She seemed to work all the time, though. And that summer night, she was at her second job of the day. The plate of salchipapas she'd left covered for me in the fridge just didn't taste the same zapped in the microwave, and I left it mostly uneaten on my desk as I looked out the window to the courtyard below.

We'd moved into the building just a few months earlier, and the only person I knew was a kid from my school, the boy from 1F. He was always in the courtyard, and tonight he was playing a game of catch with the brick wall. Over and over, he flung his blue rubber handball with his right arm, same precise windup, same overhand, and the brick wall always spit it right back to him, never missing the pocket of his left palm.

The hollow echo that rubber ball made, the way it zipped back and forth, was hypnotic. And so boring. I was tired of how boring everything was. I was young and pretty in the best city in the world on a summer night. I wasn't about to spend it sitting in my room watching a ball fly across the courtyard for an hour.

It took me less than three minutes to get outside. The boy swung his arm back but stopped just short of throwing the ball when he spotted me. He didn't say anything. He never did. Not whenever I saw him in the lobby, helping his mother carry grocery bags, or the times he avoided my gaze in the hallways at school, or the one time both of our parents sent us to check the mail at the exact same time and his clumsy fingers dropped the mailbox key *twice* before finally getting it in the slot.

He may have been the shiest boy in the world. I wasn't even sure he spoke English until we ended up in the same class the year before and the teacher struggled to get his name right during the first day's attendance.

"Vitaly," he'd said in the smallest voice. "It rhymes with Big Rally."

It was the first and last time he'd ever rhyme his name like that. The snickers that came out of Tommy Shawnessy and Ben Krudinsky, sitting in the back of the class, were quiet but deafening.

So it was up to me to say something that summer night, as he stood there with his unthrown rubber ball in his fist. Which was just fine by me. I liked to talk. "Have you kissed anyone yet?"

The ball fell from his grip and Big Rally chased after it. The kiss question may have seemed random, but it was all I could think about ever since Sof told me that she'd kissed Jayden Lavigne three days earlier. "Kissing is disgusting," Sof had said. "Jayden's mouth was like a slimy alien trying to abduct me to another planet. I can't wait to do it again."

She'd said it like it was no big deal, but to me, Sof had unlocked a new level of life. She was practically a woman now. I didn't want to get left behind. I wanted to experience life, too.

The boy from 1F continued not to say anything, and the longer he just stood there with his stupid ball and stared at me, the more I started to regret having asked the question. It was starting to feel like my first rejection from a boy, and I wasn't going to allow that. "Okay, you have three seconds to answer before I get offended."

He waited an excruciating two-point-five seconds before finally saying, "No, I never kissed anyone."

"Well, do you want to kiss *me*?"

This question seemed to stun him more than my first. He continued to stare at me, and it was getting annoying. It was too hot for me to be waiting for this silent boy from 1F to act. But then he did.

He wiped the palm of the hand that wasn't holding the ball on the side of his jean shorts and took a step toward me. I cut the distance even more, until we were standing close enough to kiss. Looking at his face, I saw things I hadn't seen there before. He had a dusting of freckles across the pale bridge of his nose. And a tiny scar along the top of his ear. "Close your eyes," I demanded.

He did as he was told and waited for me. I leaned in, and when my mouth felt his, I let my own eyes drift shut. Our lips hardly moved. They just pressed together, dry and smooth. The kiss didn't feel anything like an alien trying to suck me to another planet. But it did feel like unlocking a whole new level of life.

When I pulled away, his eyes were still closed. "I'm Jimena, by the way."

"I know."

And then Vitaly ran all the way back to his apartment.

Our kiss seemed to only make him shier, but it made me bolder, opened me up like a flower. I wanted more of that, not only the kissing part but the feeling of a boy's want, his love. Because I could tell, even though it lasted only seconds, that Vitaly definitely wanted more of me.

From then on, whenever I saw him in the building, I made sure to say hello, just to show him that he didn't need to be afraid of me. But he kept on acting like he was. I always tried to get him to laugh, which I guess meant that I'd sometimes tease him. But either way, that was how it started.

I can't pinpoint why I'm dwelling on that particular memory. I don't know if I'm just trying to grab onto a sweet moment in my life. But even that memory is colored by my status. I feel sorry for that little girl who didn't even know that her presence in that courtyard was against the law. She thought the worst thing that could happen to her was being bored on a summer night, not knowing all the things she had stacked against her. That little girl bursting with life and wonder never stood a chance.

Maybe I'm just trying to figure out how I wound up here, crumpled up in bed like a used tissue, scared and sad and unable to shake the mounting sense of dread that's pinning me down. Did it start with my plan? Or did it start with that night in July, when I was so hungry for life that I couldn't wait for the big moments to find me, I had to go out and make them happen? Back when innocence, and the desire to shed it, warred inside me.

Something buzzes deep under my covers, but I ignore it. It starts up again a second later, though, and I relent, stretching across the bed, feeling for my phone. I flip it open.

"Hello?"

"Why are you ignoring my texts?" Sof asks.

I hold my phone back to glance at it. Sixteen unanswered texts. "I was in the bathroom?"

"Don't act like you don't take your phone into the bathroom."

I do not have the energy to come back with anything quippy, so I only mutter, "Yeah." It's just one syllable, but something in it must give me away because Sof's tone changes suddenly.

"What's the matter?"

I sit up, taking a deep breath like it's enough to clear my head and my heart from all the ache they've been feeling. It's not. "Nothing."

"Jimmy. I know when something's up with you, and something's definitely up with you."

What's funny is that all I want is my best friend right now. I want to bury my face in her knee as she strokes my hair and I cry all over her lap. But how can I explain to her that last night I broke the nose of a nasty older guy who tried to extort me and threatened to call the cops on me, which could very well lead to my deportation, which means I wouldn't get to see her again and that the whole mess was my own fault and I hardly recognized myself anymore?

"Sorry. Just . . . in a weird mood."

The silence on the line is loud and clear. "Whatever," Sof finally says. "But I thought we were going to get ready for the party together."

Shit. Sof's party—it totally slipped my mind. I fling the covers off and spring out of bed. "Duh, I'm totally on my way!"

It doesn't matter how I'm feeling. I need to put my game face on for my best friend. And maybe a party is just the mindless kind of fun I need right now.

31

SOF'S PARENTS GO ON A WEEKEND GETAWAY every year. Brandon stays at Carmen's house, and this year, Sof gets to stay at home alone to prove how responsible she is. Naturally, she's throwing a party. By the time I get there, a good chunk of the guests have already arrived. Sof must still be getting ready because I don't see her anywhere, which is for the best. If she can tell something's wrong just by the sound of my voice over shitty cell service, I don't want her getting a good hard look at me.

Not that there's anything to see here, folks. There is a mirror hanging in the entryway and I check myself out in it, combing my fingers through my hair as the electronic chords of "SexyBack" waft in from the living room.

I look great.

I need a drink.

In the kitchen, I search the fridge but there's nothing. I check the cabinet where Lalo keeps the beer cases he buys from Costco. Jackpot. There's a giant bag of chips on the counter, too, and I tear into it. There's more food, little chocolate bars left over from Halloween, probably, and an open bag of BBQ corn nuts. I grab whatever party bowls I can find and start filling them between swigs of my tepid beer.

I could do this all night, stay in the kitchen, keep people fed. I can hear the party ramping up in the next room. I tear bags open and fill bowls until Sof's voice is in my ear. "Where have you been?"

"Here," I tell her. "Refreshment duty."

"Well, I need you." She pulls on my elbow until we're in the living room. "Kenz and Luce are fighting again, and you're the only one who knows how to deal with them."

I hear Kenz and Luce before I see them. Kenz is standing in front of the TV, gesticulating wildly with her hands. She's a big hand-talker. Luce is not a hand-talker. Her hands are curled into tight fists that she holds at her sides, trying to talk over Kenz.

"If you would've just said three o'clock, I would've been there at *three o'clock*," Kenz says, her stance full predatory.

Luce groans. "We get it, you like an odd number!"

"I have no idea what's going on," I whisper to Sof.

"Nobody does, just do something!"

So I gently grasp Luce's shoulder and guide her back in the direction from which I just came. Not because there's anything interesting in the kitchen, but because it's far enough away from Kenz that they can't physically continue their inane ranting.

We only get as far as the dining room when something stops me in my tracks. A frog could've been on the table, performing in top hat and coattails, for how gobsmacked I am. And yet, this is more shocking than even that.

"Is Vitaly Petrov at a party?"

"What?" Luce says, still distracted by her hatred for Kenz. But she looks where I'm looking and nods. "I guess so?"

The last time I was here, the six-seater dining room table was covered in sushi. Now it's covered in Vitaly, being held down on either side by idiot football co-captains Logan and Luke. Logan is chanting some caveman-wannabe-frat-boy nonsense while Luke funnels a river of beer down Vitaly's throat via a clear tube.

"Is this bullying?" I ask. I am genuinely concerned.

But no, Vitaly is definitely not being bullied, because when the guys let go of his arms, he sits up with a huge gurgling grin, dripping with golden beer. It's not just any smile, either. It's the lazy kind, lured to the surface by drink.

I can't believe Vitaly is at a party.

I can't believe he's having fun after the fight we had.

Of course he sees me. His beautiful smile slips. A new song starts, about hips that don't lie, and Vitaly—who is usually the one to avoid, to flee, to recede back into his shell—decides to cross the room toward me.

My own feet are welded to the floor, but I turn to Luce and say, "I think I just heard Kenz call you an unhinged introvert." It just comes out, but it does the trick. Luce's jaw drops and she spins back around, stalking toward the front of the house, muttering something about how Kenz is such an ineffectual alcoholic.

And then Vitaly and I are facing each other, close enough that we have to step back when a short freshman squeezes between us to get to the other room.

I have to raise my voice over Shakira's yodeling to be heard. "Are you drinking?"

"I'm loosening up," Vitaly says, popping the *p* at the end of his sentence. "As per your suggestion."

"Aren't you worried someone might post a picture of you like this on Facebook? Cockblock your chances of getting into Oxford?"

"Already got in."

The statement lands with a fatal thud. It's the kind of news that should be met with cheers and celebratory backslaps. If Vitaly and I were friends, I'd probably pull him in for a bear hug. But there is only a dryness in my mouth, overcorrected by the sudden tears prickling the back of my eyes. If I were a good person, I'd be happy for him. But Vitaly's news stirs up darker emotions. Jealousy for his bright, open future and grief for mine, which feels so decidedly shuttered. And there's the realization that Vitaly will be out of the country soon and out of my life. The news brings up way too many things that I don't want to deal with right now.

"I just got my acceptance letter . . ." The sting in his voice is gone, and now he sounds almost sheepish, like he doesn't want to show off. "I guess I'm celebrating."

"Congratulations," I say breathlessly. "That's awesome."

"Thank you."

"I'm really happy for you."

"Thank you."

"I should . . . Sof asked me to . . ." I trail off, but it's not like he's begging me to finish my incoherent rambling. My feet come unstuck, and I let them carry me away. They don't stop moving until I hit the kitchen island, my middle sucker punched by the marble countertop. I don't have a kitchen island. I will probably never have a kitchen island. It's such a small thing, and I don't know why that thought pops into my mind right now, but it's the truth of it, that my circumstances will never change—will never have the chance to change— that makes me stifle a scream in my throat.

Lalo keeps the good stuff in the back of the cabinet on top of the fridge. I have to drag a counter stool over to get to it. I fish out the first bottle my probing fingers can grab hold of. It's mostly empty, a caramel-colored liquid. I unscrew the top and bring it to my lips. Take a swig. Make a face. Take another.

32

I'M NOT USUALLY SUCH A FLOP AT PARTIES. I AM
the get down on the dance floor. I am the volume up on the
stereo. Fergie is on the radio, demanding I get "Fergalicious,"
but right now I am a sack of potatoes somebody dumped in the
middle of the couch. Inanimate, ignored. I half expect someone
to try and shove me out of the way for taking up valuable seat-
ing space, demanding to know who thought to bring a sack of
potatoes to a rager. As a courtesy, I try to make myself smaller,
shrinking into the cushions as much as I can. I sip from my
plastic cup. Alcohol is nothing like coffee. I don't have a toler-
ance built up and my body mocks me for it, making my head
tilt of its own accord, making my nose feel like it's not attached
to my face, making my arms feel like lead weights.

I sit between Kenz and Luce, who are facing away from
each other. They flirt with other people, but they still manage to lob the occasional snippy remark at one another. Their
words volley over my head, but I don't catch the insults. My
attention is stolen completely by Vitaly. He has set up camp at
the head of the dining room table, and I can see him laughing
as he tries to catch a wayward Ping-Pong ball.

It turns out that Mr. No-fun-follow-the-rules-no-underage-
drinking-never-played-a-game-in-his-life-loves-his-homework-

straight-As-but-still-asks-for-extra-credit-reminds-the-teacher-she-was-going-to-give-us-a-quiz-hall-monitor-couldn't-recognize-fun-if-it-slapped-him-on-the-ass is good at beer pong. What a cliché.

Even though I'm an ignored sack of potatoes, there is one person here who is paying very close attention to me. Sof looks cute in a pageboy cap over stick-straight hair. She's got at least four layers on—three different-colored tanks that come down over her fitted jeans and a cardigan, all cinched at the waist with a chunky belt. She flits around her party, chatting and dancing and laughing and being an overall perfect hostess, but when she catches sight of me her party-girl mask falls, and she stares at me like, *Why is there a sack of potatoes in the middle of my couch? And why does it look like it's hiding something from me?*

I try to keep hiding, behind my cup this time. But it's no use. At least Sof gets me moving again. Her glare singes my skin and I have to get away. I wade through the people and the thick air until I reach the kitchen. All the serving bowls I so carefully filled up are a mess of crumbs. I press the pad of my index finger into a speck of chip and then lick it off. And while I'm doing that, Vitaly enters the kitchen.

He raids the fridge, looking for something to replenish all the sweat he's losing in his beer pong game. The same sweat that's making the back of his neck glisten. He stands straight, chugging from a water bottle, and the two of us pretend that we don't notice each other.

I leave Vitaly glowing in the fridge light, but I can't avoid him. When I skulk into the dining room, he finds his way there also. When I go wait for the bathroom door to open, he's there waiting for it, too. When I slide along the hallway wall, feeling my way back to the living room, he's already there, saying more words to one of our classmates than I have ever seen him say to another teenager ever. But though he may be talking to that girl, his eyes drift over to me; constantly, inevitably.

Is he following me? Gnarls Barkley whines from the boom box on the mantel, asking repeatedly if that makes me crazy. *Does that make me crazy?* "Posssssiblyyyyy," I croon.

I need air. It's freezing outside and I am wearing the stupidest summer dress, so I set my sights on the second floor, where there aren't a million people sucking up all the oxygen. But first, I must traverse Coat Everest. Everyone's dumped their jackets at the foot of the stairs. It's an effective way to block off the entrance to the off-limits part of the premises, but it means I have to climb, which would be hard enough to do sober, let alone plastered.

I hold on to the banister and take a deep breath in. I haven't even begun to summit this mountain and I already feel like I need an oxygen tank. I pitch my foot over a fluffy mound, but it sinks like it's a snowbank. I am not deterred. I keep climbing. It's like being on an elliptical, where I take steps but they don't go anywhere. And much like with exercise, I settle into a routine. Clutch the banister, breathe in deep, take a step, wipe stray strands of hair from my eyes, repeat.

I don't know how, but I make it over. I go straight for Sof's room, perch myself on the edge of her bed, and do nothing but wait.

The door slowly opens a moment later, and he walks in. Of course. He closes the door behind his back, muffling the sounds of the party. I stand just as he crosses the room. Vitaly doesn't stop until he reaches me, or until I reach him, I guess.

My mind is too hazy to account for the order of events, to know who initiates things. My hand finds his waist and his forehead presses against my own. Perhaps the two things happen at the same time. It feels that way, like it's all happening at once: his breath, hot and forceful through his nose, my nails buried in the slick-tipped strands of hair at the back of his head. His fingers tugging, scrunching the fabric of my dress, between my collarbone and chest, like he's using my clothes to pull me closer, or can't stand that they're in the way.

In the dark bedroom, where the only light comes from the window, we can see best by feeling. And we try to see every inch of each other. All I hear is breath and pulse, so loud it feels like my heart is smashed between my spine and his chest. I want to jump out of myself, to set free something that's been bottled up since a night in July, years ago. Everything is so quick and desperate and urgent, but when I tip my face up, Vitaly catches my lips in the slowest kiss.

Things steady like a sigh, and I hold still, letting myself sink into the moment.

I thought there would be some muscle memory, because we've been here before. But this kiss isn't anything like the one we shared at thirteen. It isn't dry and stilted, and it isn't innocent. There isn't a boy attached to these lips, there is a man, and I can hear a moan from deep in his throat. The sound is small, but it triggers my own involuntary impulse to get closer to him, pulling his head down and rising on my tippy-toes.

This kiss is nothing like the one from when we were kids, but there is one similarity. In a time where everything feels closed off to me, this kiss feels like unlocking a whole new level of life.

A sudden, harsh light cuts across my cheek, and Vitaly and I rip apart. I squint at the light coming from the hallway. Two silhouettes stand in the doorframe, staring dumbly at us.

"Get out." My voice is so rough it sounds alien to my own ears.

They retreat, in search of a different, empty bedroom, but the damage is done. Vitaly's pulling his sweater back on, threading his arms through its sleeves. I didn't realize it'd come off.

Silence wedges itself between us like a battle-axe. When Vitaly's head breaks through the sweater, ruffling his hair, it takes everything in me not to reach out and smooth the tufts.

There is only one thing I want to ask him, and I'm too bold and too drunk to stop myself. "Why won't you marry me?"

I am self-aware enough to know how absolutely batshit the question is. *Who says something like that?* It's Bridezilla levels of entitlement and delusion, but I don't have time to wade through bullshit. There are a million little things I could have said to him—"Be with me"; "Stay"—but it would all build up to that much larger question anyway. Because it isn't just this kiss we've shared, it's the time we've spent together, it's the things we've told each other, the fact that he knows me better than anyone, the way I've made him laugh—and he's made me *want*—like no one else. It's that touching him is like taking a match to a striker. *Burning flame.*

We haven't been on a single date. But we amount to something.

"Is that a proposal?" Vitaly's voice is gruff, still thick with desire, I know it.

"I can tell that you like me." My eyes leave his briefly to drift farther down his body, and now both of our cheeks burn. Vitaly won't look at me anymore. Now that he's dressed, there's nothing to keep him from leaving. But before he goes for the door he takes a deep breath, hands on hips, looking like he's psyching himself up to ask me something.

"You've asked me to marry you before," he says ruefully. "Never seriously."

"I've always been serious. Every time."

But Vitaly only shakes his head, doesn't believe me. "It isn't right that you only see things in terms of—" He pauses, grasping for better words. "You only want me so you can get your papers."

No. *No.* "Vitaly." I say his name like it can reach out and touch him. It's amazing how a minute ago my hands were all over him, but now it feels like there's a force field between us that I can't breach.

"It takes more than 'like' to marry someone," he says.

I nod, mostly to try to keep the tears that suddenly spring to my eyes from spilling over. I can't even kiss a boy without spoiling it. I'm an idiot. No, I'm a maniac. I'm a menace and maybe I *should* be locked up and thrown out of the country. I rush out, head down the stairs, and try not to die on Coat Everest. But there's one more obstacle between me and the door.

Sof stands in front of me with her arms crossed over her chest. I can tell by the expression on her face that she already knows what I've been doing in her room, and who with, even before her eyes flash toward Vitaly, on the landing.

"What's going on with you?" she asks me.

"Nothing."

"Are you really going to keep lying to me at my own party?"

"Sof," I start.

"Are you with Vitaly now? And why are you hiding that?"

"I'm not with him." My voice is so hushed I wonder if she hears me.

"Doesn't look like that to me."

"I can't do this right now."

"You can't do anything, ever." Sof barely takes a second to pause. "You have been avoiding me this entire year. You know, I got so tired of waiting for you to fill out our UCLA apps with me, I had to apply *for* you?"

"You what?" I start to fill up with so much dread I might drown in it. Is some administrator going to start fishing around in my records, asking questions I don't need them asking?

"We were supposed to do that together."

"The deadline was *months* ago, Jimmy."

Did Sof use false information about me to fill out the application? She must have. Am I going to get in trouble because of it? I'm incensed that she'd do that without my permission, but I'm also terrified of what might happen now. "What did you put in for my Social Security number?"

A question flickers over Sof's face, like she doesn't get why I would ask that right now. "I left it blank. You'll sort it out later."

"You had no right to do that."

"Are you kidding me?" Sof says. "I paid your application fee—you should be thanking me!"

But I don't thank her. I push past her until I'm out the door.

33

NOT EVERYTHING ABOUT GROWING UP UNDOC- umented was bad. To some people it may all seem pretty grim, but just below the rubble of doom and gloom, in the dark part that makes you who you are, there are glimmers of good. There is sometimes something salvageable. I think growing up the way I did made me resilient. And adaptable.

I've moved so many times, all within the same New York City borough. We first lived with family friends. They were a couple with two kids, a boy and a girl around my age, and my earliest memories of America are of the toys they had. They'd left Peru for this new land and now they had the spoils to show for it. Every kind of action figure, Hot Wheel, and Barbie, with all sorts of accessories. According to my mother, we lived in their second bedroom for three months, but I don't remember anything about that living situation except those toys. They were things I'd never seen before, and to me they defined America. Shiny. Excess. Beautiful.

After that, we found another bedroom to live in, our small family of three, sharing a house with strangers. I remember having to knock on the door to the bathroom to make sure our neighbors weren't currently using it. It wasn't too long before we found somewhere else to live, a place of our own. The basement under our landlord's house wasn't like other people's homes, I knew that even as a five-year-old. It didn't have a full kitchen and the fridge fit underneath the counter, but that basement home was ours and that was all that mattered.

We've lived in our current building the longest. Moved here, somehow, after my father left. Point is, I can walk into any room—any situation—and adjust. Thrive, even. Sharing a room with parents? Fine by me. Finally have a bedroom but it's separated from the rest of the house by a flimsy curtain? I can make it work. Accidentally stumble onto the talent show stage with no discernible skills and nothing prepared? I'm taking home that trophy. So wading through my new reality of my closest friends not wanting anything to do with me should be fine.

I mean, it *is* fine. It's February. I haven't spoken to Sof or Vitaly in a month and they haven't spoken to me, and I can walk down the school hallways like nothing's changed.

I am resilient.

I am adaptable.

I am an incredible actress, because sometimes even I can't tell that I'm miserable without them.

Mondays before school I get coffee by myself, and I spend lunchtime pretending to do homework in the computer lab. Sof is angry with me, and I can't blame her. But I don't know how to make things better between us without lying to her, which is the problem.

With Vitaly, it's just like when we were thirteen: I can't seem to kiss him without making him run away. What happened at Sof's party has definitely, irreparably, ruined whatever there was between us. Vitaly retreats back into himself. I don't see him in the courtyard anymore, and if we happen to accidentally catch each other's gaze in class, he's the first to pull away. He's pretending the whole thing—whatever we were—never happened. For once, so am I.

It sucks, not talking to the two people I'm closest with, but maybe it's easier this way. They're going to move on in a few months, and I'm not going to be able to follow them. A part of me thinks it might be better this way, that if they're angry with me I can make a clean break.

And all this time alone has given me the space to think about my plan. Specifically, about quitting it. If I look at it objectively, the way Vitaly always did, I can acknowledge that I dove into this harebrained scheme without thinking it all the way through. I never considered what it would really mean to marry someone. What it would cost me. Emotionally. Mentally. Financially. What if acceptance of my circumstances isn't just the easiest thing to do, but the safest? Because the truth of the matter is that I'm in a country that doesn't want me, and I can't rely on any person or institution to protect me. What if my only means of survival is living under the radar, in the shadows, where no one will notice me?

That could be my new plan.

I'd given my mom such a hard time about not trying enough, not going through the process correctly, not hiring any lawyers, not *fighting*. And a part of me—an ugly part—resented her for having to get jobs that only paid under the table, for living her whole life carefully, walking on eggshells, making sure never to step out of line. But what I hadn't been able to see is that all of that was her method of self-preservation. My mom is just trying to survive in a system that wants to chew her up and spit her out. And she's doing it all for me.

I thought I could never be free if I was living life locked in a cage. But maybe the key is just to make my cage bigger. I can't unlock it, but someday someone will. It's time I accept my situation and give up on this dream of being free. At least for now. A lot of people give up on their dreams. It's part of growing up.

But just when I think I can go the rest of the school year without speaking to my friends again, Sof stops me in the hall between second and third period.

"My parents got me a car."

I open my mouth but nothing comes out. I'm shocked she's talking to me. I'm shocked that when she finally does speak to me, this is what she chooses to say. Though I'm not shocked her parents got her a car. "Congratulations."

"Do you want to see it?"

34

I'VE NEVER HAD A PROBLEM PLAYING HOOKY before. But having to walk five blocks to get to Sof's car feels entirely uncalled for. Sof seems to feel the same way.

"I think my parents were punishing me when they got me the car. They know there's no parking anywhere, so if I want to drive to school I need to get up extra early just to circle around for a half hour looking for a spot where they know I'll be forced to practice my parallel parking. It's really insidious, if you think about it."

"Yeah, I hope my mom never punishes me with a car." I don't have the energy to muster up the good-natured sarcasm, so my delivery is flat.

Sof stops and points. "There it is."

It's shiny and gray and honestly, all cars look the same to me. Normally, I'd fake effusiveness, but I don't really know where Sof and I stand right now, so I find myself simply nodding.

Sof clicks a button on her key fob to unlock the doors, and we get in. "Don't bother putting on your seatbelt, we're not going anywhere. I can't risk having to parallel park again." She blasts the heat so we can be comfortable for whatever conversation she wants to have.

The new car smell is overwhelming, and on the door and

dashboard there are still protective stickers covering most of the surfaces. From the glove box, a tag tells me this seat has an advanced airbag that can kill children. No wonder it feels like I could die right now.

I hug my coat to my chest while Sof flips the sun visor down to check her makeup in the mirror. She's wearing a navy-blue beret and tugs it up and down until she finds the sweet spot between her brows and hairline. I guess she's experimenting with a French look ahead of the Culture Club trip. It feels so weird that Sof's in a whole new style phase and I wasn't there for our standard trying-on-clothes-in-her-bedroom montage. Sof flips the visor back up, instantly turning the spotlight off and snapping me out of my thoughts. "You need to talk to me," she says.

It takes me a moment to process her directness. "I don't know what to say."

"You want to stop being friends, and I don't even know why. You think I deserve that?"

She definitely doesn't.

"You've been acting weird this whole year, but honestly? This past month's been the worst part. So much has happened and I don't have a best friend to talk about it with," she says.

"What's been going on?" It feels like I've lost the right to ask that, but I'm so curious. Selfishly, I want to know everything that's happening in her life.

Sof studies her French tips. "I've kind of been seeing the Dog again."

I suppress an inner squeal that would've been a full-blown howl if me and Sof were on good terms. "'Kind of'?"

Sof shrugs. "I don't think most people would consider Planet Fitness a date spot, but I'm pretty sure that to the Dog it's the height of romance."

Knowing the Dog, he'd likely take a girl there to propose, so he's definitely got it bad for Sof. "That's so exciting."

But she's got a look on her face like her heart is a balloon and I just put a needle through it. Like all she wants is to celebrate this new relationship and I can't even do it right.

"Tell me why you're hiding whatever it is you got going on with Vitaly," Sof says. "Or why you're freaking out about college. And those strange men on the dating site? There is so much I don't understand about your life right now, and I don't get why you won't let me in."

Her words fall heavy and the car feels small. Claustrophobic. If I tell Sof my secret, then that changes everything. She'll stop seeing me as just her best friend. She'll look at me like an alien. A criminal. It's what most people think about illegal immigrants. It's what her dad thinks. I just don't want Sof to hate me. I don't want her to look at me like there's something inherently wrong with me.

I can't stop the sudden onslaught of tears that pour out of me. They make everything blurry, and when I try to breathe, the air feels waterlogged.

"Whoa, whoa," Sof says, scooching closer despite the console separating us. She rests her hand on my knee. "Don't cry. Whatever it is, I'm here, okay?"

Can I trust that, though?

Why is this so hard to say? Why does this feel like the biggest, most defining thing about me? It's a grenade in my hand

and it's ready to obliterate me. Us. The person she thinks I am. Ultimately, I can't explain why this is so hard. It just is. It's the scariest thing I've ever had to do, but I'm too tired to keep lying. And Sof doesn't deserve it.

My fingernail picks at the corner of the protective film on her dashboard. "I need to tell you something." If she hates me, then she hates me. It wouldn't be so different than this last month anyway. Sof nods and stares at me with scared, narrowed eyes. I need to be out with it.

"The thing is"—I pull the film bit by bit, tugging it free— "I'm undocumented."

Sof's face changes slowly. Her forehead creases. I crumple the useless protective material into a tiny ball in my fist. *Say something.*

"What do you mean?" Sof asks.

I'm full-on sobbing now. Uncontrollable, gulping breaths, eyes squeezed shut, tears making my whole face wet. I hate this. I want to stop talking. I want to not admit this, I don't want to admit anything about myself ever. "I'm an illegal immigrant." I shrug and chance a look at Sof. The lines on her forehead deepen, and I swear I can feel her grip on my knee loosen a little bit. It's nearly imperceptible, but it's a signal of what I fear most. That I repel her, that she doesn't want to know me anymore.

"But you've been here since you were, like, three."

I don't say anything, because I'm just as confused as she is by the whole thing. It doesn't make any sense.

"Wait, are you, like, getting deported?"

I shake my head and try to sniff back the snot that's

threatening to come to this shitshow of a party. "No, I'm just . . ." I shrug again. "I'm not supposed to be here."

"Hey," Sof says. And then she does something I really don't expect. She gathers me up. As awkward as it is to reach over and squeeze her arm between me and the seat, she does it and holds on tight. "Of course you're supposed to be here. Why would you say that?"

"Because I'm an illegal alien," I sputter out. Now when I say it it's like I'm daring her. Daring her to agree, to reproach me, to *report* me. Now that the dam's been busted open, I'm letting it all out. The good, the bad, and the ugly, just to see how much she can take before kicking me out of her car and life. "My mom and I came here on tourist visas and they expired and we never left. And if they find us, they're gonna kick us out. I'm a fucking fugitive, basically. I'm not normal. I can't *be* normal. Ever."

Sof's soft palms are against my cheeks suddenly, and despite the fact that they're wet as ice floes, she keeps her hands there until I'm looking directly at her. My vision's still hazy with tears, but Sof leans in close, making sure I can see her clearly. "Listen to me," she says. "I don't see no antennas on your head. No green skin. Unless you came here from another planet, you are not an alien."

A laugh comes out of me like a dying sob.

"And you're not illegal, either."

"*Yes, I am*," I cry.

"People aren't illegal." Sof lays my head on her shoulder and strokes my hair, brushing it away from my wet face. She's trying to get me to stop crying, but I can hear her own voice going liquid, too. "I don't care where you're from or where you aren't allowed to be. I'm going to be there with you. If somebody tries to kick you out of America, then guess what? We're both going to college in Peru. Shit, I don't care!"

I laugh against her shoulder and the sound of it surprises me. Laughing is the last thing I expected I'd be doing when I got into this car.

Sof's still stroking my hair, and the rhythm of the motion is a guide for my breathing. It comes out less erratic, calmer, until I realize I'm not crying anymore. "You're my ride or die," Sof says. "We're sisters. Like Mary-Kate and Ashley."

And then, at the same time, we both say, "I'm Ashley," because we both have impeccable taste.

I lift my head from Sof's shoulder just in time for her to shove my arm. "You scared me, Jimmy! I thought you were going to tell me you killed someone!"

"Are you kidding? You'd be the first person I'd tell if I killed someone."

"Is that why you were going on those awful dates?" Sof says. "Because you're looking for a green card marriage?"

Sof gets it. No explanation necessary, no weighing the moral logic of it all. I should've just told her everything from the get-go. All she does is cluck her tongue and I know exactly how she feels about the whole thing.

I'm crying again, but for a different reason this time. And I can't believe it, but now what's flowing out of me, along with the tears, is an overwhelming sense of relief. It feels like freedom. Not the big kind of freedom, like being able to cross a country's borders, but the kind that eases my fear just a tiny bit. And maybe I can live a life like this. Collecting these small freedoms like trophies in a cabinet. Basking in them.

Because I said the unsayable thing. And now that it's out, my legal status doesn't feel like the big deal I was making it out to be. I mean, it's still a big deal, but now, with Sof by my side, it feels a little easier to face.

"Thank you," I breathe. I go in for another hug. I'm so light-headed from the relief that I need to lean on her just a little bit longer. And while I'm here, I might as well lay it all out. "I'm totally into Vitaly Petrov."

Sof gasps so hard I think the power of it physically pushes us apart. She holds me at arm's length just so she can get a good look at me. "I knew it! You like him! Tell me everything right now."

"There's nothing to tell. We're not even talking anymore."

"Why? When did this whole thing start? Are you guys in a fight? Were you like, *dating* dating or not-at-all dating? Wait, back up, can't you just marry him for your green card?"

It's all too much to get into, and I'm already emotionally drained from all the crying. I don't think this car can hold the momentous brief history of me and Vitaly. But I can answer Sof's most pertinent question. "Vitaly's going to England for college. It's not . . . it's not ever gonna happen with him."

Even that tiny statement seems like too much for the car to handle. It fills up the small space so much that it's hard for me to take in a deep breath. It's good to finally be admitting all this to Sof—to even talk honestly about something as frivolous as boys and dating. But it's surreal that there's been someone in my life who I've talked *marriage* with and my best friend didn't even know about it. I think Sof feels that surrealness, too, that our senior years have been so wildly different.

"Okay, chin up, no boy drama in my brand-new car." She opens the driver's-side door and gets out. "We're getting coffee."

Yes, please.

35

NOW THAT I'VE MADE UP WITH SOF, AVOIDING Vitaly goes from hard to excruciating. The urge to make up with him, too, is right there on the surface. Every time I see him in class, or pass him in the lobby, or catch a glimpse of him in the laundry room, I want to reach out to him. But if I've learned anything from our fight at Sof's house, it's that I'm prone to saying the wrong thing.

Plus, now that I haven't had a date in a while and I've come clean to Sof, my mind has been freed up to dwell on normal teenage stuff, like the drunk, messy, hot kiss Vitaly and I shared at the party.

In the weeks that pass, I become a poor imitation of an artist's favorite subject: girl staring forlornly out her bedroom window, just hoping to see a boy in her courtyard. I convince myself that I'm not the only reason Vitaly avoids it these days. Maybe it's too cold and he's hibernating. I wonder where he goes. I know he's not home. Not even the weather can keep him stuck there. But tonight, as I look out my window, I spot him. Instead of going straight for his patio chair, he stops and looks up at me.

I'm so startled I almost dive back into bed. I don't want him to know I was looking for him. But he's already seen me, and trying to pretend I'm not here would only make things even more humiliating.

Do I say something to him? Wave?

But Vitaly's hand is already raised, and then it subtly motions for me to come down.

I stare a few seconds longer, making sure I'm understanding him right. It's past eleven and we aren't talking. The last thing I want to do right now is show up downstairs in my pajamas because of a misunderstanding. But he's still there, gaze fixed on my window. Seemingly waiting.

I spring up and shuffle around my room, in search of a sweater. I tiptoe through the apartment, making sure my mom's asleep. If she knew what I was doing, she'd tell me to bundle up or *me va dar aire*, so I grab my coat and slip into my knockoff Uggs. When I get outside and stand a yard away from him, all Vitaly can do is stare at my pants. I've had them since I was thirteen, so they extend only to my calves, but I'm pretty sure it's not their awkward length that's caught his attention. The pj's were a gift, sent from my aunt in Peru, and they're patterned with hearts, teddy bears, and what a Spanish-language factory clearly thinks are typical English phrases appropriate for children's pajamas.

Kiss You So Much Forever. Sexy Love. Sleep with Me Party.

They're my favorite.

But I don't have time to feel ridiculous in my pj's/bubble coat/Uggs getup because I suddenly notice what's in Vitaly's hand. "Is that . . . ?"

We answer my question at the same time.

"The world's best coffee," I say. "The world's worst coffee," he says.

I'd listed the ingredients of my ideal drink for him once, while we were waiting for one of my awful dates at the café: Trenta cold brew, twelve pumps sugar-free vanilla, eight pumps hazelnut, five pumps skinny mocha, seven pumps caramel, light ice, double-blended with swirls of chocolate and jammy strawberry running along the inside of the cup. There's a big dollop of whipped cream covered in rainbow sprinkles, gleaming under a plastic dome like a snowy wonderland. But upon closer inspection I see that no, they're not sprinkles, they're something even better: nonpareils. Those magical little color bombs. I want to dip my entire face in them.

"I asked them to make it decaf because it's late," Vitaly says. "But they were ready to kick me out. So this drink will probably kill you. Not sure if you still want it."

"This a peace offering or an execution?"

Vitaly's lips twitch with the hint of a smile, and I haven't even had the coffee yet but my heart's already racing.

"That remains to be seen," Vitaly says.

I feel a million times better just standing this close to him. Talking to him. Just . . . being here, and knowing that not all is lost. I greedily accept the drink. "Thank you."

"It's not a big deal."

But I know that it is. I'm pretty sure Starbucks doesn't carry nonpareils, which means he had to go to a second location to add the topping. And that also means he was involved in the assembly. There was a lot of planning that went into this thing, and I'm suddenly wondering if there's a nonpareil jar in Vitaly's pocket and he just poured them on right before I came down, or if he did this at Starbucks, standing at the condiment station and making a mess, tiny rainbow balls bouncing all over the place. I like both scenarios.

I take a sip.

"Is it good?" Vitaly asks, dubious.

"Mhmm," I say around the straw.

He sighs, nods. "I think it's dumb that we're not talking. It's kind of killing me, actually."

The sugar rush is instant. Or maybe it's Vitaly's words that make my head spin. I stand very still, not wanting to miss a thing.

"I don't know what happened to change things so much." Vitaly stops, shakes his head, looks at his boots. He must know what happened. We were both there in Sof's bedroom. But he goes further back. "When I told you to grow up, it's because I was worried about you. It came out wrong. I'm sorry."

"When I told you to loosen up, it's because I was worried about you, too."

He tries to curb the world's smallest smirk and though it's barely visible, it warms me all the way up. Whatever deeper feelings I may have for Vitaly, at least the potential to rebuild our friendship is there. There is light at the end of this tunnel.

"Can we get back to normal?" he asks. "You can tease me about studying too much, or how boring I am. You choose."

"You're not boring."

He lets out a small laugh. "See, that's not something you ever would've said to me before."

"You want me to be honest?" I ask. "Okay. I'm sorry. Asking

why you won't marry me was kind of unhinged, but in my defense, I was very plastered."

Vitaly's already shaking his head. "No, you didn't do anything wrong. I shouldn't have followed you up to that room. I shouldn't have kissed you."

Something fizzles inside of me. I still remember the way his hands clutched my dress, the way his lips felt desperate for me, but assured. Kissing Vitaly felt like the sun breaking through clouds after the longest winter. And I know, more than anything, that it's not just me who felt that. "Are we still being honest?"

Vitaly smiles and shrugs and shakes his head to stop himself from saying something. I can sense how much he wants to get back to who we were, and how difficult I'm making that for him. So I change course. If he wants to be friends again, I'm happy to have him. It's so much easier to be near him while liking him than to be apart while liking him.

"I told Sof. About my status. It went well."

He fills his lungs so deep it pulls his shoulders back. He looks as relieved as I feel. "That's great."

"And I'm not going through with my plan anymore."

"Really?" His brow furrows and the expression on his face tightens, growing more alarmed. "Does this have to do with that dark web date? Did something happen?"

I shake my head and take a quick sip of the coffee, giving myself an excuse not to look at him.

"I just realized it wasn't working out and I needed to pump the brakes. If I'm going to get married anytime soon, it'll be 'cause it happens naturally, not because I orchestrated it."

I want to get off this marriage topic. Last time I brought it up, it nearly ruined our relationship. "Can we talk about you for a minute? Oxford! Wow."

"Oh. Yeah."

"I'm really happy for you, Big Rally."

The most sheepish smile crosses his face. "Thank you."

"So you're definitely going, then?" I fill my voice with as much sincere-sounding cheer as I can muster. "You're moving to England?"

"Yeah. I'm going."

I sip and smile. "Amazing." I grind down on a million non-pareils, feel them getting stuck in my teeth. I really am happy for Vitaly. And I tell myself it's a good thing that we're putting the kiss behind us. Vitaly and I are going in two different directions. Mainly it's him going forward and me digging my feet in the sand and sinking, slowly. One drunken kiss doesn't have the power to change that.

"Well, I just wanted to give you that," Vitaly says, pointing to my drink. "And also, um . . ."

I sip and shift my weight to my other leg as I watch him struggle to form his words.

"Prom's in a couple of weeks," he finally says. I nearly choke on the twelve pumps of vanilla. I forgot about our pact to go together and he is definitely going to say that we shouldn't go anymore.

"I would still like to take you," he says. "If you still want to go."

I swallow the icy concoction and cough and gasp at the same time. I used to be so smooth and now look at me. "Yes," I say quickly. "I mean, duh. I'm not going stag."

When Vitaly smiles this time, he doesn't try to hide it, and I don't bother hiding my smile, either.

"A-as friends, of course," Vitaly stammers.

"Of course, as friends," I say.

"Now that we're friends again."

"We definitely are frie—"

"SOME PEOPLE ARE TRYING TO SLEEP!" Mrs. Gorky shrieks from the fourth-floor window, like she's witnessing a bloody murder, not two kids speaking softly in the cold.

Vitaly scrunches one eye as he looks up at her, contrite and adorable. "Sorry, Mrs. Gorky," he whispers.

"*Old hag*," I say, less quietly.

36

I HAVE SPENT THE LAST TEN MINUTES TRYING TO
secure this bobby pin in just the right spot, but my hair keeps
coming undone. I curse under my breath until my mom shows
up behind me in the mirror, taking the pin from my clumsy
fingers and digging it deep into the strands at the back of my
head. I'm going for a half-up, half-down thing, and while I'm
usually confident about the way I look, right now I keep doubt-
ing myself.

"¿Por qué tan nerviosa? Te ves linda."

I don't know why I'm nervous, but I guess it's a big mile-
stone. Prom. I want it to be perfect, and this year hasn't exactly
been smooth sailing. Why would tonight be any different?

"Tengo tan buenos recuerdos de mi promoción," my mom
says, sighing at the memory.

"¿Tú? ¿Tuviste un prom?"

"¡Claro!" In a flash my mom scurries out of my room and
returns with a slim baby-blue photo album. She opens it for
me to see, and it's the kind of old where you secure the pictures via grips in the corners. The images in there are straight
out of the early eighties, all feathered Farrah Fawcett hair and
color-blocked eye shadow. And then I see my mother, posing

with another girl, their dates at their sides. My jaw drops. "¿Por qué nunca vi estas fotos?"

My mom shrugs, explaining that the album was always there among her things. I guess I just never looked. I'm shocked to see my mother as a teenager. I've only thought about her as the person she became in America. The hard worker. The strict mom. But in this photo stands a girl who meticulously put on makeup and styled her hair and picked out a dress for a formal dance. Her smile is megawatt and holds in it all the joy of a carefree teenage girl.

"Pensé que prom era algo Americano," I say.

My mom clicks her tongue, letting me know that America doesn't have a monopoly on typical high school rituals. She picks up the can of hair spray on top of my dresser and sprays the back of my head, and then we're both looking in the mirror. I have the urge to keep working on my hair, but my mom's hands rest over mine, settling their twitchiness. There's nothing left to be done.

"Solo falta tu vestido."

We both turn to the dress laid out on my bed, the final and most important touch.

"¿Quieres mi faja?" my mom asks.

"Ma, girls don't wear fajas here!"

My mom matches my eye roll, amusement sparkling in her eyes. "Ya, I was joking you!"

The doorbell rings, and my mom and I both look at each other and freeze. "¡Ponte tu vestido!" My mom hurries out of my bedroom and I hurry to my dress. Sof and I spent all week searching for it, and we found it at the last minute yesterday.

It's pink—azalea, to be exact—taffeta, A-line, scoop neck, floor-sweeping hem, and when I step into the living room, I know it looks fucking amazing on me just by the way Vitaly's face lights up. In the long minutes it takes him to recover, I check him out, too.

His hair is parted to the side but mercifully not gelled to oblivion as is the style with boys these days. It sweeps back, a wave of natural blond. He wears a dark suit, crisp white shirt. Around his neck is a black bow tie and around his waist, incredibly, a matching black cummerbund. I say incredibly because I never thought a cummerbund could look so good, but Vitaly sports it like it's an essential piece of men's evening wear and he's the only one in on the secret. It accentuates the smoothness of his tummy, and all I want to do is hook my fingers between the cummerbund and his shirt and now I am sure my cheeks match my dress. But I can't help it. Vitaly looks so dapper. Suddenly it's me who needs to recover at the sight of him.

"Que guapo," my mom declares, and I swear she's got stars in her eyes.

"Wappo?" Vitaly repeats the word as he hears it. "Wappo is good?"

"It's very good," I say.

He takes a step toward me, in his hands a plastic clamshell container with a tiny bouquet of azaleas and baby's breath inside. He pops the lid open and I let him snake the elastic over my wrist. "I asked Sof what color your dress would be," he says, still concentrating on the task, even though the corsage is perfectly in place. "So I could get it to match."

I bite my lip, just to keep my smile from totally giving me away. "It's beautiful."

His eyes flick up to mine. "So are you."

Just friends, my mind blares, a bullhorn right out of a cartoon. We're going to the prom as *friends*.

"¡Foto!" My mom waves a thirty-five millimeter point-and-shoot in her hand. "¡Foto!"

Vitaly and I pose in front of the door and let my mom snap away. I think of her prom photo, and the breezy, fun teen in it. My mom showing me that photograph feels like the permission I need to be the carefree girl that I haven't let myself be lately. And instead of telling me to be careful and asserting a curfew or warning me not to do anything wild, my mom only has one command for me tonight.

"Diviértete." *Have fun.*

I have no choice but to oblige.

37

THE BOYS POOLED THEIR MONEY TO SPRING FOR a limo. Kenz, Luce, and their dates Luke and Logan sit closest to the front, behind the tinted glass dividing the driver from the rest of us. Sof and I are all the way in the back by the rear windshield, gleefully watching our dates, sitting together against the side of the car, interact for the first time.

"The Dog, is it?" Vitaly holds his hand out like he's about to step into a conference room. Sof squeezes my fingers and I hold back the string of giggles that threaten to burst out of me. Vitaly is such a well-mannered old man and it is my favorite thing about him.

The Dog's paw blankets Vitaly's hand in a complicated handshake that ends with a slap on Vitaly's back, making him look like a baby who just got burped. Vitaly chuckles like even he's surprised by the unexpected shakedown and combs his fingers through his hair.

"Yo, Vitaly and the Dog look like those books for babies," Logan says from down the limo. We all stare at him, none of us understanding. "You know, like, pictures of small things and then the opposite bigger things. Like, Big Truck—Little Car. Big Mansion—Little Shack. Big Man—Little Boy."

For once, Kenz and Luce are in agreement about something,

and they nod emphatically, amazed at this SAT-level comparison. Vitaly chuckles good-naturedly but climbs over to my part of the limo, squeezing in beside me. "I'm not that small, am I?" he whispers into my ear.

I shake my head. "You're not the least bit small. The Dog is just that big." I pat him on the knee. It is a friendly pat, of course, because we are just friends.

Tonight, the school gym is alive with energy. The floor mats have been rolled away in favor of hardwood, already getting streaked with everyone's best dress shoes. Sparkly streamers, balloons, lanterns, and mirror balls dangle from the rafters. Refreshment tables off to the side boast catered finger foods, and teachers in rented tuxes guard the punch bowls. No live band, but a DJ hypes up the already-hyped crowd with the latest from Ne-Yo. The lights change with the beat, beaming blue, red, gold.

The group of us file through a balloon arch, Logan and Luke nearly taking it down, trying to see how high they can jump, but I find I'm not even annoyed at their childishness. I feel like jumping, too. And it's not just me who has a pep in their step. I've never seen Vitaly look so happy to be around people his own age. His fingers lace through mine and tug until we're next in line for the official prom photographer. I give him a surprised, questioning look, because I didn't figure him to be the prom photo type. But he just shrugs a shoulder. "I wanna remember this."

We're up, and the two of us stand in front of the shimmering tinsel backdrop, Vitaly slightly behind me and to the side, his arms around my middle, cozy as a cardigan. It is the prototypical prom picture pose, except for the fact that instead of looking into the camera lens, I turn my face toward Vitaly's, a lazy smile on my lips as I cover his hands with mine. The camera flashes and that's the photo we get.

Now it's my turn to take his hand and lead him somewhere, and we wade through the crowd until we're in the middle of the dance floor, awash in strobe lights. Usher's "Yeah!" comes on, and it doesn't matter that we've all heard this song nonstop for the last three years—everyone dances to it like it's the first time. I hike my gown up and jump, arm in the air, bare shoulders shimmying. Vitaly is still Vitaly, so he's not as quick to get down as I am, but he's trying. He pivots his upper body, juts his elbows—a caveman starting to thaw after a thousand years of no fun. Minuscule taps and twists from his shiny loafers, his head nodding like he's in total agreement with the music. Sof and the Dog dance, too, and I think seeing the Dog fully gyrate and get down to Sof's level lets something loose in Vitaly. He starts dancing in earnest now. And do my eyes deceive me or does he actually know the words to this song?

He mouths, "On a one to ten, she's a certified twenty. But that just ain't me," and I throw my head back and laugh, pulling him closer. It's not exactly dancing, but it's finally uninhibited joy, exploding from his limbs.

After five bass-heavy songs, we take a break at one of the tables bordering the dance floor, me and Vitaly, Sof and the Dog. I hook an elbow over the back of Vitaly's chair. "Didn't know you had it in you, Big Rally."

"What, my dance moves?"

"'Dance' is generous."

He leans toward me, eyes twinkling with mischief. "There was movement, though, you have to give me that much."

"That is what I'm referring to, yes."

"Were you impressed?"

"'Impressed' is generous."

His head falls forward in mock defeat, but I jab him in the side. "I'm kidding, that was amazing. Look at you." I push back a strand of hair that's fallen over his forehead. "You're sweating."

"I have been known to sweat from time to time."

"Time to time, huh?"

There's a twitch in his lips as he watches me, the mood lighting making his eyes flash red. "You want a drink?" he asks.

I nod. "And one of those mini donuts, a—"

"Pink one, I know." Vitaly slides his chair back and turns to the Dog. "Wanna come with, D-Man?"

The Dog rises from his seat like an iceberg, and Vitaly looks like a tugboat about to get crushed. It's one thing to let loose on the dance floor, but playing fast and loose with the Dog's name is never a good idea.

"I mean, do you want to come with me, *the Dog*?"

The Dog grunts and the two boys are off. Sof and I sit back, contentedly not lifting a finger as we watch our dates at the far end of the gym, piling little pastries onto gold-rimmed plastic plates. Or at least I watch them, because when I turn to Sof, she is only watching me. "What?"

She sits up and stares at me, and I'm really starting to feel like I missed something. *"What?"* I repeat.

"You touched a boy's *sweat*."

"I did?"

"I won't even touch the Dog's sweat."

"You won't?"

"No! And he sweats *a lot*!"

I look down at my fingers, vaguely clocking that I combed them through Vitaly's hair. Sof watches me, her gaze sidelong but piercing. "This isn't just puppy love, is it?"

I feel the sudden need to swallow, my mouth going dry. My throat doesn't know how to form an answer to that, and in the end, it only lets out a shaky laugh. "We haven't even been on a date."

It's an explanation. A way to shut down her accusatory claim. And it's the truth. What I feel for Vitaly can't possibly be real love, because isn't there usually a buildup to that sort of thing? Flirting and dating and kissing and years of that, even? The framework for *real love* just isn't there.

But Sof watches me out of the corner of her eye. I'm not fooling anyone. Not even myself.

The night is pretty perfect, just like the proms I've seen in movies and TV. Just as I always imagined it would be. My friends and I keep dancing, laughing, savoring every bittersweet moment of our last school dance together. Prom king and queen goes to Logan and Luce, which is great, except for the tiny fact that Logan came with Kenz and Luce came with Luke. Kenz and Luce are, consequently, no longer speaking to each other, but that feels perfectly right, too. Drama is the gas in Kenz and Luce's friendship tank, and I know they're secretly thrilled at all the ammo this scandal has provided for them.

When the DJ invites us to the floor for the last dance, I don't have to cajole Vitaly into joining me. In fact, he surprises me with the confident way he offers his hand. "Dance with me?"

I slip my fingers into his grasp and let him lead me. The lights get a shade dimmer as a slow melody imbues the room with a sleepy warmth. People clasp onto each other silently, but the air crackles with things unsaid. And it's no different for Vitaly and me. We face each other wordlessly, giving careful thought to where our hands should go, to how close we'll allow ourselves to get. But in the end the music nudges us together, settling our futile debate for us.

Vitaly's deft hand holds mine, soft against his chest, and I rest a cheek on his shoulder. We sway slowly, in time to the melody. He feels so solid. Strong and tactile somehow, in a way that makes my hands want to keep exploring the smooth planes of his suit. The curve of his neck. The sturdiness of his arm around me. It's a strange thought to have about someone—to strip everything down to the physicality of them—but maybe it's because by comparison I feel like a fizzy, fragile thing, about to float away. Vitaly holds me in place, though, steady fingers on the dip in my waist.

But it isn't just his body that feels solid, it's everything. It's how comfortable this is, how easy. There is no doubt inside of me when I think about him. There is no more lying to anyone or to myself. He is solid in the same way that I am certain. Certain in this moment, in this person, in what this is. He feels it, too, doesn't he? I pull back and search his eyes for the answer to my unasked question. *You feel it, too, right?*

There is a storm brewing in Vitaly's unwavering gaze. Compassion and lust, desire and fondness. I recognize the look in his eye, because it's everything I'm feeling, too. It doesn't need to be said, it's undeniable. And I get the sense that if I were to ask him right here and now if he'd marry me, he might just say yes.

Which is why I don't ask him. Because this thing between us? This electric moment where the people, the gym, everything disappears but us? It's big enough to make him do something stupid, like throw his whole life away.

If tonight proves anything, it's that I've rubbed off on Vitaly. I've gotten him out of his shell, shown him how to cut loose and live a little. But I think he's rubbed off on me, too, because for once I don't blurt out the first thought in my mind. I need to do the grown-up thing.

I never really understood it in the movies, when a person loves someone so much they have to let them go. It always sounded like the most backward reasoning. But it's so clear to me now. Vitaly is on a fast track. He's got his whole life ahead of him, and I'm not going to hold him back.

There's a twinge of sadness to this love song, and it's all I hear now. It might only be four minutes long, but Vitaly and I spend an eternity looking at each other—close enough to not-talk, to not-kiss, and to definitely be not-friends—and if I spend one more second like this, I don't think I'll ever be able to wrest my gaze from his. I prop my chin on his shoulder, maybe to keep it from quivering.

"It's okay," I whisper. "I understand why it can't happen for us." There's a smile in my voice, but my heart cracks in half. Slow and icy like a fracture in a frozen pond, so deep and far-reaching it will take everything down with it.

I can feel Vitaly's back stiffen, but I only hold on to him tighter. The song will be over soon and I want to stay in this moment for as long as I can. So I cling to him. I try to stave off the reality that will hit us after this slow dance ends. My hand on his back, the corsage on my wrist. I focus on it, how delicate its petals are. But I'm only reminded of how little time it has left, already plucked, long out of its cold storage.

Vitaly's solid, like I said, and holding on to him feels like holding love in my hands.

—

After prom ends, I open up my notebook with all my botched marriage plans and write down something new.

Find someone like Vitaly.

38

A WEEK AFTER PROM I GET AN EMAIL FROM SOF,
which is weird because we don't email each other. But there's
an attachment, and a simple note in the body.

We gotta go to this!

The attachment is a flyer for a rally happening this weekend. It's for the DREAM Act.

It's sweet, the fact that Sof is so invested. I don't know if she
went searching for this event or if she miraculously stumbled
upon it, but it makes my heart fill to bursting for my best friend.

Even though I'm not sure I'm ready for a rally just yet. It'd
be weird, openly supporting an issue I've so far been extremely
private about. But I've done everything to change my circumstances short of activism. It might be worth a shot, especially if
Sof says she'll be there with me.

I type out a quick reply and send it off, before I have a
chance to rethink it.

Let's do it.

Sof's excited like we're going to a block party. The front of her
denim jacket is crammed with newly bought pins, all of them

touting every possible immigration-related phrase known to man. Each saying has one random capitalized word. PEOPLE AREN'T ILLEGAL. IMMIGRATION REFORM NOW! WE ARE ALL IMMIGRANTS! She even made her own protest sign that states, in pink block letters: MY BEST FRIEND IS UNDOCUMENTED!

I don't *not* appreciate her efforts, but I also wish the biggest, most neon sign that will likely be at this rally wasn't so specifically about me.

Sof talks and snaps her gum and bounces the edge of her sign against her knees as the subway car rumbles forward. "Are you excited?" she asks. "We're going to get things done today!"

Bless her heart. I don't think anything at all will happen at this rally. I'd fallen into an internet rabbit hole after getting Sof's email, reading everything I could about the DREAM Act. The Development, Relief, and Education for Alien Minors Act is legislation that would grant legal residency to undocumented people who entered the US as minors. But, more importantly, it was proposed five years ago and it still hasn't been passed. I'm not sure a small rally in downtown Brooklyn will move the needle.

But that isn't what has me glued to my subway seat with slow-burning trepidation. This rally is a public event, and I'm going to publicly walk right into it. I have been keeping this secret about myself, my illegal status, since the moment I learned about it. And just because I've finally told my best friend doesn't mean I'm comfortable letting other people know about it.

Well, except for the Dog. Sof asked me first if she could tell him about my secret. Now that they're officially boyfriend-girlfriend, I can't expect her to keep anything from him, so I told her it was okay. And anyway, it's nice to have more people in my corner. And he's even coming to the rally with us. The Dog takes up two seats, holding a placard that could be a sheet of loose-leaf paper for how small it looks in his lap. On it is one simple word.

IMMIGRANTS

It gets the general message across.

The Dog is a good person to have with you when you're doing something daring. Like that time Sof and I stole a boat at the marina by Sheepshead Bay. The Dog was the one who untied it from the dock and figured out a way to start it and drove it while Sof and I held each other and screamed, our hair whipping through the salty spray. The Dog is really good at breaking padlocks with his bare hands, hoisting girls over chain-link fences, and pushing annoying guys against walls, so it's a comfort knowing he'll be here with me while I do one of the scariest things I've ever done: expose myself as undocumented.

I think it might be easier, knowing all the people at the rally will be strangers. But still. It's terrifying. And that's on top of the fact that the rally is taking place at Cadman Plaza. It's a green space in the middle of the metropolis, tranquil except for the fact that it's surrounded by courthouses and police headquarters. County jail is just a few blocks away. And the closer we get to it, the more I feel like I'm heading straight into the lion's den.

I'm not sure I want to do this.

"This is gonna be so fun!" Sof shouts into my ear as she pulls me off the train, past the turnstiles, and up the grimy subway station stairs to the bright light of day.

All around us there is a huge glut of protest signs and people. "Big rally," I whisper.

"Vitaly's here?"

No, though I wish he was. This is overwhelming. The whole of the quad at Cadman Plaza is stuffed. People huddle, strut, shout, all talking and walking with purpose. It would be nice to have Vitaly here. But I'm trying to maintain a respectful distance. Being with him at prom was amazing, and it can't ever happen again. We're just friends, and if that means keeping him at arm's length, then so be it. And anyway, I've got Sof, and her big Dog, too. When she threads her fingers through mine, I clutch them, grateful.

"Look at this," she says, just as awestruck as I am. "All these people. We're all here with you, babe." Sof has the ability to get me the most upset, the most excited, the most drunk with endorphin highs—and she can calm me down like no one else. My racing heart slows to a more manageable beat. And suddenly it does not matter that we are only yards away from a precinct, where cops stand outside and watch the crowd vigilantly. With Sof, and among these people here, I feel safe. I am cocooned in the warm embrace of a community that is, as Sof put it, here with me.

And for the first time it actually does feel like that—like a community. I don't know other undocumented people. It's not like we have a support group. When I hear about people like me, it's usually from the news, as statistics and numbers. But here, we're everywhere, in the flesh, not to be ignored. There is one word that pops up in most of the signs: "Dreamer." A perfectly innocuous word that may not mean much to some people, but here it has a heft to it. It belongs to me, to all of us. Being undocumented is one of the loneliest things you can be, but being a Dreamer makes me feel like I belong to something.

And now that I've claimed that word, I can step a little further out of the shadows.

"Should we do a lap around the premises?" I ask. It's our typical protocol upon arriving at a party. Might as well take the same approach here.

"We should."

So the three of us walk along the perimeter of the plaza. There is a small podium at the south of the quad, where a girl with a bullhorn is in the middle of leading a chant.

"When I say 'DREAM Act,' you say 'now.' DREAM ACT!"

"NOW!"

There are a few folding tables and booths open, displaying pins like the ones on Sof's jacket. She peruses them, even though I'm pretty sure she already owns all of them. There's a table with leaflets and petitions on clipboards. But there is one table that instantly draws my attention.

It's stacked with neatly folded black shirts, all different sizes, but each bearing the same message. I pick one off the top of the stack and hold it up so I can read the words. UNDOCUMENTED AND UNAFRAID. It's the exact same shirt I saw on that guy in the coffee shop. The shirt that took my breath away then, much the same way it does now.

"Want it?" asks the man behind the table.

All this time I've been trying to hide. To not let anybody know about my status, because I'm afraid it's the only thing they'll see when they look at me. But in this moment, there is nothing I want more than to wear this shirt, openly, proudly. I buy it.

I get a large size so I can put it on over my jean jacket. It may look a little strange, but I don't want to hide it under a layer of denim. I want it to be the only thing people see when they look at me. And also I'm incredibly stylish and I can make anything work.

And so can the Dog. I only notice he's suddenly next to me because he's drawn the attention of onlookers. He's topless, slipping his newly bought T-shirt over his head. The words on his shirt say, WITHOUT DREAMERS THERE IS NO AMERICAN DREAM. It stretches over his body like the Hulk's clothes bursting at the seams mid-transformation. He looks at me and smiles, and I can't help but lunge for him, wrapping him up in a bear hug. I'm aware that I probably look like a starfish splayed on a boulder, but I'm suddenly overcome with gratitude. For the Dog, for Sof, for the new community I can say I'm a part of. The Dog pats me gingerly on the head until I finally let go of him.

I stand in my new shirt and take a deep breath. A part of me is still waiting for a police officer to see what my shirt says and swoop in, demanding to see my papers. But no one seems to care that I'm undocumented and unafraid. When I breathe again, it's like that first breath after being underwater for too long.

The shirt is like a superhero's costume. I feel impervious in it, confident, but instead of hiding my secret identity, it does the opposite. It's a small first step, and I don't even know if I'll be brave enough to wear the shirt again after today, but for now, it's my armor and my security blanket and my favorite outfit.

"Damn, that looks cute on you," Sof says when she notices me. "Can I buy that shirt, too?"

"No," I say. "It's not for you."

"Right." She nods.

I link my elbow with hers and we take up our walk again, heading back to the southern part of the lawn. Closer to the main action, we pay more attention to the current speaker at the podium. It's a new person, yelling into his bullhorn. "We're going to win this fight! And you wanna know why?" he asks.

"He's kinda cute," Sof whispers to me.

"He has blue hair," I say.

"It looks very natural."

"Because we will not back down!" the guy with the blue hair shouts. He stops for the cheers to rise and die again, like he's accustomed to the ebb and flow of this kind of call-and-response public speaking. It's obvious he's done this before. I wonder if he's undocumented, too, though he looks like too much of a gringo to be from any place other than here, with that electric-blue hair making him look paler than any white boy even has a right to be. But I know undocumented people can look like blue-haired gringos, too.

"You are as much a part of the fabric of America as the

people who were born here!" he goes on. "Don't let anyone ever tell you that you don't belong exactly where you're standing!"

The way he says it makes me believe it. I'm cheering and clapping and smiling, and not just in response to the way he's suddenly smiling directly at me.

When Blue is done talking, he hands the bullhorn to someone else and bounds down the three short steps, not stopping until he's right in front of me. "Nice shirt!" he says.

I still feel exposed, wearing my biggest secret across my chest, so it takes me a moment to process this boy's enthusiasm. That someone can meet me for the first time and know what I am and still greet me with open kindness. "Thank you."

"Wanna grab a bite when the rally's done?" he asks.

Uh. "Okay."

39

WE'RE AT A CHICKEN PLACE ON THE CORNER OF
Fulton, sitting by the windows, where we can see the last of
the rally vendors packing up. Sof and the Dog decided to catch
a movie a few blocks away, agreeing to meet back up after my
"bite" with Blue.

We order a bucket of popcorn cauliflower to share, but
Blue's got a big appetite, and he eats the stuff like he's snack-
ing on actual popcorn. I'm not that hungry, so I let him go
to town, and really, I'm impressed by how much food he can
pack away. He is as lanky as one of Picasso's harlequins, but
the boy's got a big mouth, like Mick Jagger, or a crocodile. He
snaps it open to down anything in sight. Truly, I'm fascinated.
I'm only on my second piece and I dip it in the ketchup first,
then the mustard, and lastly a bit of mayo. Blue doesn't seem
to mind the mixed swirl of condiments. He devours his cauliflower without any accoutrements.

"So," he says, after a pelican's swallow. "You're undocumented."

"That's what it says on my shirt."

"Right! And unafraid!" Blue grins. His mouth really is
quite big, lips stretching wide enough to carve out premature
laugh lines in his cheeks.

I suddenly wonder how old he is. "How old are you?"

"Nineteen."

"Are you undocumented, too?"

He pours cola down his gullet and shakes his head. "Born and raised in Bay Ridge."

"Oh." On the surface, this is simply a casual conversation with a random guy I've just met. I've had countless dates already, and this shouldn't feel any different, but it does. Not that I'm saying this is a date, but it's surreal to be talking so openly about my status and citizenship with someone new. It's surreal to see people in the window with protest signs, heading home with their friends. My status doesn't feel isolating anymore. It isn't the lonely thing I'd forced it to be. I didn't come to the rally expecting to be blabbing about my circumstances with a random stranger, but here I am.

I'd been cagey ever since learning I was undocumented. But talking freely feels like a return to form. I don't have to watch what I say. And I can sense that old boldness of mine, which I was slowly losing, coming through again.

"Can I ask you something?"

"Shoot," Blue says.

I lean forward, narrow my gaze, and do my best Diane Sawyer impersonation. "Why did you ask me out to eat?"

"Well, you were looking at me."

"You were on the stage . . ."

"There was sustained eye contact."

"I looked at you for three seconds."

"It was at least thirty minutes."

I snort, and I can't believe I just made such an ugly noise, but Blue seems to love it.

"I've been involved with the DREAM Act cause for a while now," he says, "and from what I've seen, Dreamers fall into two categories. They're either (a): out and proud and on the front lines of protests, or (b): in the shadows. They won't tell a single person about who they really are. Undocumented and afraid."

"And you think I belong in the first category."

"Don't you?"

"This is my first rally," I say. "And you're only the fourth person I've shared my status with. I am undocumented and very, hugely, petrifyingly afraid."

Blue sits back and looks at my face like he's finding something new there. "Then the fact that you're wearing that shirt makes it even more special," he says. "I knew it was something, because it wasn't just your clothes. It was your whole aura. I had to come talk to you."

"Do you have some fetish for illegal girls or something?"

He laughs, a fit of wheezy giggles that makes him double over the small table. "You're funny, Jimena."

"For real, though. You wanna talk about seeing something special in *me* at this rally? What about the blue-haired nineteen-year-old who's giving speeches through a bullhorn in his free time? Who does that?"

"An activist."

"You could be an activist for literally anything, though. Why the DREAM Act?"

"That's kind of a long story."

I dig into the bucket between us and pluck out one of the last popcorn cauliflowers. "Good thing we ordered the bottomless bucket."

Blue settles back against his seat and sighs. "My best friend, Manny. He left Guatemala when he was five years old. His parents made a life here, had two more kids. We grew up five minutes from each other and were always at each other's houses. Then, two years ago, Manny's dad got stopped at a traffic light because he didn't signal on a turn. But, as you probably guessed, Manny's dad didn't have a real license. And that one traffic stop ended up getting him deported."

My heart crumples like a piece of paper hearing that.

"It snowballed from there," Blue says. "Manny's mom got deported next."

The ball of paper behind my rib cage only gets smaller. "What about Manny?"

"He's in deportation proceedings."

I'm so sorry for this family I've never met. But I'm also suddenly seized with fear that the same fate could find me. Like just talking about it might be contagious. I feel bad for bringing this up. Blue seemed like a chipper guy before, but now he's too sad to pop another piece of popcorn cauliflower into his mouth. I don't even know him, but I feel like I broke him. His shoulders rise and fall with a deflated finality.

"All of us—friends and people from the neighborhood—we got him a lawyer, trying to find a way for him to stay, but there's nothing anyone can do, you know? There is no form for him to fill out or legal recourse he can take. He's just in limbo. So now he's in a position where he can go back to a place he doesn't know, but at least he'd have his parents. But what about his brother and sister? They're Americans. They'd end up in foster care."

"If his siblings are Americans, wasn't that enough to keep their parents here?"

Blue shakes his head. "You can only sponsor your parents for citizenship when you're over twenty-one. They're only ten and nine."

"It doesn't make any sense."

"Yeah. Senseless. It's infuriating. It's families being torn apart." The activist part of Blue comes out in the way he squares his shoulders and jams an index finger into the tabletop with every point. "And there's nothing I can do to help my friend out. Except this, what I'm doing now. If all I can do is lend my voice, then I'm going to be as loud as I can be. I mean, I'd marry him if I could, but gay marriage isn't legal, so. Can't."

"Yeah, that's kind of been my plan."

Blue cocks an eyebrow. "Plan?"

"Ever since I found out about my status, I've sort of been looking for someone to marry me." I cough out a sad chuckle, because now that I'm admitting it, I can't believe how pathetic it sounds. But when I glance at Blue, he doesn't look at me like I'm pathetic. He reacts like I just told him a particularly interesting headline.

"I'd marry you."

I can feel my cheeks coloring as he watches me, and I smooth my hair back the way I usually do when I'm on the receiving end of what feels like a compliment. "Thanks."

But Blue scoots up to the edge of his seat, planting both his forearms on the table. "No, seriously, I mean, I will. If that's something you're interested in."

My hands freeze over my hair until they fall to my lap, numb. "What?"

"I can help you get your citizenship." He's talking like he just came up with a great new business idea, except it isn't a business, it's my life. "I can't call myself an activist unless I put my money where my mouth is, right? And if I can help even one Dreamer by marrying them, then hell yeah, why wouldn't I?"

Blue talks in big ideas and poster-speak. *Change one life, change the world*, sort of thing. It makes it hard for me to reconcile that this guy is a real, true person. And yet here he is, eyes enormous with this shiny new idea, bright even beneath the shadow of the ocean-blue wave of hair cresting over his forehead.

"Dude, I've known you for all of two minutes." While very true, I still can't believe the words coming out of my mouth. All I've been wanting is a guy *exactly like this*. He's practically on bended knee, begging me to marry him. And even if he's under some delusional spell to be the Best Activist He Can Be, I should snap him up and accept his offer.

But this little early dinner date is only growing more surreal. This guy can't be serious.

I must say that out loud, because Blue is nodding like a puppy asking for a treat. "Oh, I'm very serious. And it's just marriage. People do it all the time. What's the big deal?"

Blue sounds like an idealistic idiot. And exactly like me when I first came up with my plan. Before the reality of it crushed all the optimism out of me.

Which is the only reason I can explain my reluctance. "I could be a crazy person. I could be an axe murderer. You don't even know me."

"So let's get to know each other," Blue says.

That wondrous look in his eye isn't going away. And every vein in my body pumps with new blood.

40

A PERFECTLY ADEQUATE BOY PROPOSED MAR-
riage to me over a bottomless bucket of popcorn cauliflower
after less than an hour of knowing me. It's what dreams are
made of. Still, I need to think this through.

I give myself a week. In that time, I mull and ponder and do
the type of Facebook deep diving that should come with scuba
gear. Blue seems too good to be true. As such, I need to find out
everything about him to make sure he's for real. And according to the internet, Blue is definitely a real boy. His birthday
is October 21. He's doing the commuter thing, attending
Brooklyn College as a sophomore. And he clearly doesn't have
immigrant parents, because he's majoring in philosophy.

There are countless pictures for me to look through, some
that he's posted himself and even more that others have tagged
him in. He has pictures with friends, siblings, childhood pets,
two parents who are still together. If I go by pictures alone, Blue
seems like a socially well-adjusted guy. The only abnormality is
his hair. Its color changes frequently, with no apparent rhyme
or reason. But a penchant for neon hair dye that clashes with
his natural skin tone, while ill-advised, is not a good enough
reason not to marry the boy.

The only other red flag that comes up in my research is his obsession with do-gooding.

From the pictures, the groups he's joined, and the posts on his Facebook wall, it is obvious that "activism" is Blue's entire personality. There are photos of him at rallies, doing sit-ins outside state senators' offices, screaming into a bullhorn in front of the Washington Monument. And he doesn't stick solely to immigration stuff, either. In a throwbackthursday pic, high school Blue, sporting run-of-the-mill brown hair, sits at a card table in front of some lockers with a sign that reads FEED THE HUNGRY! He also seems to like long walks on the beach with a garbage bag and pokey stick, helping to clean up the shores. And he pitches in at a kitchen by ladling soup into outstretched bowls.

Do I really want to be with someone like that?

Blue's dedication to service and change is so commendable it kind of circles right back to abnormal. Compared to him, all I do is sit on my ass all day. I don't care about *people*, I care about *myself*. And if I spend more than an hour with him, Blue will see that.

But if I've learned anything from my research, it's that I do want to spend more time with him. Because no matter how many of his pictures I find, they still can't paint a complete picture of who he is. So when he sends me an email suggesting I come to his house next week to get to know him in his "natural habitat," I know it's something I should probably do. On the conditions that we meet in the morning and that there are other people present, of course.

So here I am, standing on his front porch. He lives on a tree-lined street in the middle of Brooklyn, in an enormous, albeit old-looking house. Is Blue secretly rich? Because if so, we can start writing up the marriage license right n—

"You made it!" Blue says, swinging open his front door. His big mouth produces a big smile, white and radiant and way too excited to see me. "We can sit outside if you want. I know it's kind of strange, coming to a guy's house when you don't even really know him, and I want you to feel safe. So if you want to s—"

But I'm already pushing past him, muttering pleasantries as I ignore everything he says. I want to get a better look at this Victorian manor. The house is old, but it's also got a foyer and a living room, and even a sunroom I spy in my peripheral vision. "This place is incredible."

"Yeah, it's great, huh," Blue says. "Though cleaning the gutters is kind of a pain."

Blue wears an NPR T-shirt with holes in the collar and a ratty pair of gray sweats. Not the outfit I expect from someone who lives in a place this large. The kind of large that tricks your mind into thinking you've left Brooklyn and walked through a portal that took you to Kansas, or wherever big, enormous houses exist. "You rich or something?"

A laugh shoots out of him. I'm beginning to notice that whenever Blue laughs hard, he holds on to the nearest durable piece of furniture, like he needs it to keep from toppling over. "Working-class kid from a working-class family, all the way."

"Then how the hell can you afford a place like this? This

is a mansion! This has a front porch with a swing on it! You have a yard!" The kind of large that makes my voice echo, and I realize I am shouting. I clear my throat and compose myself, remember I am a guest here. "If you don't mind my asking."

Blue folds his arms over his chest but he's still smiling, looking at me like I'm the darndest thing. "This place has five bedrooms."

"Now you're just bragging."

"I live with five roommates," he explains.

"Oh."

"Yeah."

"Damn."

"Yeah," Blue repeats. "There's a lot of us and things get pretty tight, and the roof leaks when it rains, but it's a great house. Splitting it up like we do makes the rent deal pretty sweet."

It's only now that I start to notice the telltale signs that this home is inhabited by college guys. There's a pile of sneakers as tall as a small child beside the door. There are heaps of clothes dotting the floor like molehills. Random dishes balance precariously on shelf and table edges. And there's the distinct *pew! pew!* of lasers coming from another room.

"Are they here?" I whisper. "The roommates?"

"Two of the guys are away at family-slash-girlfriends' houses for the weekend. Two of the guys have work, and that leaves me and Justin. Come meet him."

Blue leads me down a hallway that turns and winds until we reach a den. There's a guy on a couch, game console in hand, hunched toward the TV.

"Hey, Justin!" Blue is loud enough to counter the explosives detonating on the screen. "This is Jimena. Say hello!"

Justin briefly lets his eyes drift from the screen to give me a once-over. "You guys hooking up?"

As far as hellos go, this is not one.

"No?" I say.

"Yeah," Blue says.

I flash Blue a look and he flashes me a grin and between us, Justin only smirks and gets back to his game.

I follow Blue out of the den until we wind up at the back of the house, where the kitchen is. When I'm sure we're far enough away from Justin, I spin on Blue. "Okay. I'm going to stop you right there. If you're doing this whole thing with me because you think we're gonna be hooking up, you've got another think coming."

Blue digs a (reusable) bottle of water out of the fridge and takes a gulp as he patiently listens to me speak. "I don't think that," he says. "And I'm sorry if I offended you. But you can relax, I'm just planting the seeds."

I lean my hip against the countertop. "Seeds?"

"If we're gonna do this thing, people have to think we're actually together. You know? Be believable. If it comes down to it, Justin can provide an affidavit about the legitimacy of our . . . what should we call it . . . coupledom? Though I wouldn't bet on it, the guy can hardly write a Facebook post."

Oh. Legitimacy. That makes sense. But . . . "Affidavit?"

"Yeah, nothing like an affidavit to prove your love to Immigration."

"So, you're not expecting anything . . ." I point to myself, then at him. "Right?"

Blue sets his drink down on the opposite counter and walks over, a pure, idealistic look in his eye. "Jimena, I want to help you because I know in my heart it's the right thing to do. And I'm happy to do it. I don't expect anything from you in return. Or anything to happen between us. Though I guess, if it happens, it happens, you know?" He shrugs, and I kind of can't believe the levelheaded casualness of his thinking. It feels progressive. Liberating. Rational. Is this the kind of thing you get from a philosophy major?

"I guess what I'm saying is, who's to say what the future holds? But I think we should be free to date or not date whomever we want. With the expectation that we'd have to keep that sort of thing secret, of course. For appearances' sake."

"Right," I say. "For appearance's sake."

Blue smiles wide. "All right! Now come see what I'm all about."

41

I ALWAYS THOUGHT PEOPLE WHO WERE PASSION-
ate about making the world a better place only existed in docu-
mentaries about the sixties. But here's Blue, in the living flesh,
working the plight of child refugees from the war in Bosnia
into literally every conversation.

"Shut the fuck up about Sarajevo already!" someone who
can clearly read my mind yells at Blue as we sit in the living
room. That same someone—one of Blue's roommates, whose
name escapes me—hurls a couch pillow at Blue's head, flatten-
ing his ocean-wave hair.

Blue drops his joystick to chuck the pillow right back. "Was
I talking about Sarajevo too much?" he whispers to me.

"Is there a bigger word than 'yes'?"

Blue clamps his lips shut in a good-natured attempt at keeping quiet on the subject, at least for now.

We're in the living room of his big house, and it seems that
Blue's anti-gun stance does not extend to video games, judging
by the computer-animated violence tearing up the TV screen.
Three of his roommates are with us, one of them playing the
game, too, while the other guys sit on ancient, secondhand La-
Z-Boys, laptops propped on their knees.

Aside from his activism projects and his schoolwork, Blue's

day-to-day social circle is mostly confined to the boys who live in this house with him. I've been coming over a lot—every day after school, actually—just to get a better grasp on Blue and his life, and learning what a big part his roommates play in it.

There's Jacob, an engineering major at Cooper Union, who is permanently bent over a computer screen. There's Naveen and Asa, who are forever trying to outdo each other with terrible "Yo mama" jokes and who, I have a hunch, are secretly in love with each other. Justin is ornery and doesn't say a lot. And there's the pillow thrower, who tutors math after class.

One of the good things about there being so many roommates is that dinner duty is split evenly among them. Their meals don't stray far from the potato and noodle family, but their inventiveness with limited ingredients is commendable. They can make stews and sandwiches out of the most minimal pantry stuff. And I'm here enough to know that Jacob is by far the best cook of the bunch.

The house is a nice little corner of the world that I like peeking into. There's a lot less toxicity and, frankly, grossness, than I thought there would be. Mostly, the guys are the opposite of alpha males. They keep to themselves. They're awkward. And it's pretty clear they have no idea how to talk to human women. (I must specify the human aspect of this, because there are a lot of anime and video-game women that they are very comfortable talking to and about.)

And I'm getting to know Blue better, which is the whole point. I've known him now for a couple of weeks, enough time to be certain of one thing: We're not romantically compatible. But I still like him. Yes, his devotion to child refugees makes me feel like a monster who hates kids, and brandishing a bottle of Poland Spring in front of him will yield a lecture about how I'm contributing to the destruction of the planet, and his rants about the war in Afghanistan honestly make me want to march up to an army recruiter just to spite him. But all of that is just part of the alchemy of what makes Blue a capital *G Good person.*

His roommates, who've had to deal with Blue's stances way longer than I have, still hang out with him because despite it all, he's pretty fun to have around. They can throw pillows at his head and he'll take it in stride. And it's refreshing how he always invites me back to the house, always asks me if I want a drink anytime he gets up to go to the kitchen, always loops me into the conversation if the boys seem to forget I'm there.

He's an open book. Blue wants to know about me as much as I want to know about him. He never balks at my personal questions, like, "How many people have you slept with?" (Two, for the record.) Or my weird questions, like, "Would you eat a live bunny if your life depended on it?" (He's a vegetarian who wouldn't even eat fried chicken if there was a gun to his head.) Or even my rude questions, like, "Real talk, have you considered less flannel?" (He might, but it's so cozy.)

Blue has his quirks but it's those same quirks, to my surprise, that endear him to me. It isn't love, but I can live with someone like this. My doubts about his motives for wanting to marry me begin to melt away, along with my reservations. And if I have to spend the next two years here at his side, playing video games, breaking up fights about fracking, sharing sloppy joe recipes with his roommates, I realize that I can do that. It'd be like living with roommates in college. It's kind of exactly the adventurous, messy young adulthood I've always wanted. The same kind that most people experience. And at the end of the day, that's all I want to be: Most People.

Blue lets out a sudden celebratory howl, apparently having smoked an enemy battalion or something—it's anybody's guess. He sinks back into the couch and I sidle up beside him. Without even thinking, I lift my phone up and angle it so I'm pretty sure I've got us both in the frame. I snap a selfie.

"What was that for?" Blue asks.

I shrug. "You looked happy. And I felt like taking a pic."

"You should post that."

"I should?"

"Yeah," Blue says. Then whispers conspiratorially, *"Seeds."*

All this time I've been coming over, we haven't really spoken about what the objective of all this is. By design or mistake, us getting to know each other is happening naturally. But the mention of seeds reminds me of what we're really doing here. That it isn't just a fun new friendship we're building. It's something more calculated. It's something we're planting.

"You know, Fuko's moving out at the end of the summer," Blue whispers.

Fuko, *that's* the pillow thrower's name. Short for Buttafuoco. "He is?"

Blue nods, eyes glued to the screen as he starts a new level of his game. "He's graduating, got a job waiting for him in Palo Alto. It'd be perfect timing for you to move in."

It's all becoming more real. Living with a bunch of boys isn't ideal, but this housing situation is incredibly convenient.

If me and Blue are really going to do this, we wouldn't have to go looking for an apartment. This place is ready with a bow on it if I want to snap it up. An address to put on all the paperwork we'd have to file. And it wouldn't be made-up. We could both live here, like roommates, and the government doesn't have to know better.

"You think the guys would be cool with it?"

"The guys love you. Also, we need another roommate to make up the rent."

I nod and look at the picture I took of us on my phone. We look happy in it. No fake smiles, no poses. I am happy. And I can keep taking pictures like this for the next few years. If I look happy in all of them, then they'd be enough to convince everyone that I am.

"Cool," I say.

"Cool," Blue agrees.

That night, I sit in front of my computer and get to work, first taking the memory card out of my phone, inserting it into a USB card reader, then connecting the reader to my PC. After that, I open up my Facebook and use the Simple Uploader, which lets me browse and select photos straight from my hard drive. I find the photo I took with Blue and upload it to an album. The whole thing takes a short fifteen minutes, but I take my time with it. It's my first picture of Blue and me together. I don't add a caption to the photo, because I don't know what to say. The likes rack up, though, and I get a few comments asking who the mystery boy with the blue hair is. Sof comments with only a string of exclamation points and later, a poke. But one person hasn't acknowledged the post at all, and I keep refreshing the page to see if he'll say something, or at least like the pic.

But he doesn't.

42

THOUGH OUR GALLEY KITCHEN CAN HARDLY hold one of us in it, my mom and I stand shoulder to shoulder there, preparing dinner. My mom stakes her claim in front of the stove, frying yucas in a saucepan, while I dice tomatoes for the salad. "Qué milagro que estás aquí para cenar," she says.

It's true, I have been spending a lot of dinners away, and I haven't really told her why. But now that things are getting serious with Blue—as serious as they can get in a fake-dating relationship—it's probably time for me to come clean.

"Estaba cenando con un chico."

My mom freezes to the point where the only noise or movement comes from the fries sizzling in the pan. "¿Y quién es?"

"Just this guy."

"¿Un nuevo enamorado?"

I love that the Spanish word for boyfriend translates literally to lover. It's way too romantic and dramatic, especially considering that Blue is far from an actual boyfriend. "Not really. Pero . . . creo que he sort of . . . wants to . . . casarse conmigo."

I don't want to look her in the eye for some reason. I guess it's because what I've just said doesn't really make any sense.

He isn't my boyfriend, but I think he sort of wants to marry me.
I don't know if she'll make me explain, or just flat-out disapprove, and I don't like either option.

"¿Para darte papeles?"

I nod.

"¿Y quiere dinero?"

I shake my head.

She looks skeptical, which is totally understandable, because if Blue doesn't want money and he isn't even my boyfriend, then why is he willing to help me get my papers? I can see everything she's thinking right on her face—I've always been able to. And what my mom is thinking now is a rehash of the conversation we've had before, about not trusting anyone, ever, but especially when I'm in the situation that I'm in. Where someone can easily take advantage of me.

"Así son los Americanos," I say, trying to sum up that Americans think differently from the rest of us. More idealistic, more naive. "Solo me quiere ayudar."

I wait for my mom to voice the skepticism that's etched in every line of her face. To tell me that nothing in this life is free and to look under the surface when someone says they only want to help you out of the goodness of their own hearts. That a boy who wants to marry a girl he doesn't even love is only after one thing. I want her to tell me that I need to protect myself.

A part of me hopes, for one last time, that my mom will try to talk me out of this. She'll tell me that the only reason I should ever get married is for love. Because if anyone is supposed to tell me that, it should be my mom.

But I also know that my mom's idea of marriage is much

different from mine. I've grown up with pop culture rom-coms and meet-cutes. But even I know that "marrying for love" is a rare privilege outside of the Western world. Other people in other places know there are a million reasons to marry someone, and love is not usually at the top of the list. I guess that's exactly the kind of marriage I'm looking for anyway.

My mom's face doesn't move. Not an inkling of a smile, not a furrowed brow of concern. Just deep lines around a tight mouth. Maybe I can't easily tell what she's thinking this time around because her feelings on the matter are complicated. She could be happy that I've found a way out of this situation while also being sad that I'm in this situation in the first place. Maybe she's even feeling some guilt.

And it breaks my heart. Yeah, I'm not happy I'm undocumented, but after all this time of being frustrated and angry and blaming her, I've finally come around to understanding my mom. I spent so much time focusing on my own trauma of belonging to a place while not truly belonging to it, without even stopping to think of the trauma my mom had to deal with. She had to relearn how to live her life, multiple times, swimming against the current, just to try and give me a good life. Coming here was hard for her. Staying here was even harder. But we all have to make hard choices in life. I get that now. And putting down the axe I've been grinding makes me feel so much lighter.

I want to tell my mother not to ever feel guilty, that I understand, that I love her. But all my feelings get lodged in my throat and not a word comes out. Some habits are too hard to break.

Finally, my mom speaks so I don't have to.

"Lo tendré que conocer primero." She shoves the strips of

yuca around with a wooden spoon. "No te vas a casar hasta que conozca el chico."

I nod and continue dicing the tomatoes. It's a difficult conversation and it's already over. My mom's not yelling and neither am I, and all she wants to do is meet Blue, which is a reasonable request.

Still, it feels like I've just passed through a door I wasn't ready to go through. Any other parent might be freaking out. And any other child might stop cutting up a salad and make a fuss until they got a talking-to. But this doesn't feel like a mother-daughter argument. This feels like a talk between two adults. My heart wants my mom to tell me what to do, ground me like I'm still a little kid. But my head is thankful that she's giving me the freedom to do this. There's a struggle between those two parts of me, but I don't know what to do about it, so I just keep cutting tomatoes.

There's one more thing I need to say. One thing that might finally make my mom put her foot down and stop me from marrying this random boy.

"Tiene pelo azul," I say without looking at her.

My mom stops what she's doing so she can turn fully to me. She says her next words in English, as though trying to confirm she hasn't misunderstood. "*Blue hair?*"

I choke down a laugh.

It's only after I speak to my mom about Blue that I truly start to panic. I guess it's because until now, Blue has been my secret.

Except for the one picture I posted of us, I haven't really brought him into my world yet. I've spent a lot of time with him in his house, with his friends, and that almost makes it feel like this whole time he's been a doll I sometimes pick up and play with. But now that my mom knows about him, the floodgates are open. I overhear her talking to my tía on the phone about "a boy with blue hair." And now I'm dodging calls from my tía.

It should've been a relief, getting the whole deal with Blue out in the open, but instead of relief there's sudden, unexpected panic, sinking through my body, pinning me to my bed wide awake at five in the morning with the realization of what I am about to embark on.

I carved this journey out for myself, but that doesn't make it any less scary.

So I get out of bed and don't stop until I'm at his door, knocking and knocking and waiting for him to talk me out of this insanity.

It's Jacob who lets me in, bleary-eyed, too tired to be annoyed. He goes to fetch Blue.

"Hey," Blue says when he gets to the foyer. His hair sticks up over his ears, making him look like he's been electrocuted. I wonder if I look the same. "It's like, six in the morning," he says, squinting at me.

"I know."

"Jacob's going to kill me," Blue says through a yawn. "You, too, probably."

"I'm sorry to Jacob and for our impending deaths." I need to cut to the chase before I chicken out. "Are you sure you want to do this with me?"

"Huh?"

Blue is too out of it and tired to invite me in, so I push past him into the foyer and close the door quietly behind us. "I don't want to wake anyone. Where's a good place to talk?"

"These walls are, like, paper-thin everywhere."

So I will have to whisper. I walk to the living room and Blue follows. The place is a mess with dishes, throw blankets, notebooks on the floor. The guys never have parties and yet, the place always looks like it's hungover. Right now, it is silent and dim, a muted light coming through the bedsheets they use as window curtains. We both sink into the lumpy couch, and I fold a leg underneath me so I can better face Blue. I'm touched that he's attempting to give me all his attention while simultaneously trying not to fall back to sleep where he sits.

"You could go to jail," I tell him.

That wakes him up. He goes so still I'm not sure he's breathing. But his eyes are way open, and boring into me. "We . . . wait . . . what?"

"If you marry me and we get caught, you could go to jail. I'd get deported, but *you'd* go to jail. You get that, right?" But I don't give him a chance to answer. I just barrel right on with what I have to say. "If we're caught scamming the government, you'd have to pay, like, a million dollars."

"What?" Blue says. "No, I wouldn't."

"Okay, not a million, but a quarter of a million, at *least*," I hiss. "And you could also go to jail. You'd have a record. And even if we don't get caught, it still wouldn't be a good idea for you to go and get yourself arrested at one of your protests— you wouldn't even be able to get a parking ticket, because the government might see that and deny my application. And you wouldn't be able to ask for any government loans or benefits, you know? Because why would they approve me if we're going to need handouts all the time? And on top of everything, we'd need to hire a lawyer, probably. There's all the application fees. Your life would be scrutinized and subjected to questioning!"

I take a deep breath, slow down, but I need to be emphatic about this. I need him to know how serious it is. "You want to be a nice guy and do a good thing to 'change one life, change the world' or whatever, but I need you to realize everything you're up against if this whole thing goes south. You'll go bankrupt. You'll go to prison. Your whole future will be ruined."

I look down at my hands, useless and shaking in my lap. I know that I'm the one who wanted this, that I'm the person who pursued this arrangement between us. But this—the reality of the fallout—is an important part of the whole thing that we haven't talked about yet. And we *need* to talk about it. I don't know if it's self-sabotage or just me testing Blue—pushing his limits to see how far he's willing to take this thing. Because I don't want to come all this way just to . . . just to . . . "I don't want to get my hopes up," I say, still looking at my hands, unable to look anywhere else. "In case you decide to bail when you realize all the consequences of what it would mean to marry me."

It's all out now. Everything that was keeping me up, that jet-propelled me all the way here at six in the morning. Marrying me is a big ask, no matter who the person on the other side of the would-be altar is. But I can't imagine having this conversation with someone I actually loved. I think of Vitaly and how, for once, I'm glad it's not him who'll go down this path with me. I'd never know if he was marrying me because he truly felt something for me or because he just wanted to save me.

How can anyone truly love me if I come with all this . . . baggage?

With Blue at least, I don't have to wonder if it's real. It makes this a whole lot less fraught, and me less vulnerable. I just need to know where we both stand, that we're both on the same page. If he doesn't want to do this, I'm giving him an out. No one's feelings need to get hurt.

When I do finally glance up at Blue, I see a question in his eyes.

43

IT'S FRIDAY, THE DAY THE CULTURE CLUB LEAVES
on their four-day trip. A coach bus waits outside school to take everyone to the airport, and I don't have to stay to watch them go, but I do. I want to send Sof off properly, let her know that it isn't absolutely killing me that I can't go on the trip, too.

"You sure?" Sof asks. She searches my face for anything that might betray me. "'Cause there's nothing to be jealous about, honestly. I saw the itinerary and we have a stop at the Montreal Museum of *Cheese*. You know that's going to be beyond boring."

"So boring," I agree, even though I can feel a gaping new hole opening up in my stomach that only Canadian cheese can fill. "Not jealous at all."

"I feel kinda guilty," Sof says. "I can't believe I'm going to be meeting French guys without you."

"Hey." I pull her focus with both hands on her shoulders. "They aren't French, they're French Canadian."

Sof scoffs at that, smacking my hands away.

"Seriously, though, don't you dare feel guilty about this," I say. "Go live your life. Have fun. And don't forget you have a best friend back home. And a boyfriend—so no making out with French Canadians. You promise me that."

Sof sighs and nods. "I promise."

The bus is almost fully loaded and Kenz bangs the side of her fist against a window, trying to get Sof's attention to hurry up and board. "CHILL!" Sof shouts at her, then turns back to me. "Don't worry, Jimmy, you'll be able to travel one day. And when you do, we're going to Montreal, just the two of us."

"Screw Canada, we're going to Bermuda."

"Attagirl!" We envelop each other in the tightest embrace, which would be even sweeter if it wasn't soundtracked by Kenz's valiant attempt to break that bus window.

"I SAID CHILL!" Sof shrieks. "Bye, Jimmy."

She hurls her duffel bag into the luggage compartment below the windows and then boards the bus full of yelping, excitable seniors. I wave and watch as the coach drives down the street, taking a tiny piece of me with it. It's just a shard—a sliver, really—but I wonder how long I can stand it, losing these snippets of myself bit by bit. The tiny disappointments and missed opportunities and life unlived. How long until there are only chunks of me left, like a salt clump in a cavernous silo, growing smaller all the time?

But I don't dwell on it too long. Not just because I won't let myself, but also because something else steals my attention. *Someone* else, more like. Here I am thinking I'm the only one to watch the Culture Club go, but just on the far side of the school gates stands Vitaly. He notices me only a second after I spot him, and neither of us does anything but look at each other for a beat, me with a million questions and he, infuriatingly, providing none of the answers. But then he pushes off the gate and starts heading toward me. I meet him in the middle.

"What are—" I start. "Why didn't you get on the bus?"

"Baby tournament."

"Not sure what that means, but it sounds fascinating and unethical."

He chuckles, stuffs his fists in his pants pockets. "It's what we call the sambo tournament for the three-to-five-year-old age group. My group. It's on Sunday, so . . ." He does a lip-twisty thing as he pauses that makes it impossible for me to look at anything else. "Couldn't miss it."

I nod. Of course he wouldn't. "So everyone we know is off to Canada for the long weekend and we're stuck here, alone."

"Together," Vitaly corrects me.

"Together."

His lips relax, which means there is no explanation for why I'm still staring at them, and he better say something soon before I embarrass myself. "I know a way we can have fun," Vitaly says.

I quirk an eyebrow. "Who are you and what have you done with Big Rally?"

He only smiles in return.

44

I KNOW THAT MAINTAINING A RESPECTFUL DIS-
tance from him has been the approach thus far, but how can I
turn Vitaly's invitation down? Everyone's away except for the
two of us, and I'm really curious to know what Vitaly's idea of
fun is. I always imagined it was limited to a windowless room
containing a single textbook, so it's hard to overstate my shock
when he brings me to the beach. Honestly, I never thought the
beach in the middle of May was a viable place to go. It's chilly,
especially at night—but plenty of other people think it's a perfectly good option, considering the crowd that is already loitering by the shore.

"Vitaly Petrov, did you bring me to a beach party?" I am
more than a little surprised.

Vitaly juts his chin to the small group on the sand as we
walk through gates that are wide open. "It's more of a family
get-together. Two of those guys out there are my cousins."

I'm not too familiar with Manhattan Beach. It's so much
harder to get to than Brighton Beach, which is right off four
different subway lines. But it's a nice quiet spot, flanked by
designated picnic areas, playgrounds, and large homes. And
it's in such a far-out part of Brooklyn that the only people
around right now are the ones I see on the beach.

Vitaly and I trudge through the sand until we reach the group, four guys and three girls. Two of the guys crouch low, piling crumpled newspaper and sticks together. Vitaly greets the boys in Russian, and they pull each other into hugs and hearty backslaps.

"Guys, this is Jimena. Jimena, these are my cousins and their friends."

Vitaly starts listing off a jumble of the most Russian names I've ever heard—Vlad, Igor, Sasha, Valery—and I'm enveloped in cologne-scented hugs. One of the guys, with a buzz cut and a gold wristwatch, starts to hand me a beer can, but Vitaly stops him, declining in Russian.

"I drink, you know," I tell him. "And I happen to be thirsty."

"I got you covered." Vitaly swings his backpack to his front and unzips it to fish out a pair of beers for the both of us. "Molsons," he explains. I check the label to see what's so special about this bottle versus the beer his cousin offered.

"'Canadian lager,'" I read.

"I know you really wanted to go on the trip," Vitaly says. "I figured I could bring a little bit of Canada to you."

My lips part slightly, soundlessly, as I watch Vitaly pop the cap off with a bottle opener attached to his key chain. And in the most Vitaly move ever, he collects both caps and stuffs them into the front pouch of his hoodie so as not to pollute the beach.

"Thank you," I say.

He shrugs. "Yeah, it's nothing."

And I nod along, too, pretending it isn't. I close my eyes and bring the bottle to my lips. It's late enough that I imagine Sof has snuck out of her hotel room by now, found that Canadian dive bar of her dreams, and is just about to take her first legal drink. Maybe it's a Molson's, too. With my eyes closed, I pretend I am standing right there beside her. The lager is crisp and tickles my tongue on the way down. It's good, but I don't want to pretend I'm in a scummy dive bar anymore. I open my eyes to Vitaly and the ocean lapping at the dark shore. This is better.

Vitaly's cousins, still crouched around the nonexistent fire, begin hissing and arguing and shoving each other, until one of them calls Vitaly over. He joins them, plopping down and resting all his weight on his flat feet, arguing right back, and gesturing wildly with his hands. It all seems to be good-natured, though, and when he's the one to finally get the flames going, the rest of the boys clap him on the back and glom onto him, despite the growing fire a foot away.

All of this is new—seeing Vitaly acting so casual, with his cousins, building a fire—but what surprises me the most is seeing him roughhouse with them. It isn't just the language that's foreign to me, it's this boy, who I thought I knew only as the shy kid from my building, being gregarious and loud and joking with a group of people with whom he really seems to fit.

It occurs to me that it is because he's known his cousins much longer than he's known me. There is a different way you talk to your cousins, a shorthand that branches from the same family tree. Or I assume there is. What Vitaly has with his cousins is something else that my legal status has robbed me of, and though I'm happy they've gotten their fire going, that happiness is tainted now that I'm thinking of all the things I've never been able to do with my own cousins, thousands of miles away. I swallow another swig of beer, the taste of bitter and sweet swilling inside of me.

Vitaly comes to sit next to me on the sand, side by side but a couple of feet apart. We're close enough to still hear the conversations around the fire, but far enough away that even if they'd been speaking in English, I'd have no idea what his cousins and their friends were talking about.

We sit in pleasant silence as we nurse our lagers, listening to the ambient sounds of the tide, the party, the crackling fire. All the roughhousing has tousled Vitaly's usually neat hair. Whipping in the breeze like it is, I notice it's been a while since his last haircut, his bangs brushing the tops of his cheeks.

"It's nice to see you with your cousins," I say, more to the waves than to him. "You're different around them."

Vitaly takes another swig of his drink and considers the ocean, too, for a long moment. "You know how I learned to swim?" He cocks his head toward the group. "Vlad taught me. I was five years old, he was nine, and we were at the pool at our grandfather's building in Brighton Beach."

"A nine-year-old taught you how to swim?"

Vitaly chuckles at the memory. "He pushed me into the deep end."

Vitaly might be laughing, but I'm horrified. "Um, sorry to break it to you, but your cousin wasn't teaching you to swim, he was trying to drown you."

"He was shouting instructions at me from the edge of the pool, about how to get my bearings. I mean, eventually he had to jump in and pull me to the surface, because it was hard to hear him under all that water. But he was there with me the whole summer, showing me by trial and error."

"Trial and error?" I'm skeptical, but Vitaly's smirk is mischievous, relaxed.

"It's a Russian thing."

I can't put my finger on it, but there is something different about Vitaly tonight. He's being more easygoing than I've known him to be. Like a tenseness has melted off his shoulders. My gaze falls on those shoulders, upper body, chest—bundled in the fluffiest oversized hoodie I've ever seen. It is as white as a beacon and looks as cozy and inviting as my favorite blanket. I want to wrap myself in it. I shiver and pull my denim jacket tighter against my chest.

"I think we're just different with different people," Vitaly says. "My cousins grew up with me, they know me like brothers. I'm always going to be a different person when I'm around them. Just like when I was at that party at Sof's house? I was hanging out with people who wanted to be drunk and party, so I became Drunk Party Vitaly. Not myself."

I try not to be crushed by the fact that the guy at that party who gave me the best kiss of my life was not himself.

"But even when I'm with you," Vitaly goes on, "I'm a completely different person, too."

"What are you talking about? You're yourself with me."

"Yeah, I'm myself," he says. "But it's like a new part of me emerges whenever I'm around you. A part I didn't know was there until we started hanging out."

I watch him. "What part?"

When Vitaly turns to me, the firelight catches the side of his face, reflecting orange and gold. "I think I'm someone who usually has the answers for everything. And if I don't, I look it up. I learn and I study until I ace things. I know what I'm good at and I avoid what I'm not good at. But when I'm with you, I feel like I don't know anything. I'm not as sure of myself. I'm nervous. I feel like I fail all the time. And not just with our interactions—I fail myself, too. I'm not being real or honest."

I'm more lost than ever. "Well, why hang out with me at all, then? Everything you just said sounds awful."

Vitaly shakes his head, swallows. "See, I'm failing again. Failing to get my point across. Jimena, you unlocked a part of me that makes me *want* . . . that makes me nervous, and curious, and—" He's still shaking his head, struggling to get the words out. There is something in his hoodie's front pocket that makes it pooch, and he reaches inside it, like there's a talisman in there giving him the courage to say whatever it is he needs to say. "You're like the best math problem. You're tough and you're a struggle to wrap my head around, but trying to figure you out—and trying to figure out who *I* am when I'm with you—it's exciting and fun and . . ." Vitaly sighs, watching my face, looking deflated. Looking, I guess, the way he's trying to describe to me now. Hopeless but impassioned. Wanting but sated.

"What I'm trying to say is that I like myself when I'm around you," he says. "I feel brand-new, every time."

If I know Vitaly at all, I think that feeling would have scared him once. But he's changed. And he likes it.

"It was weird when we stopped hanging out after Sof's party," he goes on. "But then we had the prom and it was . . ."

It was everything.

"But then these last few weeks, we've been distant. I think I know why, but I don't want us to be distant. I'd rather be nervous and struggling to get a word out with you than not be around you at all. Being able to hang out with you? I consider it a gift."

I try to take in what he's saying, what it means that it feels like my stomach is in my throat and I'm trying to catch my breath. I think I understand what Vitaly's trying to say. There is a much more seamless way to say it in Spanish.

Me haces falta.

It isn't exactly *I miss you* or *I need you*. It's more, *You're a part of me, and without you I'm incomplete.*

If that is what he's trying to say, it's too big to even think about, and I pare down the moment to only what's in front of me. All I can focus on is how beautiful he looks right now, lit up, hair drifting in the breeze. I can't tell the difference between attraction and beer buzz anymore. All I know is the delicious tingling in my stomach, the cozy and lazy and needing sensation that makes me heat up with a slow burn, makes my teeth pinch my bottom lip.

But the light dancing on Vitaly's face is extinguished

suddenly. He turns from warm gold to muted blue like a light switch. It takes me a moment to realize the lost light isn't something I imagined—it's the campfire. Vitaly and I both turn to see what put it out. His cousins are kicking sand over the smoking fire pit just as a flashlight beam shines long streaks across the sand.

Distantly, approaching figures in blue yell at us to freeze.

45

MY FIRST INSTINCT IS TO RUN. THE FIRE'S FULLY
out and beer bottles get tossed and Vitaly's cousins and their
friends start to run, which seems like a very good idea. But as
soon as I get to my feet, Vitaly's hand is in mine, mooring me
like an anchor.

"It's okay." His voice is way too calm for how many cops
there are.

"It is not okay," I hiss, pulling my hand, which pulls him
up to standing.

"If we run, they'll chase us." Vitaly's already moving, taking me with him, but it isn't the sprint I hope for. Though we
aren't running, our pace isn't exactly leisurely, either. I glance
over my shoulder to see that Vlad has been the quickest, flee-
ing in the opposite direction, but Vitaly's right—a cop is on
his tail, running right behind him. I turn away from the scene
and stare straight ahead, not wanting to see the officer tackle
Vlad to the sand.

"We'll walk," Vitaly says, "get far enough away that we
don't look like we're associated with them."

"Your cousins," I begin, my question wrapped up in those
two words. Is Vitaly really going to leave his family? But I

realize that I'm the irregular variable here. If he weren't looking out for me, Vitaly would stay behind.

"They'll be okay," he says. "Don't look back."

I don't know how he can be so calm. He is coherent and levelheaded, all while there are firecrackers going off in my head. I breathe deep to steady my mind, put the firecrackers out. I blot out the shouting pair of cops behind me, zero in on the shadowed view down the beach, on putting one foot in front of the other. And on the feeling of Vitaly's fingers laced through mine. He may seem calm, but I can feel the tension in his grip, his fingers curled stiff as a claw.

"Now we're going to stop and turn around."

I don't breathe. "What?"

"If we keep ignoring what's happening, we'll look suspicious." Vitaly turns, even though I'm still too scared to. "Any other bystander would rubberneck. So we're going to turn around, pretend to be casual observers."

"Please, we need to keep going."

"Trust me," Vitaly says.

Everything inside me is screaming to keep moving. That the safest place for me is the farthest place from the police. This moment is what my mother tried to protect me from. Her fear of the cops always seemed so irrational, but now I understand. This fear that I've inherited from her is integral to my — to our — survival. I want to keep moving, but there is a louder voice inside of me, a voice that trusts Vitaly. So I turn around to look back where we came from. My stomach drops instantly.

"There's a cop coming," I say, my voice shaking.

"Yeah." Vitaly stops looking at what had been the party

and takes a step in front of me, facing me. I think he's trying to get me to stop looking at what's going on with his cousins and to ignore the cop. I think he's trying to get me to focus on only him.

"How can you be so calm?" I whisper, clutching his hand tighter.

"Because we're fine. You're not doing anything wrong."

"I exist. *Here*," I say. "To them, that's wrong."

From the corner of my eye, I can see the cop getting closer, and beyond him there's his partner, questioning Vitaly's cousins and their friends. They all sit on the sand, and it looks like the officer is collecting IDs. My mouth goes dry. I don't have an ID. What if they take me down to the station and find out who I really am? My thoughts spiral with so much fear that I'm dizzy.

I should be taking some deep breaths, counting to ten to calm myself down or something. But all I can count are the number of things we were doing wrong that the police can bust us for. Are bonfires allowed on New York City beaches? Are we allowed to be here this late at night? Is this beach supposed to be closed? Are we trespassing? Making too much noise? And the drinking. If the cop gives me a Breathalyzer, I can get deported.

One bottle of beer and I can get *deported*.

I count all these reasons on trembling fingers behind my back. I could throw up and faint at the same time. It isn't just my life flashing before my eyes, it's my future going up in flames. My entire life boiling down to a few sips of a *Canadian lager*.

How could I be so stupid?

My breaths come out shallow and the corners of my vision dim. I only realize my teeth are chattering when I feel Vitaly's hand suddenly, gentle on my jaw, guiding my distant gaze back to him.

"Hey," he whispers, impossibly soft. "We can pretend."

I latch onto his face. I concentrate on getting my breathing back, but I can't seem to fill my lungs. "Pretend?"

"We're not with them," Vitaly says, cocking his head toward his cousins' group. "We're just a couple out for a stroll on a nice night. Okay?"

I nod, even as my chin starts to quiver. But Vitaly's thumb grazes my skin, smoothing out the nervous lines beneath my lips. "I'm with you." He squeezes my hand to prove it. "I'm not going anywhere."

His gaze is so steady I think if I keep looking in his eyes I could forget anything happening beyond them. But then a cop's voice cuts through to my soul. "Hey!" he shouts.

Vitaly turns to face him, taking the lead.

"You with them?" The cop sweeps the long beam of his flashlight down the beach.

"No, Officer," Vitaly says. "Is there a problem?"

"The beach is closed. Didn't you see the signs? You're trespassing."

Trespassing. A real law. We can claim we're not with the party, but there is no denying we're in a place we aren't supposed to be. It's a funny kind of ironic, that the thing that will wind up getting me deported is the exact same crime I am technically living. Illegally being somewhere I'm not allowed to be.

"Really?" Vitaly sounds convincingly surprised. "We were just out for a walk and saw the gates open. I had no idea."

The cop doesn't buy it, though. "Can I see your IDs?"

"Sure." Vitaly fishes for his wallet in the back pocket of his jeans. His other hand stays locked on mine.

The cop accepts the card, flashing his light at it and seeming to read every bit of info before returning it to Vitaly. Then he lifts the light higher, to my face. "Yours, too."

I wince at the brightness, my heart hammering against my rib cage. All the lies I'm coming up with are sputtering in my head like a dead car battery. My palm is slick as it clutches Vitaly's. But when I glance at him, he nods, prompting me to say something, anything.

"I left my purse in his car." I manage to say it without tripping over my words, a small miracle. "I'm sorry."

And then I can't help it anymore, can't hold back the nerves and fear from gushing out of me. Something has to give, and sudden tears come spilling down my cheeks, messy and fierce. "I'm sorry," I say again, blubbering, hiccupping. I am a geyser, both exploding out of the sand and about to sink into it. Crying is making things worse, I know that. It's making me look guilty, like I'm definitely hiding something. I need to stop but I cannot stop. Nothing on this earth can make me stop. *I'm sorry.*

"Hey, it's okay," Vitaly says, one hand holding me tight while the other pushes back a wayward lock of hair that's fallen over my cheek. He guides it back behind my ear. "We didn't know we weren't supposed to be here."

One last hiccup and I decide to keep my mouth shut. And then Vitaly does the ballsiest thing anyone's ever done. He turns to the cop and doesn't plead, nor ask. He just lays out what's going to happen. "Sorry, Officer. We'll get out of your way now."

Maybe, I realize then, my crying isn't making me look guilty so much as it is making the cop feel incredibly uncomfortable. He can barely look at me as he says, "Yeah, you two need to go." And then he's heading back to join his partner, and for the first time in my life I know what it actually means to breathe.

I think Vitaly does, too. When he exhales, I realize how tense this was for him, as well. How much strength it took to keep me steady and lie to the cops and defuse the situation. He takes both my hands in his and rests his forehead against mine, and we're both too spent to move. I'm grateful for Vitaly being here, holding me up. I'm grateful for the warm press of his forehead, for the whisper of his fingers in mine.

The only movement that does come is from the gap between our mouths growing smaller. Our top lips meet first, gentle but for the electric current that sparks between them. But the words spill out of me, swift and destructive as a sledgehammer. "I'm getting married."

Saying it makes me feel as nervous as I did when I was talking to the cop. It keeps my heartbeat erratic, keeps my knees feeling like they're about to give way.

A gust of cold air hits my forehead as Vitaly peels back, eyes pried open with a searching confusion. This—more than our confrontation with the police officer—is the thing to knock him off-kilter. "You're what?"

My clammy hands are cold now that Vitaly isn't holding

them. His own hands find refuge in the front pocket of his hoodie.

"When di—" He clears his throat. "Who—" Vitaly can't settle on the right question, but I can tell that whatever the questions may be, they all border on concern. I spit out the bits of information that come to me first, just to assure him everything's okay.

"He's a good guy, just a couple years older than me. I was up front with him, about what I'm doing this for. And he wants to help."

It's not much, but I hope I've said enough to assuage any of Vitaly's fears. I want to tell him about Blue, that he really is a good person, marrying me for the right reasons, but I also have a feeling that Vitaly doesn't necessarily want to hear any more about him. I think I'm right when Vitaly shuts down the conversation with a curt, "Congratulations."

It's the last thing I want to hear. "You don't have to say that . . ." The words start off strong but die off on my lips so even I don't hear the end of that sentence.

"It's what you wanted. I'm happy for you."

The temperature has dropped so low on the beach. I'm freezing, and though he tries to smile warmly, Vitaly looks cold, too.

46

IT'S TEN A.M.—TOO EARLY TO BE UP ON A SUNDAY—
but Blue is already all over Facebook. He's been tagged in forty-seven pictures of a protest on the steps of Capitol Hill. Blue is in DC for the weekend, and I know he told me what for, but I can't for the life of me remember the cause. In the pictures, the protest looks rather paltry, with barely a dozen mismatched people holding up signs. I try to gauge the situation from the text I can make out. SENATORS, HOW DO YOU SLEEP AT NIGHT? and WHAT WILL YOU TELL YOUR GRANDCHILDREN? Still no clue.

I wonder if this will be what my weekends look like for the foreseeable future: browsing photos of protests on Facebook, spotting the righteous indignation etched into my husband's face. In all the photos, the bullhorn is never too far from Blue's shouting mouth. There are lengthy captions that I'm sure explain the day's mission, but frankly, I don't have the energy to read them. Instead, I like one photo to let him know I care.

There. I x out of the site and find my phone. A full day has passed since I told Vitaly my big news, and now: nothing. Just a big bucketful of silence from both our ends. But all I want to do is talk to him. Even if the conversation is awkward and uncomfortable. I need to reach out. I send him a text message.

> Hey, what time is the tournament?
> Want to see little baby fists smashing 2x4s.

It's corny, but I feel nakedly vulnerable sending it. Vitaly doesn't make me wait too long for a response.

> Not at all how that works.

I smile reading his message. But then he texts again.

> You don't have to come.

The smile slips off my face.

> I want to support u. I will cheer really loud.

> Thank you, but it's OK.

I stare at the texts, more than a little agitated. I know I dropped a bomb, and maybe the news of my engagement is a little shocking, but that doesn't mean Vitaly has to ice me out. There is no way he's getting in the way of me seeing tiny little babies doing flying tornado kicks.

I get out of bed and fling open my closet.

I don't remember the name of Vitaly's training gym, but I remember the train we took to get there. It was right after my date with the Canadian, and I was so down that as we rode the subway, Vitaly tried to tell me a funny story for five stops until he mercifully stopped when we got to the 25th Street station in Brooklyn.

We walked two blocks, passing the laundromat that Vitaly said he used anytime he got a cut or a bloody nose while sparring, so that his mom didn't have to see the splotches of red all over his uniform. It was when I realized what a good son he was, sparing his mom like that.

And then we got to the nondescript building with the sign over the door that said, simply, FIGHT GYM! That night it was quiet and dark until Vitaly switched on the lights to the cavernous warehouse space. Now, as I pull open the door to the place, it's full with all kinds of people. Kids training and parents watching them on the sidelines. There's a fight taking place between two teen girls in the ring at the back, and blue floor mats crammed with a million rug rats falling all over each other and screaming. Vitaly is a saint for working here.

I scan the mats for him, but I don't spot him anywhere. I glance at the ring in the back, the doors on the sides, at the people milling about. I keep looking until I bump into an adult in a blue uniform.

"You looking for someone?" the man asks.

"Yeah. Vitaly Petrov. Is he on break?"

The guy scrunches his eyebrows, shakes his head. "Vitaly's not working today. He's away for the weekend. School trip, I think."

Now it's my turn to be confused. "But what about the baby tournament?"

The confusion really is mounting between the two of us, to the point where I wonder if I walked into the right gym. I realize that perhaps "baby tournament" is a term only Vitaly uses. "Uh, the tournament for the kids' division?" I try again, gesturing to the smallest children doing very uncomplicated fighting moves on the mats.

"Sorry, miss, no tournament today. Are you babysitting one of the kids?"

I shake my head, though I'm still trying to process what the guy just said.

"You really can't be here unless you're with one of the kids," he goes on. "Unless you're interested in taking a class? Vitaly only does the kids' classes, but I teach both private and group courses. I can show you the schedule if you're interested."

I'm not sure if I answer him, but I must mutter something, because the guy is heading to a leaflet holder mounted on the wall to pull a couple of calendars and brochures for me to browse. "Uh, sorry, no," I say quickly, and make my way toward the exit.

It's only when I'm outside, the air hitting my cheeks and making them tingle, that it begins to dawn on me, what's happening. I take out my phone and write a text.

How's the tournament going?

Vitaly's reply comes quickly.

Good. Medals for everyone.

I amble back to the subway station and take the train home, every movement done by rote as my mind lingers elsewhere.

Vitaly missed the trip to Montreal. And I know—like I know that I love him—that he did it for me. So that I wasn't the only one who didn't get to go.

47

THERE IS NO AVOIDING VITALY. WE ARE CLASS-
mates and neighbors, which means I see him in pretty much
every corner of my life, without even seeking him out. But after
the roller coaster of a year we've had, where we've gone from
ribbing each other to kissing each other, we've reached the point
where neither of us knows what to say when we inadvertently
cross paths. When I bump into him in the locker bay, or when
I'm hauling a bag of recycling to the building's dumpster room
just as he's leaving it, we talk around what we really want to say.
We ask each other how we did on our finals, we talk about how
nice the weather is getting. But mostly, I don't ask him why he
lied about the reason he didn't go to Montreal, and he doesn't
ask me about my impending marriage.

We don't talk.

We are fine.

He is all I can think about.

"How about one over here?" asks Blue. He sits on a bench
beneath a tree and taps the empty space next to him. I sit beside
him and hold up my digital camera so it's facing us. Blue drapes
his long arm around my shoulders and I catch his hand to lace
my fingers through it. I snap a few pics.

We're in Prospect Park on a very narcissistic mission to

take pictures of ourselves. We're doing the typical couple thing: strolling aimlessly through a picturesque park and documenting the whole thing so we have an album of photos to show immigration agents when the time comes. For variety's sake, and to make it look like we've been together much longer than we actually have, Blue and I even have a change of clothes in our bags. Not much more than a cardigan for me and a different T-shirt (plus beanie) for him, but it will be enough to make it seem like we've been here on at least two different occasions. Make it seem like we're the kind of couple who loves nature. Make it seem like we're a couple, period.

But the trip to the park isn't just good for pictures, it's another opportunity for Blue and me to get to know each other better. Which is a nice way of saying it's a chance to learn basic trivia facts about each other.

"Childhood nickname?" Blue asks.

"My friends have been calling me Jimmy since forever."

"And you affectionately refer to me as 'Blue.' Your favorite perfume?"

"Coco Mademoiselle," I say. "And you don't wear cologne because they test it on animals?"

"No, I just don't like it. Do you sleep on your stomach?"

"My side, mostly."

"Let's say I sleep on the left and you sleep on the right side of the bed."

"Are they really going to ask what side of the bed we each sleep on?"

"According to the internet, they might even ask you my underwear preference. Briefs, by the way."

Even though I put my camera down a while ago, we stay seated like this, with his arm comfortably over my shoulders. I may not actually be with Blue, but I am relaxed enough around him that I don't feel the need to move. Our romantic relationship may not be real, but our friendship is.

Still, it doesn't escape me that this marriage is a lot to ask. I'll get my permanent residency fairly quickly, but getting my citizenship will take longer. And even with everything I know about Blue, I still can't wrap my head around why he'd do this. Ideally, we'll get divorced after a few years. But a lot can happen in that time. He could meet someone who he truly cares about. Someone who might not be okay with our situation.

"Why are you doing this for me?"

Blue is unfazed by my question. "I told you, I want to—"

"Help, I know. But we're looking at years together, Blue. Years with your wagon hitched to mine."

He laughs. "We have wagons now?"

"You know what I mean."

Blue takes a deep breath and plays lazily with the fabric at my shoulder. "You're in a tough spot. And it's unfair that there's no way for you to get out of it. It breaks my heart and it pisses me off. And when I feel like that, I can't just not do something about it."

"Yeah, but it's a whole lot of work for someone you don't love."

"I'd hate to think of doing this with someone you *do* love," Blue says. "There's no romance in filling out paperwork, meeting with lawyers, being interviewed by immigration officials. If you think about it, what we're doing would suck all the love right out of any healthy relationship. It's a screwed-up system. Love and government shouldn't have anything to do with each other."

I think about it, about this system sucking the love out of people, and I know that he's right. It gives me a whole new appreciation for Blue. I'd started my plan looking for a short-cut to love and marriage, but what Blue is saying makes sense. Even if I had found someone through those sad coffee shop dates, we definitely wouldn't have made it through the second stage of our relationship. The government-checking-that-all-our-i's-are-dotted-and-t's-are-crossed stage. I don't know if I could put someone I love through all that when they can just be free to have a normal relationship. It's what I keep telling myself.

Blue tilts his head toward me, a wild gleam in his eye. "And don't think I'm not getting just a little bit of a kick out of all this. I mean, we're subverting the broken immigration sys-tem. We're putting up a giant middle finger to all the bullshit institutions that the suits think we should live by. I mean, fuck *that*."

I nod. Yeah, fuck that.

"Your birthday's coming up, right?" Blue asks. "May thirtieth?"

"And yours is February eighth."

Blue smiles. "Yeah, but I didn't say it as a factoid. I just meant, are you throwing a party or anything?"

I shake my head. "Why?"

"Well, I was thinking we should probably announce our engagement soon, you know? It isn't really official until the people in our lives know. What if you throw a birthday party and then we surprise everyone by turning it into an engagement party? Kill a couple of birds with one stone. Get a bunch of pictures out of the deal. Then we can pretty much elope anytime after that. What do you think?"

What do I think? I think this is all moving really fast, but it's exactly what I need, and I'm not jumping off this train just as it's finally starting to leave the station.

"Sounds good to me."

48

SOF AND I STAND IN THE SNACK AISLE AT
ShopRite, stuck on what style of popcorn to get. "Salty or
sweet?" I ask.

She plucks a bag of each flavor off the shelf and dumps
them into the shopping cart. I immediately take one out and
put it back. It's moments like this when I'm most aware that
I'm the kind of person who has a limited budget for refresh-
ments and Sof is not. We're supposed to be picking up a small
selection of snacks for my birthday party tomorrow night, but
without even trying, the cart is nearly overflowing. I put the
other bag of popcorn back, too, for good measure. "Who likes
popcorn anyway?"

Sof spins on me, her face frozen in a state of alarm. I freeze,
too, briefly, and slowly retrieve the bag I just put back. "Okay,
sorry, more popcorn."

"I can't keep pretending I care about snacks right now!"
Sof's words come out shrill, unbridled. "Jimmy. Are you really
gonna go through with this?"

I already told her my birthday is going to be doubling as a
secret engagement party. She's known about Blue since the beginning, and that things with him (aka, our fake relationship)

have been moving forward for the last few weeks. The fact that we're officially tying the knot should not be a surprise. And yet, it looks like it's finally hit her, right here among the party snacks. Her best friend is seriously getting married. And we haven't even graduated yet.

It's shocking, I know. And as the sort of person who's definitely mature enough to be getting married right now, I understand instinctively that I need to give her some grace. "Yes, I'm going through with this," I say calmly, evenly. "I've made up my mind. I thought you were happy for me."

Sof shakes her head quickly, which to the casual observer may seem like she means *no*, but I know it means *Don't get the wrong idea*. "I'm super happy. I am over-the-moon happy that you have found someone who's going to help you get out of a shitty situation and join the rest of us in the real world. But. Jim. It's *marriage*. You're getting married to someone you don't love."

I lay a hand on her shoulder, truly touched that she's so concerned, but Sof isn't saying anything that I haven't already endlessly thought about. "Sof. I know."

"But what about Vitaly?"

I can feel my cheeks burn at the mention of his name, and I am embarrassed that that is my body's first response when hearing it these days. I avoid Sof's penetrating gaze. "What about him?"

"Have you tried asking him to marry you?"

It is too embarrassing to admit that yes, I have proposed to Vitaly. A lot. I can't let Sof see that all over my face. So I pick up a random snack to suddenly scrutinize. According to the nutritional facts, these cheese puffs don't have any. Into the cart they go.

"What if he were to ask you to marry him?" Sof continues.

"He hasn't." I shake my head. "He won't."

"How do you know?"

"Because Vitaly never wants to get married. He already told me that."

"Never?"

"Never. Kind of like how I never want to talk about this again."

Sof squints and I realize that my declaration might reveal way too much about how I'm actually feeling about this whole thing. I doth protest too much. I shake my head, grab more snacks, try to get us back on track here. "Vitaly will be out of my life soon. And I'll be a married woman. Time to move on."

Sof won't, though. "But hypothetically, if he did want to marry you, would you do it?"

There are not enough nutritional facts in this whole aisle for me to focus on and dodge this topic, so I decide on the hard, unavoidable truth of the matter. "No, I wouldn't marry Vitaly. I don't want to ruin his—very detailed—plans for the rest of his life. If he married me, he'd be upending his whole future. Plus, I'd never know if he truly loved me or if he just married me to 'save' me. And I don't need a martyr. I need a blue-haired activist with a spare bedroom who wants to stick it to the man."

Sof looks like she's got more to say, but suddenly I do, too. It's so much easier trying to convince myself of something when I say it all out loud and have to convince someone else, also.

"And this really isn't a fairy tale!" I say, yanking a bag of peanut-butter-stuffed pretzels off the shelf even though, *ew*. "You're thinking we'd get married and ride off into the sunset, but where would Vitaly and I even live? We'd have to find an apartment, move in together immediately—open a joint bank account! None of those things are in his five-year plan."

Saying all of it out loud is a little like taking a stiff drink. It needs a moment to go down. "If we got married . . . that would ruin our relationship."

Sof looks like I just demanded she drop everything and solve a math problem. The girl is thoroughly confused. And I have a sinking feeling that I wasted a lot of breath just to make both of us feel like crap. I grab the cart and start rolling it down the aisle, toward the cashiers. It keeps swerving to the left and I have to work to keep it on the straight and narrow. But as much as I want to move on from this topic, I need Sof to understand so she stops looking at me like I'm a wounded clown on the side of the road.

"Sof, the whole point of me getting married is so that I can be free and live a normal life. And I know that 'freedom' and 'marriage' are totally antithetical, but that's just the way it is for me. I mean, do you really think I want to be *married* at eighteen? Of course I don't. But at least this way I'll be *divorced* by my early twenties and living life without worrying that at any moment I could get kicked out of the country. I don't want the real responsibilities that come with a real marriage! That's why marrying Blue is easier. It's just us playing pretend. If I married someone I actually love, it wouldn't be pretend."

I think I've done a pretty good job of explaining myself and putting an end to this discussion, but it all may have gone over Sof's head, because she's stuck on one specific word I didn't even realize I used.

"So you do love Vitaly."

I stop rolling the cart. There aren't any food items within reach for me to read the packaging of. But I only pause for a second and then start moving again, grateful that Sof is behind me and I don't have to look her in the eye. "He isn't asking me, so there's no point talking about it."

We reach the checkout. There's no line, and we load the conveyor with our food. I think the silence signals that we're finally done with this topic. But Sof is so quiet, and so sad-looking, that I can't stand it.

"Sof, I know you think that this is, like, a crazy thing to be doing. That I'm throwing caution to the wind and being all wild and stuff. But sometimes you gotta *be* a little radical to get what you want."

Sof continues emptying the cart until there's nothing in it anymore. And when she looks at me again, it's like she's got the wisdom of the whole world behind her eyes. "I think *you* think you're being radical," she says. "But if you ask me, marrying Blue seems pretty safe. I think the most radical thing you can do is be with the person you really love."

All I wanted to do today was get a few bags of chips. But here I am, laying my life bare in a ShopRite and my best friend's words hitting me hard enough to leave a bruise.

49

THE COURTYARD IS TRANSFORMED. EVERYONE'S
here: friends from school, my mom's small group of girl-
friends, and even people I definitely did not invite, like Mrs.
Gorky, who stalks the courtyard complaining about the noise
levels even as she's the main contributor to the volume.

One person I did invite who isn't here is Vitaly. I sent him
an email because it's the courteous, grown-up thing to do. But
I understand if he doesn't want to come. *I'm* not sure I even
want him to come. He's my friend, but also, it might kill me
to stand next to Blue and announce our engagement while
Vitaly watches.

It looks like I've figured out the one way to keep him away
from the courtyard. Still, my gaze constantly drifts toward the
building door. But there's only the snack table next to it, set
with serving bowls filled with the hundreds of snacks from
ShopRite and trays of vegetable-stuffed canapés my mom
painstakingly slaved over. All of it is lit up by string lights that
twinkle from the brick walls. Tasteful latex balloons and shim-
mery silver Mylar ones float in bunches tied to the backs of
patio chairs. The decorations are all Sof's doing.

"This is amazing," I whisper to her, looping my arm
through hers as I take in the scene. "Thank you."

"Couldn't skimp on your birthday-slash-engagement party," Sof says. If she's still uneasy about my engagement, I don't hear it in her voice. Our conversation from yesterday is still fresh, but I think she's done trying to talk me out of marriage. Sof's going the supportive friend route and letting me live my life the way I need to. And I'm grateful.

"I should go into party planning. Is there a major for party planning at UCLA?"

"You'll let me know," I say.

She lays her head on my shoulder. "It's going to be so weird going to school without you."

"I know." I got my acceptance letter to UCLA in the mail. Well, acceptance pending a real Social Security number. A bitter-sweet moment. But even though there's nothing normal about the direction my life is moving in, this part—the separating-from-your-friends-after-high-school-is-over part—feels like the typical teenage experience. So even though it hurts, I cling on to it, grateful to have it. "Maybe I'll get to go one day." But we both know that for the time being, I'm staying in New York. Sof's eyes wander until they settle on the reason I'm staying put. He's currently talking to my mother by the snack table.

"Looks like your mom likes Blue."

Between the two of them, Blue does most of the talking. Even from here I notice my mom sneaking glances at his hair and trying to smooth her eyebrows into less judgmental arches. She definitely hates the color, is puzzled by his short-sleeve flannel shirt and tie, and there is a good chance that if she understands anything that he's going on about, she has a problem with that, too. But my mom is nothing if not polite, and she is positively *beaming* up at Blue, radiant smile on full display.

In her eyes I can see the way she sees him. He's the pale gringo who's here to provide me with a future she could never give me. My mom might hate everything about him, but she loves him instantly because she sees him as my savior.

I know that my marrying Blue will change my mom's life as well. When I become a citizen, I'll be able to sponsor her, so she sort of has a horse in this race, too. But as we were setting up the courtyard earlier, before anyone was here, she sat me down on one of the patio chairs, looked me right in the eyes, and told me I didn't have to go through with this. "Yo se," I'd told her, even though, in the back of my mind, I knew I would always have to go through with this. If I waited until I was forty to get married to the love of my life, it would still affect my mom's legal status. My mom's life and my marriage would always be interlinked in that way.

I hate that that's something that hangs over us, adding a whole other layer to our ever-evolving mother-daughter dynamic. But I don't blame my mother for that. It's just one more aspect of my life that being undocumented has touched and tainted. And one less thing I'll have to think about once I become a citizen.

All I feel for my mom now is love. Everything she's ever done was to protect me, to give me a better life by whatever means necessary. How can I be anything but grateful to her?

"My mom adores him," I say to Sof, just as Blue and my mom's conversation comes to an end. He searches the crowd until he spots me.

"Well, I'll leave you two to your scheming," Sof says sweetly. Blue sidles up next to me just as Sof slips away. He bends his lanky marionette body so that his mouth is level with my ear. "I think your mom just went to get me hair dye?"

My mom *does* keep a couple of boxes of Brazenly Brunette under the bathroom sink to keep the grays at bay. "She would."

"She's hilarious," Blue laughs. "Hey, when she comes back, we should probably do the announcement, right?"

"The announcement, right." I'm trying for breezy, but I think it comes out strangled.

Blue doesn't notice, though. He fishes something out of his pocket and shows it to me. There's a diamond ring in his palm, and its sparkle could rival the twinkle lights. "Is that real?"

He laughs again. "No, this was twenty bucks at Kmart, but I think it's a pretty convincing counterfeit."

I nod, getting lost in the glare of the fake ring, the word "announcement" echoing through my mind. "I'll get you a real one," Blue says. "I was gonna ask my mom if I could borrow hers, actually."

I look up at him, eyes widening. "Are your parents coming tonight?" Blue's mom and dad have been married for twenty-four years. They have three kids, of whom Blue is the middle child. I know all this because of the personal history trivia factoids Blue and I have been exchanging. And I can't believe I haven't given them much thought, but this is about to turn into our engagement party any second now, and shouldn't my fake future in-laws be here for this?

"I thought it'd be weird to invite my entire family to a birthday party for a girl they don't know," Blue says. "Yeah,

I know, we didn't really think this whole party through. But hey, it's fine, and about the ring, I'll get you my mom's, she'll be cool with it. You just have to promise you'll return it after we get divorced."

I stare up at him, my eyes stuck in their wideness.

"I know, it's kind of annoying of me to ask, but—"

"No, Blue, of course I'll return it, that wasn't what . . . that wasn't what I was—" I take a moment to breathe, collect my thoughts. It's just all hitting me now. That Blue should be saving his mother's engagement ring for a real engagement, not *me*. And what will his parents think? There is no way he's being honest with them about what we're doing here, is there? Because why would they be cool with it? Which means more people—family—are being dragged into our sordid lie. Am I going to have to act like I'm in love with their son whenever I'm around them? Am I going to have to be around them a lot?

I look back down at the twenty-dollar ring in Blue's palm. Whenever I used to think about getting engaged, I never imagined it looking like this.

"Don't give me your mom's ring."

"You sure?"

"Yeah, I'm sure." I glance at the building door for the millionth time tonight.

"Your hair looks ridiculous!"

The screechy outburst a millimeter from my ear steals both Blue's and my attention, and we look at the small older woman from which it came. Mrs. Gorky sneers at the azure waves cresting over Blue's forehead. "I knew a young man with blue hair once," Mrs. Gorky continues. "He worked in the circus! You kids these days, idiot punks treating your hair and bodies like coloring books. What's the matter with you!"

Blue cranks open his enormous mouth and starts cracking up, but I'm mortified. "Excuse me?" I say.

"This your boyfriend?" the woman asks casually, as if we've been friends for the last fifty years.

"No," I say. "*Yes,*" I correct myself immediately.

"He isn't blond."

Is this dementia? I can't believe I'm entertaining this conversation. "Who invited you?" I hiss through gritted teeth.

"What happened to the blond boy from 1F? He dead?"

I close my eyes, never wanting to open them again. "No, Mrs. G., Vitaly didn't die."

"I thought he was your boyfriend. Thought you two imbeciles were in love."

Blue watches Mrs. Gorky like she's a classic *Golden Girls* rerun and then turns to me, like I'm a guest star in the episode.

"She's senile," I explain. "She's just a senile, mean old lady."

"Aww, I think you're pretty neat, Mrs. G.," he says.

"Don't you go calling me by one letter, you don't know me! I've known this girl since she was seven years old!"

Not true.

"When *G* was the only letter she knew!"

Definitely not true.

"She earned that letter! Only reason I let her have it."

The woman is shrieking so loud people near us turn to stare, but I place my hand on her humped back and start—gently—guiding her away from me. It works, because she shuffles off to go bother somebody else. And now that she's gone, the blond boy from 1F is suddenly standing before me.

He's dressed perfectly, in a crisp baby-blue button-down. It's a small thing, but it's nice to know that he thinks my birthday is important enough for a fresh collared shirt.

"Hey," he says. He glances over at Blue, then back at me. I realize they've never met before.

"Hey—hi," I answer.

"Happy birthday."

"Thank you."

The pause is thick, smothering the rest of the party. Not Blue's voice, though. "Hi!" he says, a big, jovial bark. "Is that a plastic cup you're holding?"

Vitaly shakes himself out of his reverie to look at the cup in his own hand, and then at Blue. "Yeah?"

"You know, plastic is the single biggest cause of chemical pollution on our planet. I don't know why there are even plastic cups here. Jimena, do you? I know there are paper cups. Did you not want to choose a paper cup option, buddy?"

Vitaly stares at Blue for a long moment before turning to me and saying, "Can we talk? Privately?"

50

THE HEAVY LOBBY DOOR SWINGS CLOSED AND muffles the noise of the party outside. It's a tense, silent walk the rest of the way, except for the echo of our footsteps bouncing off the stairwell walls. Vitaly proceeds with purpose, and though I'm the one to open the door to my apartment, he breezes through, reaching my bedroom first. I shut the door behind us.

"Seriously?" he says. "Him? Captain Planet?"

I almost choke on a shocked laugh. The one time Vitaly calls someone a name and he makes him sound like a superhero.

"Blue cares about the planet, yes—why are you being so judgey?"

I was checking for Vitaly the entire night, but now that he's here, I almost wish he wasn't. It's my birthday-slash-engagement party. I should be enjoying myself, not defending my fiancé to a guy I hardly speak to anymore. "Is this why you wanted to talk privately? Because as the hostess and guest of honor, I really can't be away from my party."

Vitaly finally stops pacing, hands on hips as he fixes me with a stare. "You can't marry him."

I can't help but roll my eyes. After everything I've been through to find someone, I can't believe Vitaly's trying to convince me, once again, to drop it. Not when I'm so close to the finish line. I am nothing if not stubborn. He knows that. It was in the PowerPoint presentation he made about me.

"Is this because of the plastic cup? So he's a little fanatical about the environment, among other things, but you know what? Someone has to be! Blue is passionate about the world, about helping people, about helping *me*. He is a good Samaritan. A good guy. A good egg, even. And, I mean, the paper cups were *right there*."

I don't know if any of this is getting through to Vitaly, because he keeps pacing my tiny room like he's got too much energy to expend. When he finally stops, it's with the energy of someone who's about to run a marathon. Something on my nightstand catches his attention. He picks up the notebook, open to the page where I wrote the instructions for my plan. I can see his eyes scanning it, going down the list until he reaches the final addendum.

Find someone like Vitaly.

I don't know what to say when he turns to me. No use trying to hide the notebook now, or explain away what I've written in it. But I don't have to say anything, because Vitaly beats me to the punch. "Marry me instead."

Everything stops. My breathing, my heart. I'm too stunned to say anything, too stunned to so much as blink. Vitaly watches me like he just went all in on black and is waiting for the roulette wheel to stop spinning.

But spin is all I can do at the moment. When I do find my voice again, it isn't much more than a burnt whisper. "No."

"Why not?"

"I told you I don't need you to save me."

Vitaly shakes his head. "I'm not trying to save you."

The only boy I want has just asked me to marry him and yet—I'm so angry I feel like I'm on fire. "Well, this is really convenient."

I searched for someone to love. Then I forgot about love and searched for someone who would simply have me. And just when I thought that was never going to happen, it did. I have come to terms with marrying someone in name only. I have made it a sanitized, antiseptic process. I have made sure to take love completely out of the equation with the kind of meticulous precision a surgeon would be proud of. And here comes Vitaly, barreling through my carefully laid plans like the fucking Kool-Aid Man.

"Like the fucking Kool-Aid Man!"

"What?"

"You can't just waltz in here and ask me to marry you!" I nearly shout.

Vitaly's face tenses with hard-edged lines. His mouth, his eyebrows, the crease in his forehead, all flat and horizontal. "Why not?"

"Well, for one thing, I'm already engaged, and for another, you don't actually want to get married. You never want to get married. You told me that."

"I was wrong."

I am so mad I have to bite down hard to keep from screaming. Now I'm the one who's pacing, hands in tight fists so they don't reach for things to throw in frustration. "I can't believe you."

"Jimena, I'm serious."

I spin on him, get in his face. I swipe at a tear before it has a chance to roll all the way down my cheek. I blink them all away, actually, so I can look at Vitaly's face and be as composed as possible. "It's really shitty of you to wait for this moment. I'm about to announce my engagement. And the fact of the matter is, for the longest time, you didn't want to marry me. You never even wanted to *be* with me. And suddenly—now that I've found someone who does—you want to swoop in and do something about it?"

Vitaly shakes his head like I've gotten all this wrong, and I hate him for making me think that. For making me feel hope that I *am* wrong. But when he puts a hand on my cheek, using his thumb to wipe a rebel tear, I don't pull away.

"I have wanted you," he says. "This whole time."

I shake my head, but Vitaly only nods. "Do you know how much torture it was? Sitting outside the coffee shop, watching you on your dates when all I wanted to do was take you out on one? I never said anything, because you wanted to get married and I didn't fit into your plan. And I know what it's like to have a plan. I know not to get in the way."

"So how can you expect me to get in the way of yours?" I ask. "What about Oxford?"

Vitaly shrugs Oxford off like his whole life didn't revolve around it. "There are good schools here."

How am I supposed to believe anything he says when he's

lying right now? He's not even doing a good job of pretending Oxford wasn't his whole world five minutes ago. "You always wanted to go there," I say. "You wanted to go to the place that invented the Oxford shirt. The Oxford comma. The *Oxford English Dictionary*."

He sputters out a tight laugh, and I may be joking, but I am also completely serious. "I can't keep you from your dreams. You'll resent me."

Vitaly only exhales through his nostrils, firm in his convictions. "I'll resent myself more if I don't ask you to marry me."

I sink until I am sitting on my bed. It's almost too much. This really shouldn't be so hard. Neither turning Vitaly down nor accepting his proposal should feel like I'm getting the wind knocked out of me. But I know why it feels this way. It's because even though I need to get married and Vitaly is asking me to marry him, marriage isn't something either of us actually wants.

Vitaly is doing this because he thinks I have some burning flame inside me and this whole marriage scheme is extinguishing it. I mean—he's right. I am a different person now than I was when I first set out on this mission. I am less idealistic. I see things in a harsher light. But it's not Vitaly's responsibility to try to keep the spark in me alive. I don't want to rope him into my bullshit.

And I don't want him anywhere near this scheme. I can't mix up my real feelings for him with something as bureaucratic as a federally recognized union.

"None of this is your fault," he says. "You're in a bad situation and it has affected every aspect of your life. And maybe I didn't understand at first, but I do now, Jimena. I understand why you need to do this. But don't let your status or this screwed-up system take one more thing away from you." Vitaly glances out the window briefly, at the party below, where I'm sure Blue is wondering what's taking so long.

"With that guy? You'd have to learn random facts about him to make your relationship believable. But you already know me. You know when my birthday is."

July 3.

"You know exactly how I like my coffee."

Decaf, half a sugar packet, splash of whole milk.

"I know you know what kind of underwear I wear."

My cheeks flush as I think of the night in the laundry room when he told me he'd never marry me. *Boxers.*

"And what my least favorite color is."

"As of tonight . . . blue?"

"See?" Vitaly says. "You know me."

I look up at him through wet eyes, feeling more tired and broken than I ought to on my birthday. But I guess it's a fitting welcome to officially becoming an adult. "I can't marry you," I say. "Because if I did, it wouldn't be fake. It wouldn't just be paperwork and appearances and divorce in two years. It would be real."

Vitaly lets out a breath and comes to sit next to me on the bed. He pulls my hand onto his lap and looks at it as he talks. "I know you think I'm only asking you now, after you're already engaged to . . . that guy. But I wanted to ask you before I even knew about him."

I turn to him. I search his profile for the answers to all the new questions running through my mind. Vitaly angles his head toward me and smiles. "I was going to ask you at the beach. I had this in my sweatshirt the whole night."

Without even noticing, I see that he's fished something out of his pocket. He passes the small velvet box to me. It's rounded at the corners and maroon, the kind of size and shape that means I don't need to guess what's inside. But when I do snap the top back, the ring still manages to take my breath away. A gold band, a small gem.

Two rings in one night. Just when I stopped believing in fairy tales.

As I stare at the ring, Vitaly's voice cuts through my thoughts. "It would be real for me, too."

I take it in, and I can't believe hearing this admission from Vitaly feels so . . . scary. But I also realize something else. I used to be a free spirit. I used to throw caution to the wind. Finding out I was undocumented changed all that, but what if this is a small way to reclaim that part of myself? What if this is a chance to do something daring again? Vitaly is putting his whole life on the line for me. The least I can do is dive into this with him, headfirst. Not knowing what comes next, but facing it together.

"Two kisses?" he says. "That can't be it for us." Vitaly looks at me with a small smile pulling at the corner of his lips. "I know you think I had a perfect future planned for myself. But it's not a perfect future without you."

Oh. I press my lips to that smile, kissing him for the third time in my life. When I pull away, all I see are his eyes, looking into mine. "I love you," I tell him.

"I love you," Vitaly says.

He slips the ring onto my finger, and just like that, never becomes always.

Epilogue

THE ROOM WE'RE IN IS CIRCULAR AND BARE
except for some flags and stained-glass panels behind a
podium. It's all kind of drab, but luckily, Sof has saved the day
with some light decor. Hydrangeas aren't the most romantic,
but the selection at the bodega was limited. And anyway, I
really like the pale periwinkle petals. They're the right sort of
soft and delicate to commemorate this moment.

Sof places the small bouquet in my hands to keep them
from shaking, I think. And maybe Vitaly's hands aren't any
good right now, either, because he does not protest as Sof pins
a couple of hydrangeas to his lapel.

It almost feels like we shouldn't even be allowed in here.
But we are. We're dressed the part, me in a champagne-
colored lace dress that tickles my knees, and Vitaly in his prom
suit and skinny black tie. We got the paperwork done. Dotted
our i's and crossed our t's. At eighteen, Sof's allowed to be
our witness. Besides the three of us, there's a woman at the
podium reciting some words that totally go over my head. I
speak when I'm prompted to, and Vitaly does the same.

And just a few minutes after it starts, the ceremony is over.

It's a whirlwind, going down the elevator and out of
Borough Hall, bursting through the fresh air outside. We're

close to the same square where the DREAM Act rally took place a few months ago. The sun is high up in the sky, and Vitaly and I are giddy with what we've just done. Whenever I sneak a glance at him, between bounding down the stone steps, he's grinning, laughing, and so am I, our hands clutched tight and only a little sweaty.

Blue is outside waiting for us, clicking away on a disposable camera. He pauses only to signal with a thumbs-up and a wink. I wave, grateful to have him as my friend.

When Vitaly and I reach the ground, we stop to catch our breath and giggle like we've just gotten away with something. And I guess, in a way, we have.

We're married!

It's so grown-up!

I'm married to someone I love. But like a persistent itch, the back of my mind tickles with the thought that I've forced Vitaly's hand. The thought that he's only doing this because he has to.

I hate that even on my wedding day, my immigration status worms its way into my love story. It looms over us like a dark cloud, making me question the legitimacy of our relationship, of Vitaly's motivations. But I make a decision right there not to think about that. I decide to only focus on the fact that Vitaly loves me, and that I'm free.

Downtown Brooklyn is a haze around us, people having lunch on city hall's steps, vendors selling snacks out of their food carts, cars and delivery trucks honking in traffic, even Sof throwing pinches of rice out of a Ziploc bag. But no matter how far I try to push the fear out of my mind, it lingers.

It bears witness to my happiness, refusing to be ignored. And the more I think about what we've just done, the bigger that fear grows.

We're married.

It's so grown-up.

The reality of it feels as solid and big as the concrete I'm standing on. I wonder if Vitaly feels it, too, because our explosive giddiness settles into something quieter. So quiet the street noises cut through our bubble. Soon, it's all I hear, the abrasive sounds of people and real life. Vitaly and I look at each other as husband and wife, but neither of us really knows what those words mean.

"What now?"

Acknowledgments

THANK YOU:

Jenny Bent, for handling it all—the texts and phone calls and emails, and all the behind-the-scenes stuff I don't understand. I lucked out in the agent department.

Dana Chidiac, for guiding the book in the direction it needed to go and for putting up with all the TS song-title Easter eggs when you were probably just trying to get on with it and do your job.

Ann Marie Wong—it's a huge comfort knowing you're there and you've got my back, cheering me along.

Everyone at Macmillan and Henry Holt Books for Young Readers. Jean Feiwel, Valery Badio, Alexei Esikoff, Lelia Mander, Samira Iravani, Mariel Dawson and her team, Molly Ellis, Mary Van Akin, and their team, Jennifer Edwards and her team. It takes a village, and I am so grateful for you all devoting your time and talents to bring this novel to life.

Fili Gonçalves for the gorgeous cover art and working with us to get Jimena just right.

Librarians, teachers, and booksellers, I am so awed by the work you do for books and readers and authors. Thank you for recommending my work and putting it into the hands of those who love it most. Where would we be without you?

To every reader who has read my stuff, to those who take time out of their day to send me a note, and to those who've stuck with me from book to book, despite how much I like to skip around, genre-wise. I appreciate you more than you know.

My family: Sonia, Irina—two perfect moms who are there when I need more time to write. You guys make everything better and easier. Yasmin, Maayan, Hadas, Akiva, a constant source of joy. And Tove and Imri, I love you so much!

Alex. To me, a story is all about its big reveals. And all my biggest reveals I've saved for you. It's one of the great gifts of my life that you've handled them all with strength and humor.

Lastly, to the Dreamers. I know. I was you. You are all so close to my heart.